IN ENEMY HANDS

MICHELLE PERRY

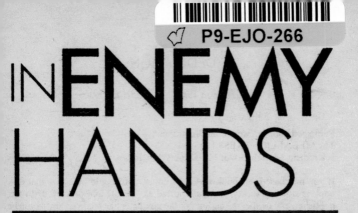

Jewel Imprint: Emerald
Medallion Press, Inc.
Printed in USA

DEDICATION:

For Theresa Gaus, a friend indeed.

Published 2006 by Medallion Press, Inc.
The MEDALLION PRESS LOGO
is a registered tradmark of Medallion Press, Inc.

Copyright © 2006 by Michelle Perry
Cover Models: Anna Ward, William Hainsworth
Cover Illustration by James Tampa

Printed in the United States of America

Library of Congress Cataloging-in-Publication Data

Perry, Michelle.
  In enemy hands / Michelle Perry.
    p. cm.
  ISBN 1-932815-47-3 (pbk.)
  1. Bounty hunters--Fiction. 2. Kidnapping victims--Fiction. 3. Children of the rich--Fiction. I. Title.
  PS3616.E7935I5 2006
  813'.6--dc22

                                2005037119

              10 9 8 7 6 5 4 3 2 1
                     First Edition

ACKNOWLEDGEMENTS:

My deepest thanks to:
Rebecca Miller, Barb Hughes, Diane Miley, Diana White,
the WWCG gang, Cat Walker, Charlina & Mavis Adams,
Tammy Layne, Beverly Campbell, Gina Baskin,
Tiffany Anderson, Debbie Walker

My family — Quinton, Chase & Selena,
Patricia Myers & the Yarworth clan, the Scissoms,
the Perrys, Kathy & Larry, Krystal Bean, Treva & Robert.

CHAPTER 1

Gary Vandergriff paused with his hand on the doorknob, trying to compose his expression into a mask of pleasant neutrality. It would not do for Father to read the wrong thing in his expression. Taking a deep breath, he opened the door to the darkened bedchamber.

The room reeked of pine cleanser; it made his eyes water when he crossed the threshold and approached his father's bed. Perhaps the maid had made an overzealous attempt to mask the second, more subtle scent in the room.

Death.

It lingered in the periphery like a spectator in a boxing arena, awaiting the results of the bout between the crusty old diplomat and the pancreatic cancer that had slowly decimated his body for the past six months.

The old man had put up a good fight, but now the cancer had him on the ropes. The doctors said he wouldn't live out the week.

Gary approached the bed. "Father?"

The old man lay still against the pillows, and for an instant, Gary thought he was already gone. Then his rheumy blue eyes fluttered open. He shot Gary a startled, faintly accusing look.

Gary swiped at his burning eyes, then was horrorstruck at the idea that the old man might think that he was crying. Franklin Vandergriff would not appreciate any tears on his behalf.

"Father, I wasn't . . . I didn't . . ."

His father rapped his stomach with a gnarled hand. For the first time, Gary noticed the manila folder that blended with the beige sheets. He spotted his name on the tab and felt the first fluttering of fear.

"You're a liar," the old man growled. "A thief!"

"Father," he gasped. "What do you . . .?"

His words stuck in his throat as the old man's palsied fingers opened the cover. Gary knew what it was in an instant. Ice water filled his veins and pooled in the pit of his stomach.

Andreakos.

Andreakos had learned of the old man's condition. This was an eleventh hour attempt to take everything Gary had fought for, everything that he would be rightfully entitled to his when his father died.

"My lawyer's coming," the old man wheezed. "You will be . . . disinherited."

Will be.

The words gave Gary hope. Maybe it wasn't too late.

Moving quickly, Gary seized a pillow from the ottoman and pressed it to the old man's face.

His father's birdlike hands beat at his arms, but Gary was surprised by how ineffectual his blows were. How easy it all was.

In a moment, it was over. Gary removed the pillow and stared down at the old man.

Finally, he let the smile that had been twitching his lips surface. He giggled, pressing his face into the pillow to mute the sound.

The old bastard was finally dead.

The sly Andreakos had almost beaten him at his own game. After blackmailing him for years, he'd tried to turn the tables at the last moment. But now Gary feared nothing. All the years groveling at his father's feet had paid off. He would possess the money and power he craved.

And at last, he would annihilate Andreakos and his family.

Gary leaned over to check his father's pulse one last time, and shook his head in disbelief when he found the old man was still dead. It seemed impossible that a flimsy little thing like a throw pillow had brought down such a creature. He'd half-suspected it'd take a silver bullet.

He giggled again.

Gary arranged the pillow back on the ottoman with the others, then held his eyes open with his thumbs and forefingers. The pungent fumes of the cleaner stung his retinas, and when tears streaked down his cheeks, Gary ran to the door.

"My father!" he shouted into the hallway. "He's not breathing."

● ● ●

Wednesday, August 3
5:28 p.m.

Somehow, Gary made it through the funeral without laughing out loud. The situation was so delicious though, that he'd had to take a couple of nerve pills before the service to mute his glee and achieve a look of slack-faced bereavement.

Back at the house, he had somehow tolerated the barrage of condolences from his father's friends, but one by one, they'd drifted away after eating and drinking their fill at the wake. Only one guest remained, and although Gary hated all his father's cronies, he took a certain perverse pleasure in speaking with this one.

"Please, General Birdsong, won't you step into the study for a drink?"

He spoke loudly, deliberately, turning to allow the old man to read his lips. The steely-eyed general was deaf as a post, but far too proud to admit it.

The general shuffled into the study and slumped into one of the overstuffed chairs. "I'm sorry for your loss, son," he said. "There will never be another Franklin Vandergriff."

"Thank God you're right about that. I've suffered enough because of him," Gary said pleasantly. He crossed over to the bar and poured two shots of bourbon.

"I beg your pardon?" the general said, and Gary smiled.

He turned and handed a glass to his guest. "I said, God knows you're right about that, but he'd suffered enough because of this."

The general nodded. "Cancer is a relentless old bitch. So quick."

"So quick," Gary agreed, and took a sip of his drink. Behind his glass, he said, "But I was quicker."

Someone rapped sharply on the study door. When it swung open, an irritated Gary looked up to see who was spoiling his game.

"Sir," the butler said. "I'm sorry to interrupt, but a Mr. Giovanni is here to see you. I told him about the wake, but he said you called this morning and requested—"

"Yes, yes." Gary quickly drained the rest of his drink. "Show him to my office, make sure he's comfortable, and tell him I'll be right with him. I have to go upstairs to get a file." He turned to his guest. "General, if you'll excuse me, this is very important."

"You're doing business on the day you bury your father?" the general asked, using the chair arm to push himself to his feet.

Gary flinched at the reproach in his voice. He was through answering to old men like him. He was through answering to anyone.

"No, of course not," he said tightly. "I'm meeting with Mr. Giovanni on a personal matter. Not that it's any of your business." This time, he made sure the general heard. Gary snapped his fingers at the butler. "Theo, will you please show the general out?"

The old man grunted when he pushed himself out of the chair. He cast Gary another disapproving glance over his shoulder while he shuffled to the door, but Gary dismissed him with a wave of his hand. He had more important things to worry about, like the performance he was about to give.

He needed Giovanni's help for the first stage of his plan to destroy Andreakos, or Branson, or whatever it was he called himself these days.

Kill the head and the body will die.

If he pulled off this plan, Andreakos would be on his knees.

● ● ●

"Mr. Vandergriff will be with you in a moment," the butler said. "He told me to make sure you were comfortable."

Dante lifted an eyebrow. Fat chance of that.

Places like this made Dante nervous. He followed the butler into an opulent, oak-paneled office.

"Would you like something to drink, sir?"

"No. I'm fine, thanks," Dante said, wondering what could be so important that a man would summon him here on the day of his father's funeral.

The butler slipped out, his feet making no sound on the lush blue carpet. Dante frowned and took a seat in a peach silk-covered chair across from the huge oak desk.

The chair was not built for a man of Dante's size. It groaned in protest when he shifted and, fearful that it was about to splinter apart, he stood. The thing probably cost more than he made in a week. Maybe a month. He had no desire to find out.

Dante jingled the change in his pocket and studied an abstract painting on the wall. No matter how hard he looked at it, he didn't get it. It looked like two peach circles with a division slash between them. What was so special about that?

The study door swung open and a dark-haired man in a gray Armani suit stepped inside. He extended a manicured hand to Dante.

"Mr. Giovanni," he said. "I appreciate your coming on such short notice."

Dante grasped the hand he offered and nodded awkwardly. "I'm sorry about your father . . ."

A sad smile creased Vandergriff' face. "Yes, me too, but at least he's not in pain anymore." His blue eyes stared at something over Dante's shoulder. "Cancer," he said absently. Suddenly, his gaze snapped back to Dante's face. "I'm sorry.

7

Forgive my lack of manners. Please, have a seat."

Dante bypassed the fragile chair by the desk and took a seat on the leather bench beyond it.

Vandergriff started toward the bar. "Can I get you something to drink?"

"No, thank you."

He paused, nodded, and walked back to his desk. Vandergriff stretched across it and withdrew a manila folder from the top drawer. He handed it to Dante, then perched on the edge of his desk to watch Dante open it.

"That's Nadia." Vandergriff pointed. "I want you to bring her to me."

Idly, Dante thumbed through the surveillance photos. The poor quality of the black and whites couldn't disguise the girl's beauty. Dante guessed her to be a little younger than himself, probably in her early twenties, with a lithe, athletic body she obviously liked to show off. In all the photos, she wore tank tops and short skirts.

But to be fair, it was summer, and a brutal one at that.

She had light eyes of some indeterminate color that were somehow shocking when framed against her dark hair. In short, she looked nothing like his usual quarry.

Dante closed the folder and held it out to Vandergriff. "I believe there's been a misunderstanding. I'm a bounty hunter, not a procurer of mail order brides, Mr. Vandergriff."

"I know who you are." Vandergriff gave him a thin smile. He raked a hand through his brown hair and it fell perfectly back in place. "I know you're the best and I need the best for this job. I'm prepared to offer you half a million dollars, plus expenses, if you can bring her to me unharmed."

Dante blinked. With that much cash, he could set up the private investigation firm he'd been dreaming of and get out of the bounty hunting business for good. But Dante wasn't the type of man to jump into something like this without knowing all the facts, a trait which had probably saved his life a time or two.

Vandergriff made no effort to accept the file Dante was trying to hand him, so Dante dropped it back in his lap. "I'm not sure I understand . . . why can't your men handle this? I saw them outside. They look capable enough. Surely this one girl can't be that hard to bring in."

Vandergriff shook his head. "You'd be surprised. The man who's threatening her did try a couple of months ago. Two of his men died. Nick Branson employs some very adept bodyguards."

"Who is she, and what do you want with her?" Dante was curious now, could already feel his blood pumping. His adrenaline addiction was going to get him killed one of these days.

Vandergriff sighed. "She's my daughter, and her life is in danger." He stared at the folder on Dante's lap and cleared his throat. "I haven't seen Nadia since she was a baby, but I can't sit by and let her die because someone wants to get back at Nick Branson."

"Who is Nick Branson?"

"When Nadia was a baby, my wife ran off with Branson." He gave Dante a cynical smile. "He was my chief of security here. What is it they say about the fox guarding the hen house?"

Dante ignored that, lost in his own thoughts. "You're a powerful man, Mr. Vandergriff. Why didn't you fight for your daughter?"

"Things were different then. The business was just starting out, and I didn't have the resources I have now. I was foolish enough to think it was simply a fling, that Maria would come back if I only let her have her space. She didn't, and they disappeared. By the time I finally tracked them down to that little hole-in-the wall in Tennessee, I'd lost my daughter."

Vandergriff's face was expressionless, but when he spoke next, his voice trembled with frustration. "For all I know, she thinks Branson is her father. She has his name. You don't know what it's like, to have your only child stolen from you, to have another man strip every trace of you from her life and not even let her keep your name."

Dante stiffened.

Was this some kind of game? Did this man know about Lara?

Vandergriff looked oblivious.

"Nick Branson has a lucrative business shipping illegal aliens from Mexico to work on area tobacco farms, and recently he's branched out into the drug business. Mexican meth, they call it. My sources say that he's involved in a turf war with a drug lord named Diego Cortez. Cortez has specifically threatened the lives of Nadia and my ex-wife if Branson doesn't close shop immediately."

Dante flexed his fingers. "You don't think Branson can handle the situation?"

Vandergriff met his gaze. "I'm more afraid for Nadia in his hands than in the drug lord's." He walked around his desk and pulled out a silver framed photo. He handed it to Dante and said, "Our wedding picture."

Dante looked it over. Vandergriff's ex-wife was lovely. Her daughter resembled her a great deal. But Dante didn't see what that had to do with anything.

Then Vandergriff handed him another photo from his desk drawer.

Involuntarily, Dante withdrew. It was hard to reconcile the fact that he was looking at the same face from the wedding photo. Thick, ropy burn scars marred one side of the woman's face, leaving a countenance that was both strikingly beautiful and tragic.

Vandergriff studied Dante with bright blue eyes. "Branson did that to her, just a few years after they married. I heard that she was trying to leave him. He threw acid in her face. I can't trust a man like him to protect a child that isn't even his."

Dante stared at the photo for a long moment. Finally, he cleared his throat. "I need a couple of days to check out your story. I'm very selective about the jobs I take," Dante said, but he knew already that he would do it if he found no discrepancies in Vandergriff's story.

It was a case that struck close to home.

"Don't take too long, Mr. Giovanni," Gary Vandergriff said quietly. "My daughter's life depends on you."

● ● ●

Back at the office, Dante sat behind his scarred desk, flipped open the folder Vandergriff had insisted he take with him, and studied the pictures of his beautiful target. Extracting the top one, a body shot, he propped his boots on the desk and leaned back in his chair to examine it. The longer he stared at her, the longer he wanted to. He found himself wishing the photos were in color, just so he could tell if her eyes were green like her mother's, or blue like Vandergriff's.

He typically favored tall, curvy blondes. This girl wasn't any of those things, but there was something about her that mesmerized him. Her body was tanned, toned, and athletic. She looked good in a mini-skirt, and he was willing to bet she looked even better in nothing at all. Although he knew he could never take it that far—never mix business and pleasure—he wanted to see her face to face. Wanted to see if the mischief in her eyes was real or just for show.

Man, he wanted to take this case.

The copy room door opened, tearing him from his thoughts. His research man, Harry Sanders, strolled in toting a stack of files.

"You wanted to see me, Boss?"

"Yeah, grab a seat."

Sanders tossed the files on Dante's desk, glanced at the open folder and whistled.

"Wowsa! Who is that?"

Dante smiled. "Potential bounty."

Harry pulled out a chair and twisted it around. Straddling it, he picked up one of the photos. "What did she do? I hope it has something to do with taking advantage of middle-aged men, because I'll be happy to volunteer as bait."

Dante dropped the body shot in his lap and laced his hands behind his head. "She didn't do anything. If the client's story is true, she's a bystander caught in the middle of her stepfather's war."

Sanders raised an eyebrow. "Beautiful *and* innocent? What's wrong with this scenario?"

Dante laughed. "Tell me about it. I'm used to dealing with thugs like Red Davenport and Johnny Fortenay—"

"Don't forget Bones Malone," Sanders added with a smirk.

Dante snorted. "I thought we agreed never to mention that name in here again. I've seen enough of that scrawny little punk to do me a lifetime."

Abraham "Bones" Malone had been his most recent—and most annoying—case. Dante had chased him from Times Square to Tijuana, and finally caught up with him after Bones was incarcerated in a Mexican jail. After a couple of nights in the company of his unconventional captors, Bones had begged Dante to bail him out. Dante had been so aggravated by that point, he'd made him spend an extra night in the hole before he paid Bones' fine and took him back to the States.

After nearly a month of chasing Bones halfway through the country, through every seedy apartment building and snake pit biker bar along the way, Dante had felt like taking a two week vacation to Bora Bora.

But unfortunately, there were bills to pay. He'd gotten behind schedule after wasting all that time on Bones. This Branson girl assignment felt like a gift from the gods. Here was this rich dude, offering him more money that he'd made all year long, just to bring in some little princess. And she was gorgeous. Man, was she gorgeous. It didn't get any better that this. The assignment would be a piece of cake. A working vacation.

Sometimes, life was good.

"Earth to boss, come in, boss," Sanders said, waving his hand back and forth like a teenager at a Bon Jovi concert.

"Uh, sorry about that," Dante said. "I was just thinking."

Sanders tapped Nadia's picture and grinned. "Yeah, and I know what you're thinking, because I'm thinking it too."

Dante laughed and swung his feet to the floor. Grabbing a pen from the chipped coffee mug he kept them in, Dante scrawled a list of names on a Post-It note.

"Check these people out for me, would you, Sanders? I

want to know everything about them, and their connection to each other. What they do, where they live . . . anything you can get me."

"Will do, Boss." Sanders accepted the note. "When do you need this? I'm working on that Milburn case you gave me—"

"The Milburn case can wait. Make this one top priority." Dante's smile faded. "Her father thinks she's in danger. If that's true, I have to get to her and get her out of there as soon possible."

Sanders nodded and stood to go. Dante waited until the door shut behind him to pick up the photograph again. He carefully placed it and the one Sanders had been ogling back in the folder. His gaze lingered on a close-up of her face.

Suddenly, he found himself thinking of Nadia Branson not as a woman, not as a case, but as a daughter. Gary Vandergriff's daughter.

"Are you really in danger, princess?" Dante murmured.

He closed his eyes, remembering all the things Vandergriff had told him, the look of frustration in his eyes . . .

Dante knew all about that frustration, that feeling of helplessness. He lived with it every day.

He closed the folder and picked up the phone. After a moment's hesitation, he punched in *67 to block his phone number. Doing that always made him feel guilty, like he was some punk kid making prank phone calls, and it was compounded by the fact that he had no intention of speaking with anyone on the other end of the line. But he figured there was no harm done. He only called once a month, and always in the middle of the day when he was sure no one was home and he never left a message.

The answering machine picked up on the third ring. They hadn't changed the message in nearly two years, and for his part he hoped they never did.

It started with a giggle. Dante smiled and held the phone tighter when Lara's sweet little girl voice came on the line.

"This is the O'Connor residence," she began. "We are un . . . un . . ."

When he listened hard enough, he could hear Sharon coaching her in the background.

". . . unavailable to take your call. Please leave your name and number, and we'll—"

"Hello?" a woman said breathlessly.

Dante yanked the phone away from his ear and stared at it.

"Hello, is anyone there?"

He quickly disconnected the call, his heart thumping in his chest.

What was Sharon doing home in the middle of the day? Was something wrong with her? Maybe Lara was sick . . .

The hell of it was, there was no way to know. No one he could ask. He pictured his future and wondered if, years from now, he'd still be sitting in this dump, propped up behind this battered desk and making pathetic phone calls to his ex-wife's answering machine because that was the only way he had of hearing his daughter's voice.

Yeah, Gary Vandergriff didn't have to tell him a thing about frustration. How much worse it had to be when you thought your child was in danger and there wasn't anything you could do to help her?

But there *was* something he could do. He could make sure Vandergriff's daughter was safe, even if he had no way of knowing the same about his own child.

Dante grabbed the file and headed back to his apartment. When Sanders called him a couple of hours later and confirmed the details of Vandergriff's story, Dante already had his bag packed. After they finished talking, he asked Sanders to transfer him to his secretary.

"Nancy, hi . . . I'm going out of town. If you need me, you can reach me by cell. Hopefully, I'll be back in a couple of days."

"May I ask where you're going?"

"I'm driving to Tennessee. I'm taking the Vandergriff case."

He took one last look at the Nadia Branson file, though he knew the information and her face by heart now. He stood over his kitchen sink and, with a flick of his lighter, lit the edge of the manila folder.

It seemed a shame to burn such beautiful photographs, but he knew that within the next few days he might be under a lot of scrutiny. Who knew how far Nadia's stepfather would go to check him out?

With any luck, he would get in there and take Nadia before Nick Branson knew what was happening. But if that wasn't possible, he had a cover story ready. He'd get her one way or another. He picked up the phone to call Vandergriff. The man seemed ecstatic when Dante told him he was taking the case. Dante asked a few more questions, then threw his bag over his shoulder and headed out.

Piece of cake, he thought again, and locked the door behind him.

● ● ●

Friday August 5
4:12 p.m.

Dante strode into the diner, ignoring the stares of the other patrons. A man of his size was guaranteed a certain amount of attention, even without the shaven head and tattoos.

Especially in a town like Sewanee, Tennessee.

He scanned the room before removing his sunglasses, then pulled up a stool at the counter. He noticed Nadia immediately; it would take a blind man not to. She was even more of a knockout than her pictures suggested.

She sat in a corner booth with another girl and two boys who could've been pinups in a teen magazine. He felt her gaze on him as the waitress handed him a menu.

Dante allowed himself a glance at her, and nodded when

their eyes met.

Another little rich girl trying not to look rich in her tight, faded jeans and purple tank top.

His body tensed in awareness of her, though he tried to act casual. Maybe she was attracted to him, too, because she was still staring.

When the waitress returned, Dante ordered the Hungry Man special and carried his coffee over to the ancient jukebox in the corner.

A ceiling fan with a missing blade beat above his head with a dull whup-whup-whup, stirring the warm air. It carried Nadia's scent when she slipped up behind him. The spicy, oriental fragrance of her perfume tickled his nose and stirred his libido.

"R 20," she said, and he caught a flash of silky black hair in his peripheral vision as she leaned against the jukebox. "That's my favorite song."

Wordlessly, Dante punched the number in. Her voice was huskier than he'd imagined it would be, the kind of voice that made a man's thoughts wander.

Amazingly, it was a song he liked.

He glanced at her and she smiled, white teeth flashing against tan skin.

Damn, but she was flawless.

Looking at her was a little like looking into the sun, and Dante Giovanni, lady killer extraordinaire, found it suddenly hard to breathe. Her eyes were green, the palest green he'd ever seen, and he could bet she knew full well the effect those eyes had on a man.

"Where are you from?" she asked, while she fiddled with the strap on her tank top.

Though it took every ounce of his concentration to keep his voice neutral, Dante said, "Not interested."

"What?" She looked taken aback, obviously not used to hearing those words.

"I'm not interested in little girls."

Instead of the anger he expected, she looked amused. The corner of her mouth quirked and Dante had to tear his gaze from those full lips.

"I'm no girl."

"Let me rephrase . . ." By an act of sheer will, he forced his eyes back to the jukebox. "I'm not interested in little princesses. Go back to your pretty boys over there before they start to cry, or break into some top 40 song or something. You're not ready for a real man, princess."

She chuckled—a deep, throaty sound that made the hair on his arms prickle. Suddenly, his mind revolted, shattering the coolness he was trying to project, when he pictured her beneath him in bed and wondered how she'd sound, screaming out his name.

"Ah, you know a real man you could hook me up with?"

Dante sipped his coffee, hiding his grin behind the cup. He'd always had a weakness for smart-mouthed women.

A shiver of warning raced through him, both hot and

cold, and he wondered if he was getting in over his head.

When he leaned down to punch in another selection, she slid in close. Her hair dusted his shoulder and her warm breath tickled his ear when she whispered, "You presume too much, Slick. If I wanted you, I could have you. I always get what I want."

A shot of pure electricity jolted Dante when she gently caught his earlobe between her teeth. She laughed and turned away, leaving him with only the fleeting sensation of the warmth of her mouth and a faint tingle in his earlobe when she sauntered back to her table.

As if she controlled his head by remote control, it swiveled to watch her walk away.

Dante's heart slammed in his chest. So much for playing it cool.

Damned if he wasn't *shaking*.

He stared at the faded, frayed waistband of her low-rise jeans and the tattoo that peeked over the top of it.

Wild Child

He wondered if it was real.

Taking a deep breath, he punched in one more song and, even though he'd already put in his money's worth, he pretended to look over the other selections, because he didn't trust himself to walk.

Keep it cool, he told himself. *She's just another little rich girl. You can't be thinking like this.*

He forced himself to calm down and strolled back to the

21

counter, where the waitress was setting his plate down.

Hungry man special. Right.

A puny pork chop, two eggs, a couple of biscuits and some mysterious white stuff the waitress called gravy.

"I'll be needing another one of these, and you can hold the gravy," he told her.

She laughed and raised her eyebrows.

"What?" He smiled. "I'm a growing boy."

The princess was over by her table, dancing in her bare feet with one of her boy-toys. To a song that he'd paid to hear. For some reason, the thought irked him. Then he caught a fleeting glance from her and almost smiled.

She was putting on a show for his benefit. Dante tried to force his attention back to his plate.

The bell above the door tinkled and he looked at the noisy group coming through the door. Farm workers, judging by their faded jeans, flannel shirts and boots. Three whites and a couple of Mexicans.

After seating them at a table to Dante's right, the waitress poured their coffee and took their orders. One of the workers, a big, hayseed-looking blond, ambled over to the counter. He tapped Dante on the shoulder.

"Can I borrow that creamer, man?" he asked.

"Sure." Dante held out the brown container.

"Appreciate it." The blond grinned.

When he reached for it, Dante noticed his hands. They were too clean and too soft looking. His nails looked like he'd just had a manicure.

Definitely not farm worker hands.

Dante had learned to trust his instincts, and they were screaming that this was all wrong. Something was about to go down.

He glanced at the girl. She stood, tucking her purse under her arm and slipping on her shades.

Getting ready to leave.

The workers stared at her when she walked by their table.

Who wouldn't? Dante thought, but his nerves were jumping.

Now he was noticing more. The tense way the men held themselves, the baggy outer shirts they wore over their T-shirts . . .

All the better to conceal weapons with, my dear.

Dante gauged the distance between himself and Nadia, wondering if he could get to her in time.

She caught his stare and blew him a kiss. "See ya later, slick."

"See ya, princess," he replied, but his mouth was dry. The workers glanced at him and he turned his head, pretending not to notice.

As soon as the door swung shut, three of the men jumped up and headed out the door. They were going after her.

Dante got up and headed the other way, toward the bathroom. At the last moment, he pushed through the swinging doors into the steamy kitchen.

The lone cook had his back turned to him. He was yelling into the phone and scribbling something on a notepad and never even looked around. Dante strolled through the kitchen and casually picked up a heavy, wooden-handled skillet full of gravy on his way out.

He strode outside and waited.

When Dante saw the blond head of the farm worker peek around the corner, he swung. The big blond screamed, crashed to his knees and wiped frantically at the steaming mess on his face. While his partner gaped at him, Dante spun and kicked the gun from his hand. Grabbing the man by the collar, Dante slammed him against the side of the building, once, twice, until he slid to the ground, unconscious.

With those two incapacitated for the moment, Dante ran around to the front of the diner, jumped into his car and took off after Nadia. Roaring out of the parking lot, he saw a red-headed man slumped over the steering wheel of a gray sedan.

The narrow country road twisted like a snake, but Dante floored it, looking for any sign of the girl. He followed a cloud of dust and what he saw up ahead made his stomach clench.

A little red sports car lay on its side off an embankment. A Suburban he assumed belonged to her pursuers was parked haphazardly on the hillside. Dante didn't see any movement anywhere.

He left his car idling on the road and scrambled down to the sports car, his gun drawn. Her three companions crouched in the backseat. One of the boy-toys screamed when he saw Dante's gun.

"Where is she?" Dante shouted.

Nobody answered.

"I'm here to help her," he said.

"She's not here!" A girl lifted her head high enough to peek out the window and point toward a section of the forest. "She took off running in that direction and those guys chased after her."

Dante scanned the tree line and saw nothing. He checked the clip in his gun. "Are you guys okay?"

"We're fine. Go help Nadia," the girl said. "I've already called the police on my cell. They're on their way."

Nadia.

Her name beat a refrain in his head while Dante slid downhill and sprinted toward the trees. The moment he plunged into the forest, a round of gunfire blasted through the quiet. He skidded to a stop, his heart sinking. Although he'd only spoken a few words with Nadia, she had already made an impression on him. The thought of her dying in the woods at the hand of some goon filled him with rage.

With his pulse pounding in his ears, Dante ran toward the sound, scared of what he would find waiting.

When he drew close, Dante saw something that made him check up in confusion. Two men burst through the trees to his left, fleeing uphill in the direction of the Suburban, and another lay writhing on the dark forest floor, clutching his leg. Before Dante could fully process what he was seeing, he heard the unmistakable click of a safety. He slowly raised his hands when a warm barrel jabbed against the base of his skull.

"You've got three seconds, Slick, to drop your gun and tell me who you work for, or I'm going to see what the inside of that lovely bald head looks like."

Nadia.

Dante's relief was so great that he dropped his hands.

She nudged him hard with the barrel. "Hey, I didn't say Simon says! Put those hands back up."

Dante did, glad she couldn't see his grin.

She sounded awfully mad.

"Hey, princess, I'm not working for anybody. I saw those guys rush out of the diner after you, and I figured you might need a knight in shining armor."

She grabbed his gun and said, "Yeah, well, you ain't exactly Prince Charming and I'm no damsel in distress. Turn around . . . slowly!"

Dante laced his fingers across the back of his head and turned to face her. His humor died when he saw the blood streaming down the side of her face.

"Hey! Are you okay?" He dropped his hands, ignoring her gun while he examined her head.

Surprisingly, she didn't shoot him.

"I banged my head in the car, but it'll be okay." She glanced at Dante and lifted her eyebrows. "I thought you weren't interested in little princesses."

He laughed. "Well, let's just say you got my attention."

He tugged his black tank top over his head.

"Holy pectorals, Batman," Nadia said.

She stared at his chest with such unabashed admiration that Dante's groin tightened and heat crept up his neck. Mottled sunlight shone through the trees, bathing one side of her face in a golden hue. One pale green eye glowed up at him like a jungle cat's.

Swallowing hard, Dante tore his gaze from her face and concentrated on the cut on her head.

"You talk all the time, princess?" he asked, using the shirt to gently scrub the blood from the side of her face.

"Yeah. My mother said I started talking at eighteen months and never shut up. Do you think I'm going to need stitches?"

"Maybe a few." He pressed his shirt to the wound. "But I don't really think it's too bad."

They were standing too close. Her warm breath stole across his bare chest, making his nipples tighten. She was so tiny. At 6'2", he was a full foot taller than she was, but Dante knew that only a fool would underestimate the woman staring up at him.

A bullet whizzed by, exploding into the tree behind them.

Dante threw Nadia to the ground, ignoring the root that jabbed painfully at his knee as he attempted to shield her with his body. Nadia pressed his .38 back in his hand, and his fingers closed around the grip.

"When I say 'go', you run for that tree," he whispered in her ear, and pointed at a thick oak a few yards in front of them.

Nadia nodded, and it surprised Dante that—even with bullets flying around them—he was conscious of the way her agile body felt under his.

Nadia shifted beneath him, breaking his thoughts.

"Go!" he shouted.

Dante fired a volley of shots into the area he'd last seen the gunman, trying to provide cover while Nadia scrambled for the tree.

He heard a muffled shout when one of his shots hit home, and he was reaching into the pocket of his black cargos for another clip when movement rattled the bushes on his right. A flash of blond hair appeared through the foliage and Nadia opened fire. Dante scurried toward her, keeping his head down.

"Where did they come from?" she asked, while he popped the clip into his gun.

"Those are the other two clowns from the diner. We've got to get out of here, before reinforcements arrive."

"Follow me," she said, and charged into the thick underbrush before Dante could protest. He fired another round in the blond's direction and took off in pursuit. Branches slapped at him, briars tore at his skin, and tree roots appeared out of nowhere to trip him. Dante lost sight of her in the thicket, and paused, disoriented.

Her hand appeared magically through the bushes and tugged at his wrist.

"Come on!" she yelled, then was gone.

She ran, fleet-footed as a deer, and it was all he could do to keep up with her. They emerged at the road several moments later.

Dante squinted in the sudden burst of sunlight when they ran across the highway. Heat beat down on his back and the thick, oily smell of hot asphalt made his stomach churn when they doubled back to his car.

Nadia threw herself into his passenger seat, laughing.

Dante blinked at her. Her green eyes sparkled with excitement, and at that moment, he knew he'd never seen anything more beautiful, even though her head was bleeding again and her dark hair was a wild tangle around her face.

"That was great!" she said, then impulsively threw her arms around his neck.

Dante wasn't ready for the kiss, or for the sweet taste of her mouth, but his arms encircled her, pushing her back against the hot leather seat as her tongue teased his.

Her breath came hard and fast, but he didn't think his was coming at all. Her skin was hot and slick, and the scent of her perfume had grown darker, more exotic as it mingled with her sweat.

Suddenly, her hands were at his chest, pushing him away. "My friends . . ." she said. "I have to see if they're okay."

Almost in response, sirens wailed in the distance. It broke through the fog she'd created in his brain. Dante shook it off and slammed the car in reverse, squealing tires when he headed off in the other direction.

"They're okay, princess, but you and I had better get out of here. I don't know how far behind Blondie is, or where the others are, so I want to make sure you're safe before we talk to the police."

She nodded, then popped open his glove compartment and rummaged through it until she found a handful of fast food napkins. Wadding them up, she pressed them against her streaming head.

"Whew, Slick, you sure are an exciting date!"

"Don't call me Slick."

"Don't call me Princess," she countered, and Dante laughed.

Some of the tension that knotted his gut relaxed. "What? It's a term of endearment," he protested.

"Yeah, well . . . it's not endearing," she replied, but she was smiling.

"I'm surprised the blond was moving," Dante said absently, while he checked the rearview mirror again. "After I hit him with that gravy."

"Pardon?" Nadia shot him a baffled look. "Did you say you hit him with . . . gravy?"

"Yeah, a whole skillet of it."

Nadia laughed.

He grinned at her and said, "Mama told me not to waste my food, and I sure wasn't going to eat that stuff."

She shook her head. "You're a nut."

"You're probably right," he conceded.

If the urge he felt to pull to the side of the road and take her in his arms was any indication, she was most definitely right.

She leaned forward to pull a cocklebur off the leg of her jeans and smiled when she caught him peeking down the front of her shirt. "Keep you eyes on the road, pal. You wouldn't want to wreck this bitchin' car. What kind is it, anyway?"

"A 1967 GTO. I'm glad you like it."

Dante reached a stop sign, and Nadia said, "Turn left. Take me to my father." She gave him a faint smile. "He's probably going ballistic by now. Flat Branch Road is a little over five miles away. Take another left when you see the sign."

She leaned back against the headrest and squinted at him. "You know, you haven't asked me why these men are trying to kill me. I find that a little strange."

Dante shrugged. "I figured you'd tell me when you had a chance. We haven't had much time for conversation, you know. Besides, whatever you've done to them, I didn't think the odds were fair." He grinned. "But it seems maybe I was wrong about that."

Nadia ignored his attempt at humor. "I haven't done anything to them," she said, bristling. "They want to get to Nick, my father. The easiest way to do that is through me."

"And he lets you walk around in the open?" Dante pretended not to notice the sharp look she shot him.

"He doesn't *let* me do anything," she snapped. "I come and go as I please. I'm a grown woman, in case you didn't notice."

Dante lifted his eyebrows and rubbed the back of his

neck with one hand. "Oh, yeah. I definitely noticed."

Nadia made a hrmmph sound in the back of her throat, but her frown relaxed. That killer smile fought its way back to the surface.

Ruefully, she said, "If Nick had his way, I'd be locked up in a nunnery somewhere."

"That would be a shame," Dante said solemnly.

Nadia punched his shoulder and laughed. Then she shook her head. "I guess I give him a hard time, but he doesn't understand that if I hide away like some scared little mouse, then this man is still taking my life."

"Why is he after your father?"

A veil slipped over Nadia's face.

"It's personal," she said, and made a show of looking through Dante's CDs. He could guess from the stubborn look on her face that she was through talking about it.

She stared at the floorboard, then said, "Fred, Jack . . . Mortimer?"

Dante frowned. "Excuse me?"

"Your name. You said I can't call you Slick, so you need to tell me something."

"My name is Dante."

"I'm Nadia. Nadia Branson. Hey, you missed the turn-off!"

Before Dante had a chance to respond, he saw them.

They came out of nowhere, surrounding them like a swarm of bees. A black Humvee, two four-wheel drives, a motorcycle

. . . and they were not the police.

A Ford Bronco pulled alongside them, and a man with a bullhorn shouted through the window, "Pull to the side of the road, turn off the ignition, and step out of the car with your hands in the air!"

Dante glanced at Nadia, but she stared straight through him with an unreadable expression on her face.

"Do as he says, Dante," she said calmly.

CHAPTER 2

Nadia swung out of the car before Dante could stop her. He climbed out slowly, raising his hands over his head. A burly redhead in a Tennessee Volunteers T-shirt shoved Dante against the side of the car. The hot glass of the window burned his bare stomach as the man frisked him.

"Geez, Waynie. No wonder I can't keep a boyfriend," Nadia complained when he emptied Dante's .38.

Dante jerked his head around to look at her and earned himself another rough shove from Waynie. Nadia shrugged and shot him an apologetic smile. Dante felt a rush of relief. They were Branson's men.

"Nadia, are you okay?" the big man asked.

"Yeah, I'm having an epic bad hair day, though, and I'd kill for a cigarette. Please tell me you have one."

"Huh uh," Dante heard a deep male voice say. "I don't think so. A bet's a bet, girl. You don't want a reputation as a welcher, do you?"

"No, Mother," Nadia said dutifully.

She winked at Dante and hopped onto the hood of his car.

"Lord knows her reputation is bad enough as it is," Waynie cracked, and Nadia administered a swift kick to his ample behind.

"Hey, Waynie, come on . . . are you going to let Dante up or not?" she asked. "He helped me get out of Dodge back there."

The big man backed off, and Dante turned to face him.

"You were kind of right about the princess thing," she admitted, and made a sweeping gesture with her hand. "Meet the royal guard. They mean well, but they watch way too many guy flicks at the Multiplex."

Six pairs of eyes bored into Dante before a dark-haired man stepped forward. Something about him looked familiar—the way he stood, the shape of his blue eyes—but Dante couldn't quite place him.

"I'm Ronnie McNamara," he said, extending his hand. "Really, we're more like big brothers trying to keep our bratty little sister out of trouble. Believe me, it's not easy with this girl."

"Dante Giovanni. And I can imagine." He shook the man's hand.

Ronnie held onto his hand for a second too long, then twisted Dante's wrist around to peer at his forearm. "Marines?" he asked, pointing at the tattoo.

"Yeah, I was in the 312th platoon. Alpha squad."

"Great!" Nadia said. "I've been looking for a few good men."

Dante grinned at her and saw that someone had snuck her a cigarette. She held it up for Waynie to light.

Ronnie never missed a beat. Grabbing it out of her fingers, he said, "No bull? My brother James MacNamara was in 312th too. Bravo squad."

"Hey, no kidding!" Dante said, recognition finally dawning. "I knew Jimmy MacNamara. He was a great guy, the most hilarious drunk in the world. He would get up and do the karaoke thing at the bar we used to go to near base."

Ignoring Nadia's protests, Ronnie broke the cigarette in half and tossed it over his shoulder. Rolling his eyes at Dante, he said, "Yeah, that sounds like the moron, all right. Do you believe he's a suit in Texas now? Military defense."

"You've got to be joking!" Dante laughed, then shook his head. "Jimmy MacNamara, a suit. Now that's hard to imagine." He pointed at the Humvee and said, "Hey, man, can I check out your ride? I love those things."

"Sure. That's my baby. I call her The Black Beast." Ronnie motioned for Dante to follow him. Nadia scowled and hopped off the hood.

Dante grinned when he heard her whisper, "Give me another one."

"Anybody gives her a cancer stick and I break his face," Ronnie said, not looking back.

Dante brushed his fingers against the door handle and peered into the gleaming black interior. "Aw, man, I'm in love. Are these things built or what? Sleek, powerful, gorgeous."

"Now I'm insulted."

Nadia leaned against front fender, her bottom lip jutting out in a way Dante found sexy as hell. When she crossed her arms over her chest, the purple strap of her tank top slipped off one tan shoulder.

"Why is it you guys have nicer things to say about vehicles than you do women?" she asked.

"Because the Hummer doesn't talk back, it doesn't get jealous if I look at other vehicles and it only takes one flick of the switch to turn it on." Ronnie grinned at Nadia and stuck out his tongue.

She rolled her eyes. "See, Ronnie, that mentality is the reason you can't get a date on Saturday nights."

"So, what's your excuse?" he shouted, and darted around the back of the vehicle before Nadia could respond.

Dante laughed. Nadia shot him a peeved look, but it gave way to a smile when he hooked his thumb under the fallen strap of her tank top and tugged it back up.

Resting his hand on her shoulder, he said, "You don't have to be jealous of anything, princess. You're as sleek, gorgeous, and powerful as it gets. You handled yourself well back there."

She gave him an uncertain smile, and Ronnie peeked back around the rear of the vehicle to see if it was safe. Seemingly satisfied Nadia wasn't going to attack him, he said, "C'mon, Dante. You can ride back to the Branson estate with us in the Humvee. I'll get one of the guys to follow behind in your car."

"I don't know, man," Dante said.

"Come on." Ronnie pushed a wave of sweaty brown hair out of his face. "It's hot as hell out here. At least have a beer with us or something. Mr. B will want to meet you."

"Yes, come with us." Nadia slipped her hand inside his. Her fingers were surprisingly cool, and when he stared down into those green eyes, Dante doubted he could've refused her anything at the moment.

He helped her into the passenger seat of the Humvee and crawled in beside her. She sat close to him, so close that her long hair tickled his bare chest. That tickling intensified when Nadia turned the air conditioner up full blast.

"Ahh, that feels so good," she said, closing her eyes.

A few moments later, she opened them and smiled up at him. A horrified Dante realized his hand was in her hair. Touching her was instinctive, and that scared him more than any gun pointed at his head.

"Now you're the one who's bleeding," she said, staring at his chest.

He looked down in surprise. A row of scratches criss-crossed his skin. Magically, they began to sting.

"They didn't hurt until you said that," he groused.

"Sorry."

He winced when she dug an embedded briar out with her bright red nails.

"Oops. Sorry again."

"Where you from?" Ronnie asked, then held up a hand. "No, wait. Let me guess. I know that accent. Queens, right?"

Dante smiled. "The Bronx."

"I'm from Riverdale."

They talked about the old neighborhoods while Ronnie turned down a narrow gravel road. Dante was checking out Nadia's head wound again when Ronnie groaned.

"Aw, crap. Anderson's working," he muttered.

They rolled to a stop at a huge black gate where an armed guard peered at them through the windshield. He tapped on Ronnie's window.

With a sigh, Ronnie lowered it.

The guard gestured at Dante. "Who's that guy?"

"A friend of Nadia's. He's okay."

"Is he on the list?"

Ronnie tapped his hand on the steering wheel. "No, but I think Mr. B will be interested in meeting the guy who helped Nadia escape back there."

"If he's armed, he needs to check his weapon here."

"Waynie dumped it. I saw him."

"I still need the gun," Anderson said.

Rolling his eyes, Ronnie turned to Dante.

"I don't have it," he said. "Waynie took it."

"Are you sure he's not carrying another piece?" the guard asked. "Maybe I should search him again. No telling what Waynie missed."

"No telling," Nadia agreed. "I think maybe we should

strip search him."

Ronnie snorted. "Spare us your twisted fantasies." Then he leaned out the window and whined, "C'mon, Anderson. Are you gonna open the gate or what? Mr. B's probably going insane right now."

The guard shook his head. "Sorry, not on my watch. I have to search him."

Ronnie dropped his head against the wheel in exasperation, making the horn bleat like a sick lamb.

"It's okay." Dante said with a resigned smile. "I've got nothing to hide."

He climbed out of the Humvee, spread his legs and laced his fingers behind his head.

"Hey!" Nadia said brightly. "You're a natural. Have you done this before?"

Dante made a sour face. "Yeah, about five minutes ago."

He jumped when Anderson got a little *too* thorough.

"Watch it, Chief," he warned, and Nadia giggled. She rolled down the window and leaned halfway out the Humvee to watch.

Cupping a hand to her mouth, she called, "Hey, Anderson. You need any help, you just holler."

Anderson yelped and seized the lower right pocket of Dante's cargo pants.

"Phone. Don't shoot, it's only a phone," Dante said quickly, earning another of Nadia's throaty laughs.

Finally, Anderson seemed satisfied. He motioned Dante

toward the Humvee, then buzzed the gate open after Dante climbed back inside. Glancing over his shoulder, Dante saw Waynie roll up behind them in his GTO. He chuckled when Anderson stepped in front of the car, preventing Waynie from passing through, and twisted around to watch the two men argue.

"Anderson is half bloodhound," Nadia commented. "None of my college friends like to visit when he's on duty, but he's good at what he does. Anybody he doesn't know would have to shoot him to get by him."

Ronnie grunted. "It's hard getting by that guy if he does know you. I've been tempted to shoot him myself a time or two." He adjusted the rearview mirror and eased up the winding asphalt drive.

Dante spotted electronic surveillance cameras hanging at various intervals on the utility poles and gate. The place was locked down tight. Maybe this wasn't going to be as simple as he thought.

He chatted with Ronnie, recalling what he could about the brother who resembled him so much while trying not to notice the heat from Nadia's skin as her bare arm rested against his chest.

His first view of the Branson estate took his breath away. Dante definitely hadn't expected to see digs like this in Tennessee. The sprawling estate sat atop a lush green hill. All around, the only breaks in the skyline were the hulking, blue-green outlines of the taller mountains. It looked like one of the expensive ski resorts he and his brother J.T. had always talked about going to but never had.

A mountain hideaway.

Built from rough-looking red cedar, the outside looked both rustic and inviting. The only sign of movement was the porch swing that swayed lazily in the afternoon breeze. Another expansive house—a long, single story made from the same red cedar— sat to the right.

Probably the men's barracks.

"What were you expecting, house trailers and outhouses?" Nadia asked, watching his face. "You know, you really shouldn't believe everything you see on television. We're modern hillbillies, running water and everything."

"I don't really know what I was expecting, but . . . wow," Dante said. "This place is incredible."

When they pulled up to the main house, a small, dark-haired man in a charcoal suit exploded out the front door and leapt down the steps.

"Nadia!" he shouted, not seeming to notice the bare-chested stranger who caught her by the waist and helped her out of the vehicle.

He seized Nadia in his arms and she brushed a kiss on her stepfather's cheek. "I'm okay, Nick." With a wink at Dante, she said, "Except you're squeezing too hard. Can't . . . breathe."

Branson released her and peered at her face. "Your head—" He groaned, and reached to examine the gash.

"—is fine," she said. "Really, it's only a bump. Ronnie

will fix it right up for me."

Dante was so busy watching them interact that he didn't notice the woman who'd slipped up behind him. Her quiet voice startled him.

"Angie called, honey. She wanted to check on you and to let you know they're all okay."

Even though he'd expected it, Dante felt a jolt when he turned to stare into Maria Branson's face. One side was perfect, flawless, an older version of Nadia's, but the other . . . A striking green eye gazed at him from a wasteland of pink, ropy scars. She ducked her head, and covered most of the scars with a fan of dark hair. In what he was sure was an unconscious gesture, she tilted her chin to present him with the left side her face, the unmarred side.

"Your eyes," he said breathlessly. "You and Nadia have the most beautiful eyes I've ever seen."

Pursing her lips, she raised her chin and stared at him as if putting forth a challenge. Dante didn't look away. Then she smiled, and suddenly looked so much like Nadia that he didn't see the scars.

"Thank you," she said.

Nadia managed to untangle herself from Branson. "I'm glad she called. I had to leave them there and I was worried about them, even though Dante thought they were okay."

"Dante," her mother repeated. "I understand you helped Nadia out. We owe you our gratitude . . ." Her smile widened. ". . . and perhaps a new shirt."

"It's nice to meet you, Mrs. Branson." Dante took the hand she offered him.

"Please, call me Maria."

"Yes, thank you for helping our daughter," Nick Branson said.

Dante shrugged. "Nadia pretty much had everything under control. I only drove the getaway car."

"I imagine you think our little family is . . . odd." Branson smiled, revealing small, even teeth.

Odd isn't the half of it, buddy, Dante thought.

Nadia yelped, saving Dante from a reply.

"Ow! Take it easy there, Ronnie!"

"Be still."

She slapped at the bodyguard's hand as he examined her head. "Some of that's still attached, you know."

"You are such a crybaby," Ronnie said, rolling his eyes.

"I'm surprised the police aren't here already," Dante said.

"There will be no police," Branson said. "I have some contacts on the local level. We'll handle this in-house."

"But the guy in the sedan—"

"He'll be okay. He was knocked unconscious. Someone's taking him to the doctor now."

When Dante said nothing, Branson nodded. "Please, won't you come in, Mr. . . . .?"

"Giovanni. Sure, I'd love to see the inside of this place. It's beautiful."

Dante blinked when he stepped inside. However rustic

the outside looked, the inside was modern. Expensive modern. The first thing he noticed when he entered was the stairway. Back in high school, Dante had briefly entertained the notion of becoming an architect. Pieces like that stairway still made him sigh.

It was straight and wide, a masterpiece of gleaming mahogany rails and red carpeted steps. At the top of it, an oil portrait of a younger, unscarred Maria Branson smiled down at them from a small landing. The true beauty of the staircase lay in its graceful curves from the landing. The steps continued in a gentle slope both to the left and right.

Maria Branson's heels clicked on the gray marble floor while she led them to a sunken den that was roughly half the size of Dante's entire apartment back in New York.

Daylight rapidly faded through the bay window and Branson clicked on several lamps by remote control. The soft light reflected off the glossy surface of the mahogany furniture. Within minutes, Dante was seated in a soft leather chair with a glass of tea in one hand and another shirt in his lap. Maria and Nick Branson sat on one white couch, and Nadia and Ronnie piled onto a loveseat.

Nadia told her version of the story while Ronnie doctored her head. Dante watched the bodyguard rub something onto the cut and carefully shave around it. Ronnie had apparently done this sort of thing before.

"So then, here comes Dante and—dang, Ronnie! Leave me some, will you?" Nadia complained as several strands of black hair fell to the floor. She looked at him and winked. "I don't want to end up looking like Dante over there."

"Then I can call you Slick." Dante smiled and took another sip of tea.

"So, where did you come in?" Branson asked him before Nadia could retort.

"Well, Nadia and I had talked a little at the restaurant. I saw these guys come in, dressed like farm workers, but their hands weren't right. Too clean."

Ronnie nodded. Dante figured he was the type to notice things too. Ronnie applied Dermabond to Nadia's wound.

Branson studied Dante. "That was very observant of you."

Dante caught the suspicion in his voice.

"I get paid to notice things, Mr. Branson."

"Really? What is it that you do?"

"A little here and there. I've been a bouncer, a security guard, then I got into bounty hunting. If you don't notice things in my line of work, you're dead."

Branson studied him with dark, wary eyes. "I see. So, what brings you to our little community? A case?"

"I just wrapped one up. Since I was so close, I thought I'd drive on up to Indiana to see my sister. Maybe take a few days off to go fishing with her old man."

Branson nodded, seeming to accept his story, but Dante knew that before the hour was up, Branson's men would be at work verifying everything he'd said.

"Okay, you're good to go," Ronnie said, and Nadia

pressed her fingers gingerly around the bandage.

Seemingly satisfied that she wasn't bald, she jumped to her feet and said, "Have you guys eaten yet? I'm starving!" She glanced at Dante and frowned. "But you already ate, didn't you? I only had coffee back there at the diner. Lee Ann told me she was making chicken and dumplings to-night, so I didn't want to ruin my appetite." Nadia rubbed her flat stomach.

"I didn't get a chance to finish," Dante said. "And what's a dumpling?"

"What planet are you from, and what the hell do they eat there?"

"Nadia!" her parents said in unison.

Nadia laughed and seized Dante's hand. He let her drag him across the living room, a bit unnerved by the feel of her hand in his. It took him a moment to realize that he was still shirtless. He held up the shirt they'd given him and said, "Hey, can I use your restroom, clean up a little before we eat?"

She smiled patiently. "That's where I'm taking you, you goof. I'm not exactly presentable myself. We'll be right there!" she called over her shoulder to her parents.

They walked past the staircase and she pushed open a thick oak door to reveal a sparkling white half-bath. Dante stepped inside and was startled when she walked in behind him and shut the door.

"Relax." She rolled her eyes. "I'm not going to ravage

you or anything. Well, at least not yet. I thought maybe we should put something on those scratches."

The soft, worn fabric of her jeans strained against her backside when she leaned across the countertop to open a section of the mirrored vanity.

As if his hand moved of its own volition, Dante's fingertips reached to brush the red letters of the tattoo visible over the low band of her pants.

"Wild child," he said slowly.

Nadia froze, and Dante stared at himself in the mirror. Although he saw his reflection, saw the brown eyes that were almost black with desire, he scarcely knew himself. He never lost it like this.

Slowly, deliberately, Nadia raised her head and met his gaze in the glass. Something powerful, something consuming passed between them in that instant, a need so dark it rocked him to the core. Dante hooked his finger in the back loop of her pants and pulled her backward against him.

Nadia gasped when his erection stirred against her bottom, and he thought he saw a flicker of fear in her eyes before she leaned into him. Dante groaned, and she smiled at his reflection.

Unable to tear his gaze from the mirror, Dante gently shoved aside her hair to expose the sleek length of her neck. Finally, he looked down and pressed his lips to her thundering pulse. He lost himself in the sweet, salty taste of her skin. A shudder raced through her body and he held her tighter. A strangled moan rose in her throat.

Dante caressed her arms with his palms, feeling childishly pleased by the goose bumps he found there. The mirror drew his eyes back.

She leaned against him, her head tilted back against his chest. Dante watched the rapid rise and fall of her chest in the glass and then slipped his hands underneath her shirt. Nadia's eyes flew open when he ran his fingers over the smooth, hard plane of her abdomen.

She groaned and shut her eyes again, rocking against him.

"Nadia," he whispered. "Look at me."

Her eyes opened to half slits, watching his hands move beneath her shirt. When he dipped his head to kiss her neck again, she whispered, "I can't . . . I can't do this."

Instantly, Dante dropped his hands and took a step backward. Nadia swayed and stumbled to the door.

Shooting him an apologetic look, she said, "Not here. Not now. My parents . . ."

Swallowing hard, Dante nodded.

Nadia tugged at the hem of her shirt, then yanked the door open and propelled herself out of there.

A little stunned by what had just happened, Dante locked the door behind her and rested his back against it before sliding down to sit on the bathroom floor.

"Get it together," he told himself roughly. "You've got a job to do."

He pulled his cell phone out of his pants pocket, fished

a business card out of his wallet and shakily dialed the number printed on back.

Raking a hand down his face, he said, "This is Giovanni. I'm here."

Gary Vandergriff's anxious voice blasted through the phone and Dante had to hold it a couple of inches from his ear.

"You're inside the Branson estate? Is Nadia okay?"

"She's fine. We were attacked, but we managed to get away unharmed."

"Attacked? What happened?" Vandergriff fairly screeched.

"Some goons ran her off the road. But she's okay, I swear."

"When are you bringing her to me? When do I get to see my daughter?"

Dante stared at the tile floor. "It's not going to be that simple. The security around this place is tight. I'm going to have to make them trust me first."

"You have to hurry!" Vandergriff said. "I can't sit by and let her die because someone wants to get back at Nick Branson."

"I understand. I'll do everything I can."

The line fell silent and Dante was about to hang up when Vandergriff asked, "Did you see my ex-wife?"

Dante frowned. "Yeah, I saw her."

A wave of anger washed over him, hot and black, when he thought of Maria Branson and recalled how small and birdlike her hand had felt in his. Unlike her spunky daughter, she seemed so fragile.

How could a man do that to his wife? What kind of life

did she and Nadia lead?

"Nick Branson is a monster," Vandergriff said. "A cold-hearted, cold-blooded monster. He took everything from me when he stole my wife and baby away to Tennessee. I know things will never be right between Nadia and me, too much time has been lost, but I have to do what I can to protect her. You'd do the same if it was your child, wouldn't you, Mr. Giovanni?"

Dante flipped open the worn brown wallet and smoothed his thumb over the plastic screen that protected Lara's baby picture. "Yeah," he said. "Of course I would."

"Does Nadia call him Father? Does she know anything about me at all?"

"I don't know." Dante shifted against the cold, white tile. "She calls him Nick, but she also calls her mother 'Maria'." He heard voices outside and glanced at the door. "Look, I've got to go. I'll be in touch soon."

Dante clicked the phone shut and stared down at Lara's picture, at the real reason he'd taken this case. He wondered where she was tonight and if she was safe. If Lara was in danger, he'd give his life to save her.

When he'd accepted this job from Vandergriff, he had as much as promised the same, to lay down his life to protect Nadia. To do that, he was going to have to shove aside this crazy attraction he felt for her before his distraction got them hurt.

Nadia Branson was only a job.

Nothing more. He would just have to remember that.

He quickly washed up in the sink and joined the Bransons in the dining room. Nadia was already sitting at the table. She didn't look up when he took a seat across from her.

A plump blonde in an apron bustled through the other doorway, carrying a steaming pot. Nadia hurriedly moved a vase of fresh flowers out of the way and the cook set the dish on a flowery tablemat.

"It smells like heaven, Lee Ann," Nadia said, and she was right.

The scent made Dante's mouth water and, much to his embarrassment, his stomach rumbled loudly.

Lee Ann grinned. "I hope they taste like heaven too. Sounds like your young man here is in need of some nourishment."

Nadia flushed. "Damn Yankee doesn't even know what a dumpling is," she grumbled. "Can you believe that?"

She finally glanced at him and Dante smiled. He received a faltering smile in return.

"Hey," he said. "I'm not above a little educating. I'm not afraid to try anything that smells that good."

"Well, I hope a big boy like you has a big appetite," Lee Ann said with a wink. "I don't like messing with leftovers."

"I'll try to do my part, ma'am," he promised.

Dinner with the Branson's was a strange affair. Dante couldn't get a read on their relationships. Nadia and Nick seemed to have a close relationship, but what bugged Dante was the vibe between Nick and Maria.

They were a quiet couple, but seemed comfortable with each other, and she didn't have the demeanor of an abused wife. People forgave each other for horrible things every day, but to forgive such cruelty seemed inconceivable. But then again, maybe Maria Branson was just a good actress.

Dante stared at Nadia across the table. Her sudden shyness disturbed him. He was afraid he'd hurt her some way, scared her, and it nagged at him because he'd had no intention of doing either of those things. But then she cleared her throat and looked at him.

"Dante, you'll have to spend the night here." She patted her mouth with a napkin and gave him what looked like a forced smile. "It's too late to head to Indiana now, after the exciting day you've had."

This was what he'd been hoping for, but he made a show of protesting. "I don't want to impose. I am tired, though. If Ronnie or one of the guys will take me back to my car and direct me to the nearest motel, I'd be grateful."

"Nonsense," Maria said. "We insist. We have plenty of room, and besides, there's not a decent motel for miles."

Nick Branson didn't look too happy, but he smiled and said, "Of course. Please let us do this little thing to repay you, Mr. Giovanni."

Slowly, Dante nodded. Conversation lapsed after that. Dante lifted his glass to take a sip of tea and even the clink of ice in his glass seemed loud in the silence.

Finally, Lee Ann came to clear away the dishes and Nadia stood. Brushing the napkin against her mouth, she said, "Come on, Dante. I'll show you to the guest room."

Dante was still getting this weird vibe from her, like she'd thrown up a wall between them, and he couldn't stand it anymore. She walked quickly up the stairs in front of him, and he waited until they reached the hallway to catch her wrist.

She froze.

"What?" she asked without turning around.

"Look at me."

Her shoulders contracted. She took a deep breath and slowly turned to face him, plastering on another of those false smiles.

"What?" she repeated.

"I'm sorry for what happened in the bathroom. If I hurt you, if I scared you . . ."

With a nervous laugh, she said, "You scare the hell out of me."

He thought he saw the glimmer of a tear in her eye before she ducked her head, and he wanted to know what caused it.

"I didn't mean—"

She silenced him by pressing a fingertip to his lips. "It's okay." She leaned against him to brush a soft kiss on his cheek. "It's a good kind of scared."

She turned and started walking again. Dante decided not to press the issue.

"This is it," she said, and pushed open a door to reveal a

king-sized bed with a royal blue comforter. The battered duffle bag from his trunk lay at the foot of the bed.

"Do I get a map?" Dante joked. "I'll be afraid to go to the john. If I get lost in this place, you'll have to send a search party to find me."

She gave him a patient smile. "There's a bathroom connected to your room. You should find towels and whatever else you'll need inside, but feel free to holler if you need me. I'm only three doors down."

She blew him a kiss and sauntered down the hall. Once again, Dante found himself unable to look away.

Finally, he let himself in and shut the door. Something felt off with this whole thing, but Dante wasn't sure if his instincts were true, or if his perceptions were off because Nadia made him such a wreck.

He placed the duffle bag on the bed, tugged his T-shirt over his head and pulled out his phone to call his office. When the machine picked up, he remembered how late it was and dialed Sanders at home.

"Hello?"

"Hey, Sanders. This is Giovanni again. Sorry to call you after hours."

"Not a problem. Diane's got me cleaning out the garage, so I need rescuing. What can I do for you?"

"It's about Nick Branson." Dante paused, perching on the edge of the bed to tug off his boots. "Tell me again what you know about him."

"Um, okay. Hang on a minute while I go inside to get the folder." Dante heard the phone clatter, then, a few moments later, the rustling of papers over the line. "Okay. Let's see what we have here . . . my sources say Branson had a pretty good business going, shipping illegal aliens from Mexico to work on tobacco farms, but he's branching out into new and naughtier things. Sources say they'd probably classify him as a mid-grade dealer, Mexican meth, but he's got his eyes on the prize. He's involved in a turf war with a drug lord named Diego Cortez over a section of business in Grundy County."

"Okay." Dante sighed and raked a hand over his face. "That's pretty much squares with what Vandergriff told me. And you didn't find anything at all on Vandergriff?"

"No, nothing. He looks clean. A few speeding tickets, but nothing out of the ordinary. His company makes those little foam thingies that keep my beer nice and cold this time of year."

"What about family?"

"No close relations, now that his father is dead. He has an aunt and a couple of cousins in Maine. One ex-wife, who is now the honey of our notorious Mr. Branson. One daughter, the lovely Nadia, who was three months old when Maria walked out."

"Okay, thanks, Sanders. I only wanted to be sure about all this."

Dante clicked the phone shut, grabbed a change of clothes and headed to the shower. He wasn't sure how he was going to manage it, but as soon as he got a chance, he had to get Nadia out of here.

● ● ●

Gary Vandergriff stared at the phone and contemplated making another call to his bounty hunter.

Not yet. Don't push him, the voice in his head whispered. *It's simply a matter of time now.*

A shiver of anticipation stole through him when he thought of how perfectly his plan was working. His Trojan horse was inside, quicker than he'd ever dared to hope. He didn't know if that was a credit to the bounty hunter, or a chink in Andreakos' armor. He preferred to think the latter, because it pleased him to think his old enemy was slipping when he himself had never felt more cunning. More alive.

Andreakos had started this war, for years holding him powerless with his cowardly blackmail, but Gary had known his patience would pay off eventually.

So many times he'd been tempted to call Andreakos' bluff because he knew his father. The old man had cloaked himself in religion, but the god he served was himself, and the number one commandment was "Thou Shall Not Tarnish the Family Name."

If Andreakos had gone to him when the old man was still in power, he would've been signing both his and Maria's death warrants. But also because he knew his father, and the fact that he harbored a strong sense of self-preservation, Gary had bided his time and made his plans.

This time, he would not be denied.

CHAPTER**3**

Nadia crawled under her bed, straining to reach the pack of cigarettes stashed below the headboard. Her fingertips grazed the cellophane wrapper, but it remained just out of her reach.

Muttering to herself, she wiggled back out and yanked a clothes hanger from her closet. Resuming her position on the floor, she finally fished the pack toward her and blinked in surprise at the yellow Post-it note stuck on front of it.

It read, "Sorry, loser. A bet's a bet."

"Damn you, Ronnie," she said, and crumpled the empty pack into a ball. She tossed it at the waste can and missed.

If there was ever a time she needed a cigarette, it was now.

Nadia couldn't sleep. Her head was pounding like a drum, and the events of the day wouldn't let her mind shut down. She felt hyper, anxious, and it had everything to do with the man down the hall.

After futilely searching her dresser again, Nadia placed

both palms on her dresser and stared into the mirror.

She didn't like what she saw.

The wan reflection gazing back at her looked scared and confused, and it made her furious.

She thought about how Dante had looked at her in that mirror, like he could see into her soul—like he *knew* her. But that was impossible. No one knew her.

Because if he did know her, he wouldn't want her.

She was nothing. She was empty.

With another growl of frustration, she yanked open her door and wandered downstairs in her bare feet.

The mansion was oddly built, a result of Nick's obsession with security. An outdoor garden was situated in the very center of the house, visible through three sets of sliding glass doors. Nick had built it for her mother, a place where Maria could feel safe when she tended to her flowers, but it had become Nadia's favorite place, a place where she went to sort out her thoughts.

She felt better the moment she walked outside.

Pale marble statues glowed in the moonlight, reflective of Maria's passion for Greek mythology. Nadia had never felt alone under their watchful stares.

Poseidon, god of the sea, presided over a cascading fountain, looking so real that sometimes Nadia could almost swear she saw his robes flutter. She gazed into the rippling water for a moment, standing close enough that a faint spray of water covered her face.

Her father had taken to throwing pennies in the bottom of the circular fountain when she was only a girl.

"Make a wish," he'd say, then he'd send the coin sailing into the clear water. Although she had no coin to offer tonight, she made a wish anyway.

"Let him be the one," she whispered, then flushed with embarrassment.

What a stupid little girl wish that was, because there was no "one". Not for someone like her. Nadia wiped the mist from her face with the back of her hand and continued down the walkway.

The white cobblestones were smooth and cool against the bottoms of her feet as she wandered deeper into the garden. She trailed her fingers down the muscular arm of Ares when she passed and tried to enjoy the warm summer breeze that ruffled her hair. The scent of her mother's roses hung heavy in the air around her.

Nadia sat on a marble bench beneath a bronze replica of Rodin's *The Kiss*. The embracing lovers should've seemed out of place among the other statues, but somehow they didn't. She stared at them and then up at the full moon, and found herself thinking again not of the man who had tried to kill her, but of the man who had rescued her.

"Nadia?"

Magically, Dante appeared behind her, looking like a Greek god himself in the moonlight. His shirt was gone again, and Nadia stared at the chiseled planes of his body for a beat with total objectivity, the way an artist appreciates a fine sculpture.

That objectivity vanished when he sat beside her. Her heart twisted when Dante withdrew a single orange rose from behind his back and presented it to her.

"Stolen flower," he said with a smile.

Nadia took it from him and buried her nose in the soft petals. She inhaled deeply, and whispered, "Maria Stern."

"Sorry?"

"That's the name of the rose. Nick had them flown in from Florida because they share my mother's first name."

She remembered how he'd tickled her mother's face with one and sang, "Maria Stern, for when my Maria is stern with me."

The memory made a lump in Nadia's throat because she wanted what they had, and it could never be hers.

"It reminded me of you. Beautiful, vibrant, surprising."

Nadia wasn't sure how to respond to that. He only saw the outside. He didn't see what was cold and ugly and empty.

She broke off the thorns and tucked it behind her ear. The emotions she felt when she stared into those whiskey-colored eyes unnerved her. Her whole life, her relationships with men had been superficial. Nothing ventured, nothing gained, and that was okay. She'd had fun and she'd been in control, always the one who walked away before things got serious. She wasn't sure she could do that with Dante.

"I couldn't sleep, either," he said. "I hope you don't mind. I saw you come out here and thought I'd join you."

His gravelly voice rolled over her like scotch over ice, causing heat to pool in her belly.

"No," she said. "I don't mind."

Abruptly, she stood and turned her back to him, pretending to inspect the pink blooms of a nearby bush.

"You're doing it again," he said.

"What?" she asked, although she knew what he meant.

"Talk to me. Tell me about yourself."

With a shrug, Nadia said, "There isn't much to tell. I'm just a princess, and this is my cage."

She winced. Why on earth had she said that? She'd meant to say castle. Panic spiked through her when she sensed him stand.

"Do you feel trapped?" he asked, walking toward her.

She shut her eyes and forced a laugh. "Yeah, right now. Can we please change the subject?"

"Why do I scare you?"

"Don't push me, Dante," she said quietly.

"It was only a question. I want to know."

He was at her back, so close she felt the heat of his body and his breath on the back of her head, but he didn't attempt to touch her.

"Why are you afraid of me?"

Taking a deep breath, she faced him. It would be better for him to find out how crazy she was now than before they got in too deep.

"Because I feel you."

63

He opened his mouth, then clamped it shut again.

Nadia hugged herself, but she couldn't stop the words that seemed to burst from her chest. "I do things . . . I've jumped out of an airplane, skied off the top of a mountain, bungee-jumped off a bridge. I do all these things, just for that moment, for those few seconds when nothing else matters and I can *feel* something. I'm cold inside, numb. I don't feel much of anything, but when you touch me . . . I feel you."

Sudden, unthinkable tears stung her eyes, horrifying her.

Nadia Branson did not act like a babbling idiot in front of some guy she'd just met and she most certainly did not cry. But she had, and she was.

The shocked look that crossed his face shamed her, and she looked away.

Silence fell over the garden. Even the crickets seemed to wait on his response.

Dante touched her shoulder, his big fingers brushing against her bare shoulder. "Nadia, I understand what you're saying," he said.

Was he making fun of her?

Her eyes narrowed, and she pulled away. Dante grabbed her chin and forced her to look at him.

"I . . . understand," he repeated.

Nadia searched his eyes and saw the truth in their brown depths.

Oh God, he did understand. Somehow, that terrified her more than anything.

Dante folded her into his arms and she buried her face against his bare chest. "What are we getting ourselves into?" he murmured into her hair.

Nadia didn't answer, because she didn't know. How could she have just met him?

"Would it make you feel better to know you scare me, too?" he asked, and a helpless laugh burst from her.

"I bet I do," she said. "Because I'm scaring myself right now. This is not me. I don't talk like this. I don't *cry*."

His arms tightened around her, and she clung to him. Slowly, in the safety of his arms, with his heart pounding in her ear, Nadia began to calm down. He held her for a long time. She thought he would have probably held her all night if she'd asked.

She wanted to ask if he felt her, too, but she wasn't feeling quite that brave. So, instead, she changed the subject.

"Okay." She pushed away from him with a smile. "There's only so much of this touchy feely stuff I can take in one night. Let's start over."

She walked to the bench and sat down, staring up at him expectantly.

Dante looked puzzled for a moment, then he grinned. "Oh, okay . . . let's see here." He cleared his throat and stuck his hands in his pockets. "Hi, there, Miss Branson. I couldn't sleep. May I join you?"

She giggled and patted the bench beside her. "Yes, you may."

"I love this garden. It's a beautiful place."

"This is the place I come to think."

They sat in silence for a few minutes, then Dante asked, "What were you thinking about, before I so rudely interrupted you?"

"I was thinking about kissing you."

His eyes widened and his jaw dropped a fraction. Then he laughed. "You're a straight shooter, aren't you, princess?"

"Does that bother you?" she asked, feeling a little defensive. She knew her personality did bother some men.

"No, it's kind of . . . refreshing."

Nadia smiled, but didn't look up. He was sitting close, with his leg pressed against hers, and somehow even that small touch was comforting.

"There's one thing about me, Dante. Despite all my faults—and there are many—I never lie."

"Hmmm, that could be a good thing to know," he teased, and finally she looked up at him, into the velvety depths of his eyes.

"What were you thinking about our kiss?" he asked, then a funny look crossed his features, as if he were surprised he'd asked that.

Nadia stared up at the bright moon and sighed. "I was thinking that I'd like to kiss you again."

She heard Dante's sharp intake of breath and suddenly his rough fingers skimmed her face. With a tenderness that belied his appearance, he caressed the line of her cheekbone with his thumb. Part of her was screaming "run", but another part had already lost that battle by the time his lips brushed against hers.

He caught her lower lip between his teeth and gently sucked it. When his tongue began its hesitant exploration, Nadia parted her lips, welcoming him. She groaned when Dante's hands grasped her hips and pulled her into his lap.

Touching him was a marvel. Hard muscles covered by warm, soft skin. She ran her hands over his head, enjoying how the faint rasp of new hair tingled against her palm.

The force of her desire stunned her. Everything in her wanted this man, and she knew little more about him than his name. She should pull away, save herself while she still could, but her body betrayed her.

Dante's mouth hovered at the racing pulse on her throat. The feel of his labored breathing against her neck and the heat of his hands through her flimsy silk nightgown were driving her to the brink of insanity. His rough fingers glided across the material, caressing her hips.

An alarm blared, shattering the silence. Nadia jerked and nearly fell out of his lap. Dante's hands closed around her waist, and he gently sat her aside.

"Stay here until I see what's going on," he commanded.

Nadia rolled her eyes.

Right.

She jumped to her feet and followed him. Dante turned to frown at her, but then she saw the resignation cross his face.

When they went back in the house, she wasn't surprised to find Nick already downstairs, barking into the intercom.

He barely spared them a glance as he demanded, "Somebody talk to me. What's going on out there?"

"Sorry, boss," Waynie's sheepish voice crackled over the intercom. "It's only me. I didn't get the code punched in time."

Nick sighed and pressed the button. "All right, Waynie. Go to bed." His eyes narrowed when he turned to them. "What are you two doing up?"

"Insomnia," Nadia said quickly. "I was showing Dante the garden."

Not to mention what I might've shown him if Waynie hadn't tripped the alarm, she thought, glad the room was dark and her father couldn't see the blush creeping up her neck.

"Go try to get some rest. You can show Dante around tomorrow."

"Okay, goodnight, Nick." Nadia hurried up the stairs, conscious of Dante's gaze burning into her back while he jogged up the steps behind her. She found the courage to face him when they stepped into the hallway.

She pointed to the oak doors and forced a smile. "This is me, that one's you."

To her surprise and disappointment, Dante turned without another word and walked toward the guestroom.

"What, no goodnight kiss?" she blurted.

He stopped and slowly twisted around to smile at her. Something unreadable flashed in his dark eyes.

"Still afraid of me, huh?" she joked, but her heart pounded in her ears when he strolled back to her.

Her breath caught when he gently removed the flower from behind her ear. He traced the bloom along her face, down her throat and Nadia shivered, not from the whisper of the rose across her skin, but the desire burning in his eyes.

"No. I'm afraid of me. Afraid if I touch you again, I won't be able to stop. Goodnight, princess."

He handed her the rose and walked to his room. He slipped inside and shut the door behind him before she could even muster a reply. Not that she had any idea what to say to that anyway.

Nadia slipped inside her room and shut the door behind her. She closed her eyes and leaned against it for a moment, reliving his kiss and the feel of his hands on her body. With a sigh, she crossed back to her bed and slipped between the cool, crisp sheets.

She sniffed the rose again before laying it on the nightstand and tugging the sheets up to her chin. Closing her eyes, she willed herself to sleep, but thoughts of Dante kept intruding.

What would tomorrow be like? For the first time in a long time, she couldn't wait to find out.

● ● ●

Saturday, August 6
8:30 a.m.

Dante slipped out of the guest bedroom and shut the door be-hind him. He stopped by Nadia's door and lifted his hand to knock, but then decided against it. The emotion of the night before still had him reeling.

I feel you.

He'd known exactly what she meant.

Ever since he'd lost Sharon, when he'd known he'd lost Lara forever, he'd felt it. The same void, the same restlessness inside that provoked him to do crazy things just for that one surge of adrenaline, that one moment he felt alive. All these things, this mindless attraction to Nadia . . . he finally recog-nized it for what it was.

He felt her too.

What kind of life had Nadia led to make her feel the way she did? What could make such a beautiful, electrifying woman feel cold and numb inside?

His mind was like a movie screen and only one feature played there. Visions of Nadia in the garden, her silver silk nightgown sliding on his bare skin, the way she tasted, the scent of her perfume. The raw, vulnerable look in her eyes.

He was in serious trouble here.

If he kept on, he would hurt her. She needed someone she could trust, and he wasn't it. How would Nadia feel if she knew he was here to kidnap her, even if he was doing it for her protection? But no matter how many times he vowed to keep his distance, his resolve crumbled at her touch.

Troubled, Dante wandered downstairs, through the dining room and into the kitchen. Nick Branson sat with his back to him, outside on the patio. He was talking on a cell phone, and Dante guessed from his animated gestures that the conversation was an important one. He slid the door open a crack to listen.

"I want him dead! Whatever you have to do, whatever the cost. I'm sick of worrying about my family. My daughter was nearly killed yesterday. Yes, yes, I know that, but you have to find a way to get to him. No, I don't blame you . . . no. It was a good plan, but it came just a little too late."

Footsteps sounded in the foyer behind Dante. Not wanting to be caught eavesdropping, he yanked open the patio door, making sure Nick heard him.

Nick twisted around to stare at Dante, then said into the phone, "I have to go. I'll be in touch soon."

Clicking the phone shut, he smiled and gestured at an empty seat across from him. "Please, Dante, join me for breakfast."

"Thanks."

Plates heaped with eggs, bacon, and fresh fruit covered the table. Dante filled a plate as Nick poured himself a cup of coffee. The strong smell beckoned Dante, sharp and enticing, reminding him of how little sleep he'd gotten the night before. "Is Nadia up yet?" he asked.

"Not yet," Nick said. "Actually, I'm glad we have a

chance to talk without her. I have a proposition for you."

Dante waited while Nick dumped a teaspoonful of sugar into his cup and stirred it. Nick frowned, tapping the spoon against the side of his cup. "As you saw yesterday, I have major security problems. My family is under attack, and to be honest with you, Ronnie's the only man I have that I can fully trust to protect Nadia. But he's just one man, and he can't be on duty all the time." Nick waved toward the house. "My wife isn't really a problem. She doesn't leave the house much anyway, but as I'm sure you can imagine, I have my hands full with Nadia."

Dante sipped his coffee, wondering if Mrs. Branson stayed home by choice, or because she was afraid to go against her husband's wishes.

"I'd like to offer you a temporary job as Nadia's bodyguard. I know you have your own business, with its own expenses, but I think you'll find my compensation more than enough to cover your downtime. I need someone with your experience to keep her safe until I can neutralize the threat against her. Are you interested?"

"I'm interested." The wheels in Dante's mind were spinning. This was a perfect opportunity, but he didn't need to look too eager. "I need a little time to think about it, make arrangements."

"Fair enough," Nick replied, then leaned back in his chair. "There is, however, one stipulation."

"What's that?" Dante asked, but he already knew what

the man was going to say next. Resentment settled in the pit of his stomach like a rock.

"I want you to keep your relationship with Nadia strictly business."

There it was. Same story, different faces.

Men like Nick Branson were all the same. They expected him to die for their daughters, but he wasn't good enough to date them. Dante remembered the fury on Sharon's father's face when he'd caught the teenagers kissing behind the garage. Russ Martin had fired Dante on the spot, but it had been too late. Sharon was already carrying his child.

"Please don't take offense," Nick said.

Dante remained silent.

"I can't tell Nadia not to see you, because she's so rebellious it would be like spitting in the wind. She needs someone who would be a stabilizing influence on her. Somehow I don't think you're it."

"You don't know anything about me."

The words slipped out before Dante could stop them. He should be playing along, agreeing with whatever Branson suggested, but Nadia's stepfather had managed to tear the scab off a wound that had never quite healed.

"Don't I?"

Nick's sympathetic smile infuriated Dante. "Let's see . . ." He flipped through the file in front of him. "You signed up for the marines when you were 18 and served a four-year stint. In the past three years, you've lived in Texas, Los Angeles, Chicago,

Japan, and recently returned home to New York. Always looking for action, the next big adventure. I simply don't want to
see my daughter hurt the next time you blow out of town."

Dante struggled to keep his face impassive. He took another sip of coffee before replying. "Fine."

The fact that Nick Branson lied about his real reason
didn't make it go down any easier, but Dante knew he couldn't
blow this opportunity.

"Hey, guys. What's going on?"

Dante looked up to see Nadia standing at the patio door.

● ● ●

Nadia leaned in the doorway, suddenly feeling self-conscious
in her blue jeans and white T-shirt. Maybe she should've
dressed up a little more. Or maybe she should've stayed in
her room and prayed Dante would be gone by the time she
came out. She didn't know what to think, or what to feel.

Dante's eyes were on her and, although physically he was
several feet away, his gaze felt like a touch.

Her father turned to smile at her. "Good morning,
sweetheart."

"Good morning. You guys save me anything to eat?" she
managed.

"What would you like?" Nick asked.

For my hands to quit shaking, she thought, but replied,
"Um, I think I'll just get some cereal. Anybody need anything

while I'm up?"

They both shook their heads and she fled into the kitchen. While she poured herself a bowl of Raisin Bran, Dante came through the doorway, juggling a couple of plates and his coffee cup.

"Here, give me those." She took the dishes from his hands and stacked them in the sink. "You didn't have to mess with that. I would've gotten them, or one of the maids—"

"I'm a big boy. I can clean up after myself," he said with a slow smile that made her heart flutter. She hurriedly turned away to retrieve a carton of milk from the refrigerator.

He cleared his throat and said, "Look, Nadia . . . about last night . . ."

Her stomach pitched at the serious tone of his voice. Here it was. He wasn't any different after all. Nadia slammed the carton on the counter and closed her eyes.

"So, I guess you're leaving. Today? Right now?"

"That's what I wanted to talk to you about," he said, and cupped her shoulders with his big hands. Nadia tensed when he bent to kiss the top of her head. "Your father offered me a job."

"What?" she asked, hardly daring to breathe.

"He wanted to know if I'd be your bodyguard."

"What did you tell him?" The thought of being around Dante, day in and day out, was as exhilarating as it was terrifying.

He laughed, that deep, sexy laugh of his that sounded like

the rumble of thunder. "What do you want me to tell him?"

"Say yes," she blurted. "Say you're not going to Indiana."

"Okay, I'm not going to Indiana."

"Easy as that?"

"Easy as that."

He released her, and she poured milk over her cereal. Then she laughed.

"What?" Dante asked, smiling.

"You're going to protect me?"

"That's the plan."

She tucked an errant strand of hair behind her ear and smiled up at him. "So, who's going to protect you from me?"

● ● ●

Who indeed? Dante thought a few hours later when Nadia skipped down the front steps in a pair of short, faded cut-offs and a yellow bikini top. Standing outside the barracks, Dante struggled to ignore her and listen to Nick Branson explain the guard rotation.

Despite his best efforts, his gaze sought her out over Nick's shoulder. Nadia gave him a secretive smile before taking a sip from the glass in her hand. She strutted over to the carport where Waynie was watching Ronnie check the oil in the Hummer. Nadia leaned into the big man and whispered something. Waynie gaped at her and vehemently shook his head.

She set her glass on the Hummer's hood and clasped her

hands together in a pleading gesture. Ronnie scowled and snatched the glass away, rubbing the Hummer with the tail of his T-shirt. Waynie shot her a beleaguered look and shook his head again. Dante turned his attention back to Branson, wondering what she was planning.

He didn't have to wait long to find out. Waynie jogged over to them.

"Mr. B," he said breathlessly. "I've messed up my computer again. Do you think you could help me fix it?"

"Do you mean right now?" Branson asked, lifting an eyebrow.

Waynie shifted and tugged at his scraggly red beard. "Well, yeah, if you're not too busy. As soon as you can anyway. I've got a paper due in Sociology Monday, and there's an online poker tournament in a couple of hours that I'd like to get in on."

A paper due? Dante didn't know what surprised him more: that the burly redhead knew how to use a computer, or that he was taking a sociology class.

Nick sighed. "I suppose I can. We were almost finished here anyway." He frowned at Dante. "If you have any questions about anything, ask Ronnie."

That's exactly what Dante intended to do.

So far, all of Dante's fishing with Nick had turned up nothing. Nick wanted him to protect Nadia, but he was very vague about from whom. This whole situation felt off in some way, and Dante didn't like it.

One thing was becoming crystal clear, though. Nick Branson wasn't the kind of man you messed around with. Although Dante was still puzzled by Nick's relationships with his family and bodyguards, he'd glimpsed the coldness behind those dark eyes. Dante didn't have to guess what would happen if he was caught trying to kidnap Nadia. Nick Branson would kill him without hesitation.

Nadia slipped up behind her stepfather and linked her arm through his.

"I'm going for a swim," she announced. "Ronnie said he'd go with me. Waynie, are you coming?"

"Would be a nice day for a swim, but I can't," Waynie said grumpily. "Mr. B is going to work on my computer for me. It's started freezing up again. I guess *Dante* will have to go in my place."

Nadia glared at him emphasis, and Waynie dropped his head. He sighed. "I'm going to boot it up now."

Branson's eyes narrowed. As Waynie shuffled inside the barracks, the corner of Branson's mouth twitched. He snagged Nadia's ponytail and gave it a gentle tug. "You think you're a clever girl, don't you?"

She stared up at him with twinkling green eyes and an impish smile. "Apparently not as clever as I thought."

Nick laughed and seized her in a brief, fierce hug. Then he kissed the top of her head and shooed her away. "Go, before I change my mind, you little sneak."

Dante watched with amusement. Whatever Vandergriff

thought about Nick, he was wrong about one thing. Nick loved Nadia. He felt the connection between them. But Nick wasn't the real threat—the meth dealer was. He was going to have to remember that.

A laughing Nadia pushed Dante toward the barracks. "You heard what the man said. "Go change. Ronnie and I will meet you behind the house."

Inside the room Nick had assigned him, Dante remembered he didn't have any shorts in his duffle bag. He hadn't exactly figured on a pleasure trip. But Nadia was waiting, so he sat on the edge of the bed and sawed the legs of his blue jeans off at mid-thigh with his pocket knife.

He found her in the backyard, adjusting her ponytail holder. A white bottle of Coppertone peeked out from the loose waistband of her shorts and, when he drew closer, the wind carried her sweet coconut smell to him. Her tan glistened in the sun, and once again Dante's mind filled with thoughts he had no business thinking.

"Hiya, handsome," she said with a wink. "I hope you don't mind us stealing you away. Nick's had you busy for hours, so I thought a rescue mission might be in order."

Dante grinned. "Thanks. A swim sounds great. But where's the pool?"

"Pool?" Nadia scoffed. "You're not in New York, mister. We do things different around here."

"Nadia, you do have a pool," Ronnie pointed out, and Dante jumped. He hadn't even noticed the bodyguard standing there. Man, he really had to focus.

She wrinkled her nose. "Yeah, but what good's an indoor pool in the summer? I like to feel the sun on my skin, the wind in my hair—"

"You just like to make me freeze my ass off in that running water," Ronnie grumbled. He lifted the digital camera slung around his neck, snapped a picture of the big oak tree at the corner of the house, and headed to the woods.

Nadia slid her hand in his, and Dante felt a little jolt at how good it felt there. How natural. He thought about Nick's stipulation, but he couldn't bring himself to pull away from her. Instead, he gripped her hand tighter.

Trailing behind Ronnie, they entered the woods.

"It's a waterfall," she said, staring up at him with those jungle eyes. "Not a big one, but it's still amazing. The most gorgeous thing you've ever seen."

Dante squeezed her fingers. "Somehow, I doubt that."

Her cheeks flushed, impossibly rendering her even more beautiful. She was such a strange combination of seduction and innocence, woman and child. He didn't know what to make of her, but he knew he liked her. Liked her a lot.

If he lived to be a hundred, would he ever hold another woman without seeing Nadia's face?

I don't feel much of anything, but when you touch me . . . I feel you.

He'd had women tell him they loved him—one or two of them might have even meant it—but none of their declarations had affected him like that one simple statement. He wanted to believe it was just something physical—that's all it could be, right? But looking down at her, he thought, *I could love you.*

Man, he was seriously losing it.

They stepped into a clearing. Nadia released his hand and wandered over to an old bridge. He stared at her back, finding even her the jut of shoulder blades exciting.

"The main road used to run through here," Ronnie explained, drawing Dante's attention to the faded gray road with weeds growing through the cracked asphalt. "But then they added the interstate a couple miles north of here and bisected this section out." He leaned to peer around Dante. "Hey, Nadia, get down from there."

Dante glanced back to see her climbing onto the metal guardrail. Her shorts, shoes, and bottle of Coppertone lay in a pile near her feet.

"Relax, Grandma," Nadia said, and began walking the rail heel to toe like it was a tightrope. She staggered once and threw her arms out to balance herself. "Whew!" she said, and shot Ronnie a triumphant grin.

"Nadia!" Ronnie said sharply. "I'm not kidding. Quit screwing around and get down from there."

She jerked her hand up to salute him, and lost her footing. Dante's heart did a crazy dance while she flapped her arms wildly, struggling to regain her balance. Before he could move, she screamed and fell over the side.

Dante ran to the rail and stared down. He barely registered the flash of Ronnie's camera as he stared at the creek some thirty feet below. For a moment, he saw nothing. Then Nadia bobbed to the surface like a cork and waved at him.

"Hey, Ronnie. How was it?" she shouted.

"Not bad," Ronnie yelled back. Looking at the screen on his digital camera, he said, "Not as good as Waynie's, but still . . . not too shabby."

Dante stared at him open-mouthed. "You mean . . . you did that on purpose!"

Ronnie grinned. "*She* did that on purpose. All I can tell you is the girl's got a messed up sense of humor. She nearly made Waynie cry doing that."

Dante scowled down at Nadia. "How deep is that water, Ronnie?" he asked.

"Deep enough. Waynie jumped off there day before yesterday and didn't touch bottom, so you'll be okay. Just keep to the center."

"Ready or not, princess, here I come," Dante yelled down to her, and took off his shoes. After he climbed on the rail, he looked at Ronnie. "You coming?"

"I don't dive," Ronnie said. "Not when there's a perfectly good trail over there." He shook his head and scooped up their things. Walking off, he muttered, "You and Nadia need to switch to decaf."

Dante stared into the crystal blue water below. Nadia butterflied backward, giving him plenty of room.

He jumped.

Wind roared in his ears and adrenaline surged through his veins like electricity. He sliced through the cold water and managed to keep himself from bobbing to the top. Propelling himself through the water, he scanned the surface above him, searching for Nadia.

When he thought he was going to have to give up and come to the surface for a breath, he saw her. Her lovely legs treaded the water to his left, looking unnaturally white in the dark water. He kicked up to grab her.

She sucked in a breath the instant before he dragged her under, but then she looked at him and bubbles of laughter escaped her mouth. Dante let her go.

He popped to the surface and she clutched at his neck, burying her face in his chilled skin.

"You dog," she gasped. "You scared me."

"I scared *you*?" he said incredulously, and she laughed again.

"Damn, baby, this water's c-cold," he chattered.

She wrapped her legs around his waist and he opened the arms he was hugging himself with to pull her against his chest.

"I'll keep you warm," she said, and crushed her mouth to his.

Her hot mouth was a shocking contrast to the bitter cold that enveloped the rest of his body. Like she'd flipped a thermostat, Dante's blood surged, flooding him with warmth. He waved his arms at his side to keep them adrift while she clutched at his shoulders.

"Still cold?" she asked coyly, her nose bumping against his.

"Huh uh." He caught her lower lip between his teeth, and then found himself enveloped in another firestorm of a kiss. By the time they separated, they were both panting for breath.

Nadia gave him a seductive smile and pushed a chunk of damp hair out of her face. She slid her cheek against his until her lips hovered at his earlobe. She whispered, "I've been day-dreaming about that all day."

The thought of her wanting him as badly as he did her caused an unexpected, savage thrill to race through him.

"Hey, Dante!" Ronnie called, and they guiltily broke apart.

Dante scanned the banks, but didn't yet see him. Then Ronnie's white shirt appeared through the greenery.

"What do you think about the waterfall?" he yelled.

Dante laughed and lifted his eyebrows. To Nadia, he said, "What waterfall?"

Nadia pointed over his shoulder. He twisted his head to look at the white, foaming water spilling over the rock wall.

"Oh." He grinned. "It's great!" he yelled back at Ronnie.

Ronnie peeled off his shirt and tossed it on a rock along with the pile of their shoes. He dove into the silvery blue water and Dante took advantage of the moment to give Nadia another quick kiss.

"I wish we were alone," he said.

Well, most of him wished that, but another part of him wondered how the hell he was going to walk away from her now, and they weren't even lovers yet. Not that he wanted to walk away, but he had the feeling she'd leave him no choice when she found out his true mission. Nadia made it painfully clear that she valued honesty and directness, and he'd been neither with her. But looking into her smiling face, he granted himself a short reprieve from the doubt and worry. For the next couple of hours, he was simply going to enjoy being with her.

After they exhausted themselves swimming and playing beneath the waterfall, Nadia announced she was getting out. Dante followed her to the rocky shore. She sat on a long, smooth rock.

They lay on their sides, facing each other. Dante trailed his fingertips down her side and she smiled. Ronnie emerged from the water a few minutes later and stretched on a grassy bank several yards away. With an exaggerated yawn, he turned away, giving them a small measure of privacy if they talked softly enough.

"Your old man would kill me if he found out about this," Dante whispered, caressing her hip.

Nadia's laugh was low and husky. "Well, I'm not telling, and Ronnie won't say anything either. He's like a brother to me, and he wouldn't narc me out unless he thought I was going to get hurt." She propped her head in one hand and stroked his face with the other. "You won't hurt me, will you?"

Dante twisted his head to kiss her palm. "Not on purpose. Never on purpose." He cleared his throat. "So, tell me what it was like growing up here. How long have you been under lock and key?"

"Well, let's see." Nadia glanced up at the sky, pretending to count. "The fifth of next month will be . . . forever." She smiled and trailed her fingers over his Adam's apple down to his necklace. Dante shivered and she bit back a smile as she toyed with the medallion that hung from it. "Please tell me all about New York," she said. "I've always wanted to visit there . . ."

Dante grinned. "There you go again, trying to turn it back to me. Why won't you tell me about yourself?"

Her playful smile faded and he caught a glimpse of pain in her eyes, though her voice was deadly calm. "There's nothing to tell. What you see is what you get. Sometimes I feel like I'm trapped in one of those snow globe things. Everything around me looks perfect and still, but it's all an illusion. My life isn't real." She wrinkled her nose and smiled. "I want to see the world. I want to *live*."

Come away with me.

The stupid words swelled in Dante's heart and nearly escaped his lips. For just a moment, he dreamed of stealing her away from both her fathers. He wanted to be the one who showed her the world and all the amazing things he'd found in it. He wanted to hold her hand while they walked the white, sandy beaches of Mexico, see her face lit by the gorgeous orange and reds of an African sunset, and get snowed in with her in some cozy little cabin in South Dakota.

It wasn't simply her beauty that called him, though it scorched him like the sun. It was the hunger in her eyes. He wanted to be her lover, her guide.

He wanted to be her everything.

"What?" she asked, her smile returning. "What are you thinking about?"

"That's easy. The only thing I've thought about since I walked into that diner . . . you."

Nadia leaned into him, pressing her soft, sweet mouth to his. Her skin was slick from the residue of the coconut scented oil and water, and his fingers glided down the curve of her spine. His lips parted to welcome the slow, sweet invasion of her tongue.

Her bikini top felt cold and clammy against his bare chest, but the skin around it burned like fever. Since his divorce, he'd been reckless with many things, but never his heart. As her hot, lithe body melded to his, Dante felt in danger of losing not only his heart, but his very soul.

Dante caught her staring at him. Mesmerized, he couldn't look away, giving himself over to the desire in the jaguar green depths of her eyes as they kissed. Never had a simple kiss felt so intimate. So consuming.

Come away with me, he thought again. *Run away with me forever.*

Drugged from the heat of the sun beating on his back and Nadia's intoxicating kiss, Dante's mind drifted, again carrying her with him to all the exotic places he'd been.

Nadia broke the kiss, trailing her lips along his jaw to his ear. His breath caught when she nipped his earlobe.

"If your lovemaking is as good as your kisses . . ." she

whispered huskily, ". . . I'll never survive it."

Funny, he'd just had the same thought.

"Ahem."

They both started at the loud cough behind them.

"I am *not* looking," Ronnie said, "because I don't want to go blind or anything, but we'd better get going if you want to make Charlie's tonight. I know how long it takes you to get ready."

"Charlie's?" Dante asked, but Nadia didn't seem to hear him. She scrambled to her feet.

"Ooh, right." She rubbed her wrist where her watch usually rested. "What time is it, anyway?"

"Ten till six," Ronnie answered.

Nadia shimmied back into her shorts with a little wiggle that made Dante's blood pressure spike and slipped her pretty feet into her white tennis shoes. Her eyes gleamed when she looked up at him.

"We're going to have some fun tonight, boys," she promised.

Dante grinned and squeezed her shoulder. "I can't imagine any time spent with you not being 'fun', princess."

The climb out of the swimming hole was a steep one. Ronnie scaled the nearly vertical terrain like a mountain goat. Although Dante thought he could've probably kept the same pace, he hung back with a panting Nadia.

She gasped, "He always . . . leaves me." Putting her hands on her hips, she stopped and straightened for a moment, turning her face up to the sky. "Hey, Ronnie," she yelled.

"You see this? A real gentleman waits on a lady."

"Yeah, yeah," he called, with a dismissive wave over his shoulder. "Smoke you another one."

She made a rude gesture at Ronnie's back and Dante laughed.

Sweat trickled down Dante's back by the time they reached the top. Nadia bent over at the waist, clutching her sides.

Ronnie grinned at them and nudged Nadia with his shoulder. "What a loser. You're sucking wind like Waynie."

"Shut . . . up," she panted.

He snapped a picture of her reddened face and turned to Dante. "You should've seen him the first time. He crawled the last five or six feet to the top and lay there like a beached whale. I seriously thought he was dying. We ended up having to go back and get a four-wheeler to haul his sorry butt home. He's getting better, though. The last time he didn't start begging us to call 911 until he was halfway up."

Dante laughed and Nadia gave a grudging smile.

"It's a fun trip down, but . . . whew." Dante rubbed a hand across the top of his head.

Ronnie snapped another picture of them and they headed into the forest. Nadia slipped her hand inside his, and Dante stroked her fingers.

He released her when they emerged in the backyard. He hated to let go of her, but he couldn't risk getting fired. It was a pretty safe assumption that Nick Branson would not tolerate insubordination lightly. They crossed the yard and wandered around the side of the house.

"I'm going to get a shower." Ronnie pointed at Nadia. "*You* get to tell Mr. B we're going out."

She came to an abrupt stop. "*Me?*" she whined. "Why me?"

Ronnie grinned. "Hey, he's your Pops."

Nadia rolled her eyes and he snapped his shirt at her. "Ah, quit pretending like you don't know how to work him. Dante's already seen your scheming."

He twisted up his shirt to pop her again and Nadia snatched it out of his hands. She balled it up and tossed it at his head. "Gee, thanks, Ronnie. You're a real pal."

He stuck out his tongue at her and walked off, leaving them standing by the barracks.

Dante smiled and lifted his eyebrows. "I guess I'd better get cleaned up too. What is Charlie's? I hope it's nothing fancy, because I don't do so good with fancy."

"Charlie's a campus bar and grill. A beer and peanuts kind of place." Nadia did a half-twirl. "Do I *look* like a fancy girl to you?"

Dante smoothed a twig of her damp hair between his fingers. "You look like a beautiful girl. A perfect girl."

Nadia flashed him a dazzling white smile and it was all he could do not to take her in his arms right there, Nick Branson be damned.

He forced himself to take a step backward. "Okay," he said. "I'd better . . ."

She nodded, but remained still, watching him with her

arms crossed over her chest. Her cheeks and the tip of her nose were pink with sunburn. The rosy flush made the green in her eyes flare to life like kryptonite.

Superman was going down for the count, and there wasn't a thing he could do about it.

Damn, but she was beautiful. Dante forced himself to take another step backwards, then another. She grinned at him like she was reading his mind. He turned away and smacked headfirst into the one of the barracks' porch posts.

"Smooth," he muttered, rubbing his forehead and feeling his face turn as red as Nadia's.

"Are you okay?" she choked out.

He glared at her and she giggled behind her hand like a kindergartener. He tried to scowl, but he couldn't quite make the corners of his mouth turn down.

"Stop it," he said, pointing at her while he climbed onto the porch.

She pressed her fingers to her mouth and gave him a wide-eyed "what?" look.

He tripped going in the doorway, but didn't look back. The sweet, musical sound of her laughter followed him inside.

He was turning into such a spaz. It would've been demoralizing if it wasn't so damn funny.

Ronnie walked by with a towel and pair of blue jeans slung over his shoulder. He looked at Dante, smiled, rolled his eyes and kept walking.

"The shower on the other end is open, Romeo," he said.

"I'm taking this side."

"Thanks," Dante replied.

Waynie sat on the sofa, munching a handful of potato chips. He squinted at Dante. "*Dude*, what happened to your head?"

Dante grinned and shook his head. "I don't know, man."

He wandered off in search of his room. The ceiling fans pushed cool, conditioned air down on him. He caught the sweet scent of coconut and brought his forearm to his face. He could still smell the scent of her where his arm had rested against her body.

Man, the next thing you knew, he'd be—well, hell, he didn't know what he'd be doing. This was unknown territory. He was afraid to guess what stupid thing he would do next.

After showering and changing, he joined Ronnie and Waynie on the front porch. They seemed to have been waiting on him, because immediately they wandered to the main house.

"How did you do in the poker tournament?" Dante asked Waynie while they climbed the front steps.

"Got busted on the last card. It was a bad beat, man. Some amateur. Getting an eight on the river was all that would save his butt, and what do you think he got?" Waynie rolled his eyes heavenward and tugged on his goatee. "I finished five spots out of the money."

"How many people were playing?" Ronnie asked. "Six?"

"Ha ha. I'll have you know, there were over eighty people in that tournament. Some of them were big shots too."

"Here we go." Ronnie rolled his eyes. "Are you going to tell us you played Elvis again?"

"It was the king, man," Waynie said earnestly. "He knew stuff only the real Elvis would know."

"Great." Ronnie shouldered past him. "The next time you talk to him, tell him I want Lisa Marie's number."

Waynie shook his head. "Sorry, I already thought of that, man, but he said he hasn't spoken to her since the whole Michael Jackson thing. He said that if he *had* been dead, he would have rolled over in his grave."

Ronnie smacked his forehead with his palm, then rubbed his hand down his face. "Do you see?" he asked Dante. "Do you see what I have to put up with around here?"

Dante laughed and clamped a hand on Ronnie's shoulder. They entered the living room together.

Dante paused at the sight of Nick and Maria Branson together on the leather sofa. She lay back against the chair arm with her legs propped in his lap. He whispered something to her and she chuckled softly as he stroked one of her nylon covered feet with his thumb. Dante coughed, feeling like an intruder.

"Hey, boys, come on in," Maria said.

"Sorry to interrupt, Mrs. B," Ronnie said.

"You're not interrupting anything." She smiled and swung her feet to the floor. "Nick and I are being lazy. Are you guys hungry? Lee Ann made chili . . ."

Ronnie made a face. "Chili? In this heat?"

Nick laughed and nudged Maria. "Ah, ha. See there?"

She gave him a grudging smile and he looked at Dante.

"That's what I tell them all the time, but they insist that anything she cooks would be hot. It's not the same, is it?"

"I think you should only have chili during the winter," Ronnie said, plopping into a chair and brushing a wave of dark hair out of his face.

Nick opened his mouth to speak, but paused when Nadia skipped down the stairs in a bright red halter top and faded jeans. Her dark hair curled around her face, and makeup accentuated her features, though Dante didn't think she needed any help at all.

"See ya later, guys," she said, looking at her parents. "I'm taking the boys with me. We'll be back in a little while."

Nadia grabbed Waynie and Dante's hands and pulled them toward the door. Both Nick and Maria jumped to their feet.

"Nadia, where do you think you're going?" Nick asked, his voice edged with panic.

Nadia blew a piece of hair out of her face and turned around. "Remember, I told you the other day I had a gig at Charlie's."

"Surely you can't mean to go sing in some bar tonight?" Nick sputtered.

Nadia folded her arms across her chest. "Well, as a matter of fact, I do."

"Honey, that's crazy," her mother said, pressing a hand to

Nick's back. "You were almost killed yesterday."

A flash of impatience crossed Nadia's face. "So, when do you two propose I venture back into the real world? Tomorrow . . . next week . . . next year? Heck, maybe never. Maybe I'll just stay here the rest of my life, holed up with you guys."

"Nadia, that's not fair," Maria said.

"No, it's not," Nadia said sharply, then she softened her tone. "Look, I'm not going to hide. Yes, if he kills me, he wins. But he still wins if I cower here in the shadows, afraid to go outside. I'm not going to let him control my life."

Nadia crossed over to her parents and hugged them both.

"I love you guys, but I can't live like this," she said gently. "I'll be okay. Dante and Ronnie will be there, along with the others. I have a whole platoon following me around. What could happen?"

When they didn't reply, she pivoted toward the door. "I'll be back around midnight, okay?" she called over her shoulder, and pushed out the door before they could protest. Dante followed.

She jumped off the porch, not bothering with the steps, and strode toward the garage in the moonlight. Dante glanced back at the house.

Maria Branson stood in the doorway watching, her hand twisting the gold chain around her neck. He felt a little sorry for Nadia's mother, even though he could see Nadia's side of it too. Nadia was a lot like him, he suspected, and the worst thing anyone could do to people like them was to cage them up.

"Ronnie, Waynie!" Nadia yelled. "Are you coming?"

"Yeah, yeah. Hold your horses," Ronnie called from the house.

Another bodyguard stumbled out of the barracks, tugging a black T-shirt over his head. Waynie started toward the Hummer clutching a bag of Fritos and Ronnie waved him away.

"Huh uh. No, you don't. I just vacuumed this thing. You and your Fritos have to ride with Jacobi."

Waynie made a loser sign on his forehead with his thumb and forefinger and Ronnie flipped him a bird. Finally, Dante found himself in the back of the Humvee with Nadia. She leaned in close to press her face to his shirt.

"Geez, Dante, what kind of cologne is that?" she demanded.

He hesitated. "Uh, it's called Diesel Green. Why? Does it smell bad?"

"No! It's wonderful." She gave him a wicked smile and ran her freshly polished nails up the back of his neck. "Makes me want to scratch and sniff."

She reached over the driver's seat and rapped Ronnie on the head with her knuckles. "I think that's what I'm going to buy you for Christmas. A whole case of Diesel Green. Maybe then you can get a girlfriend."

Ronnie grunted and adjusted the rearview mirror. "No, thanks. Now that I know it's a proven attractant for annoying little pests like you."

"Better a pest like me than no pest at all."

"I'm not so sure about that."

Ignoring him, Nadia turned back to Dante. "You know, I forgot to ask. What did Nick have you doing all morning?"

Dante shrugged. "Nothing much. He showed me around and explained my duties. Stuff like that. He warned me about you too. About how much trouble you could get into."

The amber glow from the streetlights lining the drive illuminated her face and Dante grinned when she rolled her eyes.

"Not hard to do around here, believe me." She leaned back in the seat and pressed her leg against his.

"Does he know you jump off bridges too?" he teased.

"Sure he does," Ronnie said, wagging his eyebrows in the mirror. "I have the picture to prove it."

Dante laughed. Nadia leaned against him, resting her head in the crook of his arm.

And she'd talked about *his* cologne.

She was wearing that perfume again. It enveloped Dante like a drug, stealing his common sense. Nick had told him to ignore her, to pretend he wasn't interested. He wondered how on earth he was supposed to do that.

Her hands lay in her lap and he picked one up, tracing his fingers over her palm. "I find it hard to believe you don't have a boyfriend, princess."

"Believe it," Ronnie said from the front seat. "She ain't even had a date in awhile."

Nadia frowned. "It's been a few days."

Dante caught Ronnie's wink in the rearview mirror and

tried to hide his smile.

"You know, now that I think about it . . . you haven't had one in a few weeks, huh?"

"No." Nadia stretched to pop Ronnie in the back of the head. "But thanks for clearing that up for us." She smiled at Dante. "You know how it is. I've been biding my time, waiting on a real man."

He laughed, remembering their first conversation.

Glancing at three pairs of headlights following them down the drive, she said, "Geez, I bet the president's daughter doesn't have this much security. I'm sure to fill the house tonight, since I'm bringing most of the audience with me."

"So, that's your job? You're a singer?" Dante asked.

Ronnie snorted. "To qualify as a job, it's supposed to be something that makes money."

"Hey, Charlie paid my bar tab last time," Nadia protested. Turning back to Dante, she said, "Nah, this is only for fun. When I was a mean little kid, my grandma would take up for me, saying, 'That girl's got ants in her pants. She doesn't mean to get into everything. She's only working off energy.' That's what I'm doing. Working off energy."

Dante squeezed her shoulder and kissed the top of her head.

She glanced out the window and said, "I can't stay cooped up in that house like they do. I know this makes them nervous, but I really don't do much. I even go to college here in Sewanee because Nick's afraid somebody will assassinate me on campus. This last semester, he started sending people *in* the classroom with me. I walked into Psych class one day and there sat Waynie." She chuckled. "Hey, Ronnie. How did Nick manage to get Waynie enrolled in that class anyway?"

"I don't wanna know," Ronnie replied. "But you should've seen Waynie doing his homework."

"Your father must be very afraid of this man," Dante commented, wondering how long this had been going on. Had Nadia always lived under armed guard?

"He's evil," Ronnie said matter-of-factly, and Nadia nodded her head in agreement.

"Why is he after your father?"

"He thinks Nick took what was his."

Then she changed the subject, talking instead about the term paper Waynie had done for the course, *Slobs Who Live With Obsessive Compulsives*.

"He did not!" Ronnie accused, staring wide-eyed in the rearview mirror.

"He most certainly did. He had a hypothetical that mentioned two roommates, Dwayne the slob and Ronald the neat freak. Ronald was all uptight and tense, taking out all his aggression on his poor roomie Dwayne, who was just your average guy. He blamed Ronald's compulsiveness on his lack of female companionship. Said he was sexually repressed."

Ronnie nearly wrecked. Dante slung a protective arm around Nadia to keep her from being pitched into the floorboard. She was laughing so hard she was almost in tears.

"I'm gonna *kill* that moron!" Ronnie shouted.

● ● ●

Leaving Nadia to get ready for her set, Dante strode down the corridor and reentered the bar using the stage door. A sense of relief stole over him as he surveyed the crowd. Charlie's was a pretty small bar. There were probably no more than fifty people here tonight, and they all looked like they belonged. A bunch of college kids, a couple of roughnecks . . . no farm workers with fifty dollar manicures.

This was the kind of joint he was comfortable in. Peanut shells crunched underneath his boots, and the place smelled like pizza, beer, and cigarette smoke. Dante walked past the blaring jukebox, past the crooked tables with mismatched tablecloths and took a seat at the bar.

A flashing pink sign above the bar advertised a beer he'd never heard of, and the bartender caught him staring at it.

"You want one of those, hon?" she asked.

Dante shook his head. "I'll take a Coke, though, when you have time."

The bartender nodded and snapped her gum. She had teased red hair, thick blue eye shadow, and a name tag that read "Flo". Dante smiled when she walked away, thinking of the waitress from a TV show he'd watched when he was a kid.

Ronnie hopped up on a barstool beside him.

"Wait till you hear Nadia sing. She's great." He winked. "Just don't tell her I said so."

"Okay." Dante smiled.

The bartender slid Dante's drink to him. He thanked her and reached for his wallet, but Ronnie shook his head. "Put it on my bill, Flo."

Flo nodded and walked off.

"Thanks, man," Dante said, lifting his glass.

"No problem. We're co-workers now." Ronnie was quiet for a moment, then he said, "Nadia likes you, you know?"

Dante paused, wondering if Branson had told Ronnie about their arrangement. Maybe not, since he hadn't been fired yet. He weighed his answers and, in the end, decided to be honest. "I like her too."

"I've been working for Mr. Branson for eight years now. Nadia was a kid when I started. I taught her how to drive." He looked at Dante over his own glass and said, "All I'm asking is, don't hurt her, man. Nadia ain't as tough as she acts."

Dante nodded, thinking about the vulnerable little girl he'd glimpsed beneath her cocky exterior last night.

Ronnie continued, "She's been through a lot of crap in her life. I wasn't lying about the little sister thing. All of us guys are real protective of her." He gave Dante a faint smile. "I'd hate to have to beat you up."

"Understood," Dante said with a nod. Then he said, "So, tell me . . . how did you end up rooming with Waynie?"

Ronnie scowled. "I drew the freakin' short straw, that's

how. You don't think it was because I had a choice, do you?"

Ronnie started on another tirade and soon Dante was laughing hard as Nadia had on the way down.

"Hey, Ronnie," Flo said. "Quit your yapping and get that jukebox for me, would you? It's almost time for Nadia."

"With pleasure." Ronnie drained the rest of his drink and set the glass on the counter. "I hate this song."

He walked over to the jukebox and yanked the plug.

Nadia walked onto the stage. "Hey, guys!" Nadia yelled into the microphone.

Catcalls and whistles greeted her while the band assembled behind her. Dante recognized the two boy toys from the restaurant and said a fervent prayer that Nadia was not a pop singer.

She gave a little bow and said, "I'm feeling magnanimous tonight, so you guys know what that means . . ."

"I have no idea what that means!" Waynie shouted from across the room.

"Moron," Ronnie muttered.

Nadia laughed. "Okay, Waynie. I'm feeling *generous* tonight, so here it is. This is request night. I'll sing whatever you want me to, but if you make me sing bubblegum crap, no more request nights. Okay?"

Someone shouted out a request and the band began to play. Dante had to admit, they were pretty good. Then Nadia began to sing.

She was better than good.

Her smoky voice filled the room and the whole place got quiet. Nadia was a presence on the stage. In other bars, people did their own things and hardly paid attention to the band, but Nadia had them under her spell.

She impressed him with the range of songs she was able to cover. She sang mostly rock, contemporary, and classic, then a drunk cowboy threw his hat on the stage and shouted out a request. Without missing a beat, Nadia donned the hat and cued the band.

Soon, she was singing and prancing around the stage, doing some of the most inspired wiggling and jiggling Dante had ever seen. He couldn't help but laugh.

The girl was a firecracker, and she was having a ball. The crowd roared their approval.

"Whew, thank you!" Nadia paused between songs to get a drink of water. "This song here is for my friend, Slick."

The band broke into a frenzied version of the old Joan Jett and the Blackhearts song, *I Love Rock and Roll*. Nadia blew him a kiss when she sang about meeting a guy by the record machine.

Dante laughed, remembering their first meeting. Remembering the first time Nadia had knocked him off his feet. Hadn't part of him known even then that he was going to fall in love with her?

The thought sobered him.

He wasn't falling in love with Nadia. He couldn't. He was here to do a job, and he'd best get that through his thick head.

No way he could be falling for her. He'd only known her for twenty-four hours and Dante had never been much of a believer in love at first sight. But no woman he'd ever known made him feel like Nadia did.

Not even the one he'd married.

Why was he thinking of all this?

Dante Giovanni wasn't steady relationship material. He'd been told that more than once, and knew it to be true. So, why was he dreaming about happily-ever-after with Nadia?

He needed to get her to her father soon, before both of them got hurt. Because no matter what his head told him, his heart wasn't listening when he was around her.

Maybe tonight.

Dante could guess how Nadia would react if she knew about Nick's stipulation. She'd go nuts. He could talk her into leaving with him. She could be safe and sound with her real father in a matter of hours.

You ruthless jerk, he thought.

His stomach rolled when he realized he was contemplating using her attraction to him to his advantage. But what other choice did he have?

Ronnie's shout tore him from his thoughts. Dante glanced up to see the drunken cowboy charge the stage.

CHAPTER 4

"Let go . . . of me," Nadia gasped when the cowboy grabbed her waist and pulled her to him. The stench of beer and body odor made her eyes water.

"Come on, baby, just one little kiss," he slurred. "That's all I need."

Nadia planted her hand under his chin and forced his face away from hers. She groaned when she heard Ronnie's shout. Waynie's heavy footsteps thundered across the stage.

She'd have to move quickly to keep them from killing the poor slob.

Glancing down, she stomped on his instep with the heel of her boot. The cowboy howled and abruptly released her. Before he could do anything stupid, Nadia hooked her foot behind his ankle and sent him tumbling to the floor. He made no attempt to get up.

"You ought to be ashamed of yourself," she said, standing over him. "What would your mama think if she saw you acting like such an ass? Now, get over there and get yourself some coffee."

Ronnie chuckled. "Gee, Nadia. You already beat him up. You're going to nag him to death too?"

He moved around her to haul the drunk to his feet.

"You okay?" Dante asked from behind her.

He placed a protective hand on her waist and Nadia started at his touch. She covered it with a smile.

"I'm fine. Told you, I'm a big girl. I can take care of my-self." Nadia winked at him and leaned down to pick up the microphone. She winced at the microphone backfeed and announced, "Hey, guys. We're going to take a short break."

Almost immediately, the jukebox roared back to life.

Hopping off the stage, she headed toward the bar with Dante trailing behind. He gave her a surprised look when she ordered a soft drink.

"What, you expected me to be a sot or something?" she asked. "I don't drink much." She leaned forward and whis-pered, "The stuff makes me *crazy*."

Dante laughed. "I can't imagine."

Nadia took a sip of her soda and hopped back off the stool. Dante chuckled.

"What?" she demanded.

Dante scratched his chin and grinned. "Ah, nothing, princess. I was only wondering if you were even capable of sitting still for five minutes."

"Nope. Come on, let's dance. Ronnie steps on my feet,

and Waynie . . . well, look." She pointed to the dance floor. Waynie was swaying by himself to the song blaring from the jukebox, hilariously out of time with the music. He caught their stares and raised his glass in a toast.

Nadia lifted an eyebrow and said, "See what I mean?"

"Yeah, I do." Dante's brown eyes twinkled, and she didn't need alcohol to make her feel tipsy. "But will you beat me up if I try to kiss you?"

"Hmmm." She leaned in close, like she was going to kiss him, then pulled away. "I guess it depends on how nice you ask."

"No fair," he said, and let her lead him to the dance floor.

His big body dwarfed hers, and Nadia discovered she liked the feeling of him surrounding her.

Liked it a lot.

Being this close to Dante—touching him—left her shaky, a little unsure of herself. It was sensory overload. The soft skin that covered the hard slabs of muscle, the deep timbre of his voice, the wonderful scent of him. It was an intoxicating package.

Since he was so much taller, Nadia opted to wrap her arms around his waist and rest her face against his broad chest. One of Dante's hands wound in her hair and the other caressed the bare skin on her upper back.

"It's hard, dancing with the munchkin queen, huh, Dante?" Ronnie reached around them to grab a handful of peanuts from the bowl on the counter.

"Go away, Ronnie," Nadia murmured, too content to even muster up a good insult.

"Just so you guys know, the music's stopped," he continued.

"Go away, Ronnie," Dante said, smiling down at her.

"Fine, I can tell when I'm not wanted." Ronnie grabbed the bowl and wandered off into the crowd.

Someone fed more money into the jukebox, and they slow danced to another song. Nadia stared up at Dante. He was too quiet, too tense.

"What's wrong?" she asked.

He looked away. "Nothing."

"I can tell that something's wrong."

He frowned and rubbed the bridge of his nose. "Okay. Yeah, something's wrong. Can we go somewhere to talk?"

Nadia's heart fluttered in her chest. Was he already tired of her? Was he going to tell her he'd made a mistake by staying?

"Let's go outside," she said.

Ronnie lounged by the door, and she held up a finger, indicating for him to give them a moment. He nodded.

A slight breeze was blowing, stirring the hot August night, and Nadia slipped her hand inside Dante's. It gave her little reassurance when he squeezed her fingers.

When they walked by Waynie's pickup, Dante surprised her by lifting her up and setting her on the hood.

He stood between her open knees and rested his palms on the metal on either side of her. Nadia held her breath when he leaned forward.

He kissed her hard, with a fervor that both shocked and thrilled her. She wrapped her legs around his waist, tugging him closer. When they finally broke apart, they were both breathing hard.

Dante pressed his forehead to hers, and she raked her fingernails lightly over his scalp. He shuddered, making them both laugh.

His fingers gently massaged the back of her neck as he asked, "What are you, some kind of witch?"

Nadia gave a startled laugh. "Well, I guess I've been called worse . . ."

"I barely know you, but I can't stop thinking about you. I don't usually let myself get so . . . distracted. Must have something to do with those green eyes of yours."

Nadia couldn't stop the idiotic grin that spread across her face at his words. "Yeah, well, just so you know . . . making out in bar parking lots with big, bald strangers isn't exactly a habit of mine, either."

"I'm not all that strange."

"Ah, well. That makes me feel better." She pulled back to look in his eyes. "I need to talk to you too. I want to ask you . . ." Nadia hesitated.

Her heart threatened to pound out of her chest, but she smiled again and stroked his jaw. "I need to know if I can trust you. If you woke up in my bed tomorrow, would you break my heart?"

Dante abruptly pulled away from her.

"I can't do this," he muttered, and pulled a hand down his face as he paced underneath the pink glow of the neon sign.

Nadia's mouth went dry. It took some effort to force the words out. "You can't do what?"

A burst of gunfire shattered the night around them.

Nadia screamed and Dante threw himself at her. He jerked her off the hood into the gravel beside him.

"Stay down!" he shouted, and grabbed a gun from his calf holster.

Gunfire peppered around the truck when the bodyguards stationed in the parking lot returned fire.

Nadia watched in horror when the bar doors burst open. Ronnie and Waynie led the charge. A big red flower appeared on Waynie's shirt.

Then he went down.

"Waynie!" she screamed.

She started crawling to him. Sharp gravel bit into her palms, nearly slicing them when Dante seized her ankle and yanked her backward.

"Are you trying to get yourself killed?" he demanded.

"Let go of me. I've got to help Waynie."

"Waynie would want you to be safe. We've got to get out of here." He yanked open the door to Waynie's pickup and pushed her inside. "Keep your head down."

Dante reached around her, fumbling for the switch. He cursed and Nadia realized the keys were missing.

"Help them," she said. "I can do this."

Without waiting for his reply, Nadia jerked a handful of wires from underneath the dash. Dante slid out of the cab and she heard the report from his weapon when he moved around the side of the truck.

She worked fast. Red, purple, green. The wires sparked and the engine roared to life. She scooted behind the wheel when she heard Dante fumble with the passenger side door. Dante threw himself in the seat and Nadia stomped the accelerator, sending up a spray of gravel when they rocketed past the neon sign.

"How did you do that?" Dante asked. He ejected an empty clip onto the floorboard and reloaded.

"You'd be surprised at the things I can do," Nadia said absently, checking the rearview mirror.

A pair of headlights swung out of Charlie's parking lot, but she had the jump on them. She tromped on the gas. The needle on the speedometer hit 90, and the little truck began to shimmy.

"I bet. But I know hotwiring cars. It's not like the movies, not that quick of a process. How did you know which wires?"

"You're assuming I haven't hotwired this truck before," she said. "Waynie . . ." Sudden tears stung her eyes, and she couldn't finish her sentence.

Dante's voice was soft, concerned. "I've got my phone. Do you have Ronnie's cell number?"

Nadia nodded and blinked back tears. Now was no time to cry.

She rattled the number off to Dante. Her mind was racing. She had to shake their pursuers. Nadia almost missed the turnoff before she realized where she wanted to go.

Wheeler Town. That would be perfect. She twisted the wheel and shot down the narrow back road.

"Ronnie? Hey!"

Dante grunted when she threw him against the dash. He dropped the phone and pawed around the floorboard for it. "Yeah, I'm still here, and we're both okay. It's only Nadia's driving." He placed a hand on her shoulder and gave it a gentle squeeze. "Waynie said you'd better not wreck his truck."

"Oh!" Nadia's breath left her in a rush. She pressed a hand to her mouth. "Waynie's alive?"

"Yeah, but we won't be if you don't put both hands back on the wheel. Ronnie wants to know where we're going."

"Hold the phone up here so I can talk to him."

Dante obediently held the phone to her head.

"Thanks," she murmured. "Ronnie, are you there?"

"Nadia, where you headed?" he asked. "Don't say road names over the cell."

Nadia tried to think. "Do you remember where we hid from the state trooper that time—"

"That's not far enough. You have to go much farther. Two of the cars behind you are not friendlies. Drive out of town. You know where Henderson wrecked his motorcycle? Go at least that far. Give us a chance to take care of these guys."

"Okay. Got it."

"Call me back in fifteen." Ronnie paused. There was a catch in his voice when he said, "Take care, little sister."

Nadia's throat ached with the emotion caught there. "You too."

She nodded at Dante, who clicked the phone shut.

"Hotwiring trucks, outrunning state troopers . . . what kind of delinquent are you?" he asked, twisting around to face her.

She appreciated his effort to make her smile, and tried to hold up her end of the conversation. "Waynie's always losing his keys. As for the state trooper . . . well, I'll put it like this . . . if I get one more speeding ticket, my driver's license will make a very interesting coaster."

Nadia no longer saw headlights in her mirror, but she took another detour, just in case. The narrow road was cratered with potholes. Dante muttered something when she crashed through one of them and made him bang his head on the back glass. Nadia tried in vain to hide her smile.

"What's so funny?" he demanded, rubbing his head.

"Nothing." She glanced in the rearview mirror. "Hey, I think we've lost them."

She'd been riding these back roads all her life. They'd never find her if she didn't want to be found.

Dante's cell phone rang.

● ● ●

He flipped it open. "Giovanni."

"Is Nadia okay?" Gary Vandergriff's anxious voice asked.

"She's fine."

"Who is it, Dante?" Nadia asked.

Holding up his hand, he indicated for her to wait. He turned his head, ignoring the impatient look she shot him.

"Are you bringing her to me?" Vandergriff asked.

The more Dante thought about the situation, the more he realized he had no choice. Nadia would be furious, but Nick couldn't keep her safe. Twice in a matter of days, his men had been outgunned. Dante had to do what was best for her, even if she hated him for it.

"Yeah," he told Vandergriff. "Where do we go?"

"To my place on Rock Island, where you and I met before. Do you remember how get back there?"

"No problem."

"Wait! Do you need back-up?"

"No, we've got it covered."

Dante clicked the phone shut, switching the ringer off as he did. He looked at Nadia. "Change of plans."

"Who was that?" she asked, glancing at him.

Dante couldn't meet her eyes. He stared out the window as he shoved the phone back into his pocket. "Your father," he said. "He's afraid it's not safe for you at home. He wants me to take you somewhere until things settle down."

"Oooh, you and me? Alone?" Nadia laughed. "Looks like my luck's changing for the better."

Dante chuckled, but he was troubled. He didn't like lying to her.

"Which way are we going?" Nadia asked as they drove out of the city limits.

"McMinnville."

"Wish I'd known that before. We're going off the wrong side of the mountain. But it's no big deal. I'll go this way and catch the interstate to Tullahoma. A little out of the way, but it'll be better than driving back through the middle of town."

During the next half hour, Nadia made several attempts at conversation, but Dante couldn't keep up his end. He was sick inside, nervous.

All over one lie.

It was crazy. In his line of work, he told lots of lies. So many, in fact, that sometimes it was hard to remember what was real and what was fantasy.

He shook his head, tried to clear his thoughts. This was different. He was doing this for Nadia. To keep her safe.

So, why did it feel like a betrayal?

He didn't know what Nadia knew about her father or what she didn't, but the fact was that—in a matter of minutes now—the life Nadia knew would be changed forever. He had seen the bond between her and Nick Branson. If she didn't already know Gary Vandergriff was her real father, she could be crushed.

"What's wrong?" Nadia's voice was quiet. "Talk to me. Tell me what you're thinking."

Dante sighed. "I'm thinking it was too close. Thinking I'm really lucky you're not dead right now. It was stupid, to have you out in the open back there."

"We're okay," she said. "Stop beating yourself up. It was my fault we were out there." She gave him a lopsided grin and said, "How's that old saying go, only the good die young? I think both of us are probably safe."

Dante reached underneath her hair and gently rubbed the nape of her neck. "That's all I want, Nadia, for you to be safe."

"Before the shooting started, you said you couldn't do this. What did you mean?" she asked.

Indecision tore at him. He'd come close to spilling the whole story in the parking lot—the *real* story—and he wanted to now, but he didn't know how Nadia would react to the news. Better to just stick to the plan and deliver her to her father. Maybe after he had a chance to explain, she could forgive him.

"It's about your father," he said. "When Nick hired me, he had a condition to my employment. I'm supposed to keep my hands off you."

She blinked, and turned to him with wide eyes. "He did *what*?"

"He didn't think I was the right guy for you."

"It's not his choice to make," she said finally. The shock faded from her voice, replaced by fury. She violently shifted gears.

Dante shrugged. "I've been through it before. Not too many daddies are happy to have a guy like me hanging around with their little girls."

"I told you before, I'm no little girl. If Nick thinks he can treat me like one, he's crazy." She gave him a suspicious glance. "You're not going to listen to him, are you?"

Dante smiled. "You mean like I've listened so far? Baby, you're like gravity or something. How am I supposed to stay away from you?"

Nadia's frown relaxed, and she actually smiled. Shaking her head, she said, "If he fires you, I'll move out. I've wanted to since I was eighteen, but I never pushed it. He's not going to tell me who I can and can't see."

Dante touched her neck, and realized Nick was right. Nadia had no business with a guy like him. No way around it, she was going to be hurt. She would hate his guts.

He smoothed her hair. They were almost there and he couldn't keep his hands off her. After tonight, Nadia would probably never allow him to touch her again.

"Turn left there, at the Lyons Ferry Dock sign."

Nadia peered out the window, staring out over the silvery, moonlit river and the huge, rocky crags surrounding it.

"I didn't know Nick had a place here or I would've come sooner," she said. "We used to come here sometimes when I was a kid. There's a swinging bridge over at the state park, a treacherous looking thing. I used to stand in the middle of it and make it shimmy. Nick would nearly have a stroke, convinced I was going to fall into the gulf below."

Dante managed a faint smile at the image. "I imagine you were hell on wheels when you were a kid."

"A brat," Nadia confirmed, pulling into the launch area.

Dante squinted at the dock. The hulking shapes of two men standing on the ramp materialized from the shadows.

Dante fought the urge to tell Nadia to turn around and drive away. To leave before her faith in him was destroyed. Instead, he unhooked the wires to shut off the engine and kissed her.

Holding her in his arms and breathing in the sweet scent of her, he felt his heart break. How would she feel about him when she came face to face with her real father?

"What was that for?" she murmured against his throat.

Dante swallowed hard. "I thought I told you already. I like to kiss you."

"That didn't feel like an ordinary kiss." Nadia's fingers splayed over his cheek as she stared into his eyes.

She was stunning in the moonlight, a creature too beautiful to exist even in dreams, and already part of him was dying.

"Good," he said, his mouth dry. "Because I don't want you to think my kisses are ordinary."

Nadia frowned and reached for the door handle. Her eyes searched his again before she opened the door. Her voice was so soft he thought he might have imagined it when she said, "It felt . . . like goodbye."

● ● ●

August 7
12:10 a.m.

Dante shivered as he helped Nadia slip on an orange life-jacket. His sudden chill had nothing to do with the warm summer night. He fought against the anxiety rising in him, not trusting the instincts that had served him so well in the past because he knew what scared him.

He was afraid of losing her.

His hands shook when he clicked her safety straps closed.

The wind picked up, and the boat ride was a choppy one. Dante and Nadia shared a seat on the little fishing boat, and he twisted his hand in the straps on the back of her lifejacket to keep her from bouncing over the side.

"What river is this?" he asked, not really caring, but trying to keep from thinking about the confrontation to come.

"It's the junction of the Collins River and the Caney Fork. Good walleye fishing in the spring," the man beside them answered.

The other man had yet to say a word. He simply watched them with a blank expression on his face.

The river was nearly deserted at this hour. In the fifteen minute ride to Vandergriff's house, Dante only saw one other craft. A couple of old men in an aluminum boat were fishing under a bridge, and one of them lifted a hand in greeting when they passed.

Dante returned his wave and tried to ignore the heart that threatened to beat its way out of his chest. Finally, they arrived at the private dock.

While one of the men tied off the boat, Dante hopped onto the swaying wooden structure and reached for Nadia's hand. The fingers that slipped inside his were cold, and he wondered if she'd caught some of the anxiety that rolled off him.

A set of handmade wooden steps snaked their way up the side of the bluff. Nadia wordlessly released his hand and started up.

Wild honeysuckle grew in clusters around the bank, perfuming the night air. It was usually a scent Dante liked, but tonight it was cloying, almost overpowering. He was sweating and almost nauseous by the time they reached the top. Nadia stopped to stare at the house before her.

"This is my father's place?" she asked. Her voice sounded funny, tight. Maybe even scared.

"Yes," was all Dante could say.

Two armed guards stood on the front lawn. They stepped aside when they recognized their comrades. Dante placed a steadying hand on the small of Nadia's back as they stepped onto the sprawling porch.

This is wrong. This is wrong. This is wrong.

The words screamed in Dante's head, and once again he had to resist the urge to grab Nadia and bolt.

The porch lights came on and the front door swung

open. Dante shielded his eyes and blinked at the uniformed servant standing in front of them.

"Mr. Giovanni, Ms. Branson. Won't you please follow me?"

The servant turned on his heel and started walking. The men behind them crowded in closer and he and Nadia had no choice but to move forward.

Nadia glanced back at him with a troubled look on her face, then walked on ahead. The heels of her boots made a soft clacking sound on the gleaming oak floor, and all around them hung the scent of lemon cleanser. Dante watched her body stiffen when she scanned the room.

Gary Vandergriff stepped out of a shadowy doorway. He smiled and said, "Welcome, Nadia. Welcome to my home."

Dante heard Nadia's gasp.

She spun on her heel to face him, and her horrified expression hit Dante like a physical blow.

"You bastard," she whispered.

CHAPTER 5

Nadia hurt too much to be afraid. She stared at Dante and he stared back.

Then her hurt gave way to fury.

Closing the distance between them, she took a swing at him. Dante didn't even try to dodge it. The wild hay-maker caught him square in the mouth.

The mouth that had lied to her and kissed her and made her believe there really was someone out there for her. Someone like her, someone she could love.

Some chance at happiness.

At that moment, she hated him worse than she could ever hate Gary Vandergriff.

"Nadia, don't," he pleaded, and touched his lip.

His fingers came away wet with blood. It streamed down his chin, and Nadia felt a cold satisfaction.

But it wasn't enough. Not nearly enough.

"How much did he pay you, Dante? Or is that even

your real name?" she screamed. "How much was my life worth to you?"

"Nadia, what are you talking about?" Dante reached to touch her, but she slapped his hand away.

"She's confused." Vandergriff interrupted, his voice smooth and controlled. "And no wonder. No telling what kind of lies they've told her about me. Nadia, honey, it's all right. You're safe here. You're safe with me."

Nadia glared at Gary Vandergriff and wondered what kind of game he was playing. He was the only thing she could ever remember fearing. He was the boogeyman in her closet, the monster under her childhood bed.

A murderous demon with a lying tongue.

"I only wanted you to be safe," Dante said, holding out his palms. "Your father was afraid that Nick couldn't keep you safe, so he hired me to bring you to him."

Nadia whipped her head around. "What are you saying?" she demanded. "You think *he's* my father?"

"Did they tell you I wasn't?" Vandergriff asked. He moved closer to her and Nadia took a step backward. He grabbed her wrist.

"Don't touch me!" Nadia jerked away from him, and inadvertently stumbled toward Dante. He reached out his arms to steady her and, God help her, she wanted to hurl herself in those arms.

"I'm sorry you had to find out like this," Dante said softly. "And I'm sorry I lied to you. I never wanted to hurt you. I swear, all I ever wanted to do was protect you. The money doesn't mean anything to me now." He stared over her shoulder at Vandergriff. "You can keep it. All of it. The only thing I want is your word that Nadia will be safe."

"His word!" Nadia spat.

She was shaking, and she tried to force herself to calm down. To remember what she'd been taught.

Show no fear. Look for a way out.

But there was no way out. Not this time.

"He's lying, Dante," she said desperately. "He is *not* my father."

Vandergriff frowned and snapped his fingers. His butler stepped forward and gave a slight bow. "Yes, Mr. Vandergriff?"

"Theo, will you take Mr. Giovanni into my study? I would like to speak to my daughter alone. I can try to clear up some of this mess."

Abruptly, Nadia's fury was washed away by fear at the thought of being left alone with Vandergriff. "Don't leave me, Dante!" she cried when one of the men from the boat took his arm and started to lead him away.

Her breath caught when Dante yanked his arm from the man's grasp and stalked back in her direction.

Vandergriff moved quickly to stand between them.

"Please, Mr. Giovanni," he begged. "Just give me a few minutes alone with my daughter, that's all I ask. You'll be right in the next room. And you know what I'm saying is true. I know you had my story checked out. Now, let me convince Nadia."

Dante hesitated and shifted his eyes back to hers. He studied her for a long moment and sighed.

"Nadia, try to hear him out. I'll be in the next room." He pointed at Vandergriff. "You have fifteen minutes. If Nadia still doesn't want to stay, I'm taking her with me."

Nadia watched helplessly while he walked into the next room. As the door swung shut, she shouted, "My father was protecting me—"

A jolt of electricity arced through her body. Nadia's legs collapsed, and she crashed to the floor.

Vandergriff squatted beside her, watching her face. Nadia opened her mouth to scream, but she couldn't make a sound.

As if he were reading her mind, he said, "Scream all you like. He's in a soundproof room."

He seized her by her hair and dragged her to the over-stuffed sofa.

It didn't even hurt.

The only thing she felt was her wildly contracting muscles, and it took her several minutes to clear her head. To realize what had happened.

A stun gun. The jerk had used a stun gun on her.

Dazed, Nadia realized she was sitting on the sofa.

Vandergriff leaned toward her. His mouth was moving and she realized he was talking. She tried to understand what he was saying.

"You're not my . . . father," she managed, and Vandergriff laughed.

"Of course not, but you do belong to me now."

He stroked her cheek, but Nadia couldn't feel his touch. She was numb except for a weird tingling sensation underneath her skin. Then her shoulder started to burn.

"Maybe you'll bear me an heir. Replace the one your mother and I would have had if it hadn't been for your father. Wouldn't that simply kill them both?"

Tears stung Nadia's eyes when the hopelessness of her situation sank in. She'd always been so flippant about her father's warnings, so sure that Gary Vandergriff could never get to her. Now, she was at his mercy. No one could save her, not even . . .

"Dante," she whispered.

"Yes." Vandergriff smiled and glanced at his watch. Raking his hand through his hair, he leaned back into the brown sofa. "How amusing. What happens to the bounty hunter is entirely up to you. I really have no quarrel with him. He did an excellent job."

Nadia found herself unable to look away from those icy blue eyes.

"So . . . it's up to you, Nadia." He paused, wrinkling his brow. "One, you can pretend I'm your long lost daddy, and let him walk out of here. Or two, you can tell him what a bad man I am." He twisted a lock of her hair around his finger. "And I'll have his heart cut out and prepared for your dinner."

126

"Go to hell," she rasped.

"Been there, babe. Thanks to your parents. But things are definitely looking up." Vandergriff grinned at her when the study door opened.

Dante stepped through the doorway, and the worried look on his face shattered Nadia's heart into a million pieces.

Out of concern for her, he had done what he thought was best.

Out of love for him, she would too.

"Nadia, are you okay?" he asked, and crossed the room to stand before her.

Slowly, she nodded. "It was just such a shock."

Vandergriff's grip tightened on her arm, and she realized what she'd said. She dropped her head and tried to figure out what to say. Dante looked so strong, so invincible. But he was only one man against an army.

If she blew this, he would die.

Dante jerked his head at Vandergriff. "Do you believe him? Do you believe he's your father?"

"Yes." Nadia swallowed hard, hating the taste of the lie on her lips. "I believe him. He has . . . proof."

She wished there was something she could say. Some way she could tell him to go quietly, to get her father to help him. But her mind was still foggy, and she couldn't risk getting caught by Vandergriff.

Dante rubbed the back of his neck. "So, what do you want to do? We can leave right now. I can take you—"

"I'm staying," she interrupted, and Dante looked at her in surprise.

"I'll stay here with you then. I can help guard you."

"No. I need time to sort this out. I need time alone with my . . . father." She mustered what she hoped was a reassuring smile. "I'll call you when things settle down. When I work things out."

"You don't hate me?" He gave her a hopeful smile that melted her.

She wanted to tell him she could never hate him. That she thought she might even be falling in love with him. But that would give Gary Vandergriff too much ammunition to use against her.

All she said was no.

"Well, here. Write down my number and call me whenever you need me." Dante picked up a pad of paper lying on the coffee table and held it out to her.

"You write it," she said.

She still felt jittery from the shock she'd taken and doubted she could grasp the pen.

Dante wrote down the number and tore off the page. Folding it carefully, he crouched beside her and tucked it in her hand. She somehow forced her slack fingers to clutch it.

Nadia's heart froze when he hugged her, enveloping her in his strong arms. The scent of him and his damned Diesel Green surrounded her. She wanted to hold him, to pull him close to her one last time, but she still couldn't lift her arms.

All too soon, he let her go.

He brushed a kiss on the top of her head. "It's going to be all right," he said. "I promise."

She managed a nod and looked away before she burst into tears.

"I'll have one of my men take you back to your vehicle," Vandergriff said, standing to shake Dante's hand. "Thank you, son, for bringing her to me. The money—"

"I don't want the money," Dante said again.

"It's already been wired to your account. I authorized the transaction as soon as the boat docked outside. Do with it what you will." He smiled at Nadia. "You've earned it."

Vandergriff walked Dante to the door. Before he went outside, Dante glanced at Nadia.

"It's going to be okay," he repeated.

"I know," she said, even though she knew nothing would ever be okay again. Vandergriff shut the door behind him and turned the lock. He peered out the peephole a moment before turning back to her.

"Good job!" he said. "But I should have known that any child of Maria's would be a born liar."

He crossed over and flopped back on the couch beside her. Snatching the paper out of her hands, Vandergriff shredded it and tossed the pieces over his shoulder. He rubbed his hands together gleefully, like a child at Christmas. "I bet your daddy is going nuts right now. Can you imagine? Maybe we'll call him later."

He made a move like he was going to kiss her and Nadia turned her head. Vandergriff seized her chin and whipped her face back around.

"Don't you ever turn away from me," he growled, and crushed his mouth to hers.

Nadia squirmed, horrified by the feel of his kiss. She bit his lip.

With a howl, he shoved her backward. She never saw the slap coming, but it rang in her ears, rattled her throbbing head. His face swam before her eyes, and it was a moment before she was able to focus on him again.

Vandergriff touched his lip gingerly. Then he smiled. A bloody, maniacal smile that made him look like a cannibal.

"My dear . . . didn't your mother tell you?" he said. "I *like* it rough."

Angry tears stung Nadia's eyes. She wished she could wipe her mouth. "She didn't talk about you . . . at all," she managed.

It was true. Her mother never mentioned Gary Vandergriff, like he was a curse that could be avoided if she never uttered his name aloud. Whenever anyone else spoke it, she would get up and leave the room.

Anger simmered in Vandergriff's cold blue eyes, and his mouth tightened.

You can't stand it, can you? she thought. *You can't stand to think that she survived you, that you aren't the focus of her life.*

"Well," he said casually. "I can't believe she didn't mention how we'd met. It was such a memorable encounter."

Nadia felt sickened by the gleam in his eye, even before she heard what he had to say.

"I bought her services for six hundred dollars," he said.

"Liar!" she spat. "My mother is not a whore."

Vandergriff grinned. "Maybe not at first, but she was a quick learner. My father owned a tobacco farm in Kentucky. Maria worked in the field, along with her father and brothers. I think her mother died giving birth to one of them or something." He waved his hand dismissively. "Anyway, she wasn't around."

"You're lying again," Nadia muttered. "My mother was an only child, just like me."

"Are you sure?" he asked, with a wink. "Are you absolutely sure about either of those things?"

Confused, Nadia lapsed into silence. What was the point of all this? Did he really think she was going to believe a word he said?

Vandergriff rubbed his hands together. "The first time I saw her, I knew I had to have her. All that long dark hair, and those green eyes . . . I'm really glad you look like her instead of Andreakos. He's such an ugly bastard. This makes things much more pleasant for me, almost like a walk down memory lane."

"Who is Andreakos?" she snapped.

Vandergriff chuckled. "My, my . . . haven't they told you *anything*? Andreakos is your father's real name. But he hasn't called himself that in all these years that he's been hiding from me like a cockroach in the walls."

Nadia opened her mouth to deny it, but then frowned as a tinge of memory intruded. Hadn't she heard that name once? Hadn't she even written it?

Suddenly, she pictured herself at a school desk, painstakingly writing the name across a sheet of big ruled paper. It had been a real pain to try to fit it on that little black line. Was that a true memory, or was her dazed mind accepting Vandergriff's fabrication as truth?

It didn't matter. So what if her father had changed his name? Her parents had had ample reason to fear, and to hide. She closed her eyes, and Vandergriff grabbed her shoulder to shake her. The movement made her eyes feel like they were marbles rattling loose inside her skull.

"Hey, no fading out on me. We have so much to talk about. Don't make me zap you again."

With some effort, Nadia opened her eyes once more. Nothing he said mattered. His words, she could endure. His touch was something else entirely.

"What was I saying? Oh, yes . . . your mother. Maria was beautiful. All that long, dark hair. I spotted her in the field, and tried to get her to go into the barn with me. She wouldn't speak to me. She kept shaking her head, no, no, like a freaking mute. Nobody tells me no. I grabbed her arm and she pulled away. She spat on my shoes." Vandergriff laughed. "I threw her on the ground. It didn't make much difference to me if she wanted it rough and dirty."

Bile rose in Nadia's throat and she started singing a song in her mind, trying to block out the vileness she felt was coming. Maybe she couldn't endure his words, after all.

"Her father and brothers were working in the rows behind her. They came running when she screamed. She looked so grateful to see them that I decided to teach her a little lesson about who I was and *what* she was. I dug out my wallet. I still remember exactly how much money it had in it, six hundred twenty dollars." He shrugged. "Not a bad sum back then. I flashed it at her old man. It was probably more than the old drunk made in a month. 'Half an hour,' I said. 'This money is yours if you give me half an hour in the barn with your daughter.' One of her brothers lunged at me."

Vandergriff paused. Staring at something over Nadia's shoulder, he giggled. "It was the funniest thing I've ever seen. He lunged at me and his father caught his arm. He'd never taken his eyes off the money, you see. I took it out of my wallet and pressed it in his hand. 'Just half and hour,' I repeated. The old man stared at the ground and whispered, 'You won't hurt her?' I managed not to laugh in his face. I'd already decided that little bitch was going to pay for her disrespect. 'Of course not,' I told him. You should have seen the look on Maria's face. She kicked and screamed and scratched when I grabbed her arms and dragged her to the barn. Her family simply stood there."

Vandergriff scratched his chin and gave her a speculative glance. Nadia hoped her slack face didn't reveal the horror she felt inside.

"I always wondered if that six hundred dollars felt like Judas's thirty pieces of silver burning in her father's pocket while he stood in that barnyard and listened to her screams."

Vandergriff leaned forward, suddenly red-faced and angry. He jabbed Nadia in the chest with his finger. "I had her any way I wanted her, and I took longer than thirty frigging minutes. I left her lying there, battered and bleeding and bruised, and by the time I left, she wasn't saying 'no' anymore. She was saying, 'Please don't kill me, sir.'"

An evil smile curled his lips and the bile in Nadia's throat burned like acid, threatening to choke her.

"I had to go back to college the next day. I figured I'd never see any of them again, but four months later, when I was home for winter break, I found my father waiting up for me one night. As soon as my key hit the front door lock, he summoned me into his study. Maria's father and oldest brother were inside waiting. I don't think I've ever seen my father so furious. He pointed at the old drunk and said, 'This man says his daughter is pregnant with your child. Could that possibly be true?' I shrugged. I figured he'd take care of it for me, so I said, 'Yeah, it's possible.' He busted me one across the mouth and launched into a tirade about how I was a Vandergriff, and what did I think I was doing sleeping about with white trash like her. Her father sat there, afraid to say a word, but her brother got in Father's face. He swore that Maria was a virgin before I 'used' her, a fact I was forced to admit, and that no man had known her since." Vandergriff shook his head.

"When my father was raging like that, he'd scare the tail off Satan himself. I was shocked, but not entirely displeased when Father said I would be marrying her. No Vandergriff had ever been born out of wedlock, apparently not even to servants. After the baby was born, a blood test would be performed to confirm paternity. That was all they had back then. Father made it clear that they would pay with their lives if they were lying."

"My father paid her father twenty thousand dollars in cash for her silence. He and her brothers were to leave that night, and never darken our doorstep again. Maria would be a Vandergriff, lost to them forever. So, once again, her father sold her to me. She was only fifteen, such a pretty little toy, and to be honest, I looked forward to taming her." He winked and brushed his hand in Nadia's hair. "Much the same as I look forward to taming you. I forgot how fierce those green eyes could look."

Nadia looked down. The barely restrained glee in his face was more than she could stand.

"Effective immediately, Maria was moved into the main house." Vandergriff leered at her. "Would you like to know what my father did to your grandfather and uncles?"

"No," Nadia said.

Vandergriff propped his feet on the coffee table. Lacing his hands behind his head, he smiled at Nadia. "Come now, don't be a spoilsport. I'm going to tell you anyway. They all lived in the same camper. You know, one of those little round silver things. That night, my father and I watched his men surround it. One of them padlocked the door, the only way out. A dog couldn't have fit through those tiny windows. They poured gasoline under it and struck a match. Whoosh!" Vandergriff spread his fingers wide. "You should've heard them screaming. I always wondered what it must have felt like inside that thing. Did you ever see any of those old fashioned popcorn cookers, the kind people used before microwaves? I used to love to do those on the wood stove. The little covered aluminum pan with a handle that you shook over the stove until its top popped out like, well, a pregnant woman's belly." Vandergriff laughed at his own joke. "I figured it might've felt like that, or maybe a can of sardines with a blowtorch beneath it."

"The baby," Nadia asked softly, trying to rid her mind of the horrible visual images of death and suffering he invoked. "What happened to the baby?"

Vandergriff shrugged. "Your mother's sweet little teenage body was made for a lot of things, but apparently childbirth wasn't one of them. Our son died. She nearly died. She labored for over fifteen hours. I can still hear her screams. I think it did something to her, mentally. Stole the fire right out of her. She was never quite the same after that."

How had her mother survived it? Nadia wondered. The scars on her face were nothing compared to the scars she must carry on her soul. How very strong she must be. He hadn't broken her. He hadn't destroyed her. But it must've been so hard for her. How could you survive such things, and still have the ability to love? How strong the bond between her parents had to be, to withstand so much trauma.

Nadia remembered one time when her mother was sick with the flu. She'd cried and begged and screamed in her delirium. Her father had never left her side. He'd held her hand, mopped her forehead with a cool washcloth and whispered reassurances in her ear.

Nadia's heart swelled with a new love and respect for her parents. For them, she would not let Vandergriff defeat her.

He reached for her again.

Someone coughed behind them and Vandergriff drew back his hand.

"I'm sorry to interrupt, sir—"

"What is it, Theo?" Vandergriff snapped without turning around, without looking away from her face.

"It's Andreakos. His men are on the move. We think . . . Peterson thinks they might be heading this way. If they are, they could be here in a couple of hours."

Vandergriff flinched.

"There's no way he could know about this place," he said, but Nadia caught a glimpse of fear in his eyes. "Have you talked to Underwood?"

"No, sir."

For a moment, hope surged within her. Her father was

coming to rescue her.

Then Vandergriff said, "Tell Peterson to get the plane ready. He's going to accompany the girl back to California. The compound is more secure. There's no way they'll be able to get to her there."

The butler paused. "You're not going, sir?"

Vandergriff sighed. "I wish I were. I'm so sick of this godforsaken place." He wrinkled his nose at Nadia and smiled. "But if I leave, who will be here to greet our guests?"

❀ ❀ ❀

The ride back across the river seemed endless. The churning waves only increased the churning in Dante's stomach. He kept picturing the look on Nadia's face. The pain in her eyes.

Would she ever forgive him? He would never be able to forgive himself if anything happened to her.

"Here we are." Vandergriff's man grabbed hold of the dock and pulled the boat close so Dante could jump off.

Dante glanced across the parking lot. It was empty except for Waynie's truck. The sight of that battered little pickup made his throat ache.

Dante stood and slowly unfastened his lifejacket. Dropping it into his empty seat, he moved toward the tow. The boat lurched and he leaned forward to keep his balance.

Vandergriff's man never saw Dante's punch coming. Without so much as a grunt, he crumpled to the bottom of the boat.

Dante moved quickly, sawing through the straps of the lifejacket with his pocketknife. Using them, he secured the man's hands and feet. He pushed his burden onto the creaking wooden dock, pausing only to strip the man of his cap and walkie talkie. He pulled the cap snugly on his head and clipped the walkie talkie to his waistband.

Swinging the boat around, Dante opened up the throttle and headed back the way he'd come.

He had known something was wrong as soon as he'd stepped out of that study and seen the pain in her eyes. Nadia had told the truth when she said she wasn't a liar. No matter what she'd said back there, or how calmly she'd said it, she couldn't hide the desperation in her eyes. Her terror was raw, palpable, and grotesquely disproportionate to the situation. When he'd held her, he'd caught the scent of ozone . . . the smell of burnt flesh . . . and he had known.

It had nearly killed him to walk out that door, but if they were going to have any chance at all, he had to catch Vandergriff and his men by surprise.

As he zipped along the black water, the walkie talkie crackled to life.

"Base to North."

Dante hesitated. They were calling for his escort.

He'd listened to their radio conversation as they'd made the first trip across, but he didn't feel confident enough to impersonate the man.

"Base to North. Come in."

He had no choice.

Keying the device, Dante counted on the crashing water to muffle his voice.

"This is North. Over."

"Drop off your package, North?"

"Affirmative. On my way in."

"What?"

"Affirmative," Dante repeated.

"Go to Cahill when you get back to get an update. We've got company coming tonight, 10-4?"

"10-4."

The radio was quiet after that and Dante could only hope he didn't have an ambush waiting for him.

No doubt who the company was. Dante only prayed Vandergriff's men weren't already on red alert.

No one was waiting on him when he arrived back at the dock. He secured the boat next to the others and hopped off. Tugging his cap lower, he skipped up the wooden steps, heading back to the main house.

Hoping the guys who were monitoring the cameras weren't paying too much attention, Dante headed toward the men's barracks adjacent to the house. It struck him how similar the set-up was to Branson's.

A distraction. He needed a distraction.

Then he spotted it.

A red lawnmower sat next to the front steps. Beside it was

a can of gasoline.

Whistling, Dante grabbed the can and liberally doused the back of the barracks. The fumes made his eyes tear when he flicked his silver lighter and tossed it into the pooling gasoline. With a loud whoosh, the weathered wood burst into flames.

Dante ran down the front porch of the building, rapping on doors and shouting, "Fire! Fire!"

Men emptied out of the building in various stages of undress. They came from around the house. Inside the house. An alarm began to blare.

Dante took advantage of the pandemonium and burst through the back door of the main house, startling the cook. The tiny Mexican woman dropped the pan of rolls she was pulling from the oven.

She opened her mouth to scream.

"*El fuego. La casa es se quemar,*" Dante said quickly. His Spanish was rusty, but the woman seemed to understand. She shut her mouth, nodded at him and ran out through the back door.

Dante checked the clip in his gun and pushed his way through the swinging doors into a deserted dining room. He had almost reached the other door when he heard the loud voices outside it. He scurried under the low-hanging tablecloth a moment before the doors burst open.

"I want to know what's going on, and I want to know right now."

Vandergriff sounded furious. He stopped right beside

Dante's hiding place. If he'd wanted to, Dante could've touched his black loafers. Sweat beaded on Dante's forehead and he struggled to control his rapid breathing.

"Stewart, go upstairs with the girl until I call you down. Blow a hole through anyone who tries to open the door. Theo, you come with me."

Dante waited until he heard the soft whish of the swinging doors before he took off after Stewart.

He was starting up the stairs. Dante rushed him. At the last moment, the big man turned and stared at Dante with huge, shocked eyes.

Stewart reached for his gun.

Dante never slowed. He crashed into him, driving Stewart backward into the steps. The wind left the fat man's body in a rush and he heard a sickening crunch.

Shoving his gun under the man's chin, Dante said, "The girl. Tell me where he's got the girl."

"Mister . . ." the man wheezed. "I can't. I'd be better off . . . with you pulling the trigger. . ."

Knowing he was running out of time, Dante slammed Stewart's head against a step, knocking him unconscious. He crawled over the man's bulky body and sprinted up the stairs.

Four identical doors greeted him. Dante started at the closest one and began trying them all.

The third was locked. Dante launched himself at it, kept launching himself at it until it splintered beneath his shoulder. He stumbled through the doorway and found himself staring into Nadia's stunned face.

She was tied to the headboard of a huge oak bed.

Dante clamored up on the bed and whipped out his pocketknife. He began sawing through the ropes.

"You came back for me," she said.

She looked so glad to see him that Dante felt his guts knot. This was all his fault. He had done this to her.

A faint, purple bruise darkened her cheek. "What did he do to you?" he demanded.

Her frantic eyes searched over his shoulder. "It's nothing. Please, just hurry. We have to get out of here."

Dante ran to the balcony doors and flung them open, searching for another escape route. The house was built on the edge of a cliff and Dante found himself staring into the black, swirling waters of the river below.

At the very least, it was a fifty foot drop.

When Dante heard the angry shouts outside the bedroom door, he realized he was too late. Gary Vandergriff and one of his gunmen exploded through the doorway.

"Execute him!" Vandergriff shouted.

Dante's brain cataloged the next few seconds in slow motion.

A burst of gunfire.

Nadia's scream.

The impact of the bullet slamming him against the railing.

The wood splintered, and he pitched backward into nothing.

CHAPTER **6**

Get in position.

Dante's military training took over before his mind could adjust to what was happening. With some effort, he straightened his body against the force of the freefall while the wind whistled around him.

Head back. Feet down. Arms crossed.

His shoulder felt funny, numb almost. The pain would come a little later, he had no doubt.

It's only a jump, he told himself when he glanced at the rushing black water beneath him. All he could do was hope there were no surprises beneath the rippling surface. No hidden rocks to crush his legs or snap his spine. Adrenaline raced through his veins, telling him that he was alive.

Invincible.

Hopefully, that would hold true once he hit the water. He braced himself for the shock. Running water was always cold, even in the heat of summer. He took a deep breath and closed his eyes.

The water closed around him like a cold, wet fist and Dante resisted the shock of it, the almost overwhelming urge to expel his breath.

He sliced through the water neatly. Expertly. Exactly like he'd been trained to do. The pressure squeezed his body, but after that initial jolt he was able to adjust to the temperature.

When Dante fought his way back to the surface, he discovered his true struggle would be against the current. For a moment, he let the choppy water carry him while he surveyed his surroundings. Then he began to swim, fighting his way to the rocky shore. His left arm hung uselessly, lacking the strength to be effective against the pressure, but he knew the bullet hadn't done that much damage. He could still flex his fingers.

Besides, he didn't have time to die. He had to rescue Nadia.

Still, Dante was beginning to wonder if sheer stubbornness was going to be enough this time. The rocky shore seemed like an optical illusion. The harder he swam toward it, the further away it appeared.

Finally, his fingers skimmed the surface of a huge rock. He clutched at it, hugging himself to it while he fought against the water that threatened to peel him away. With a lunge, Dante hoisted himself atop the rock and lay there for a moment, thankful to be breathing, even though he was having to work at it.

In basic, he'd learned to ignore the pain. To lock it behind a wall and move beyond it. Right now, he was even grateful for the sadistic SOB he'd trained under.

The few. The proud. The tortured.

He could remember his sergeant's favorite saying.

Pain is just weakness leaving your body.

Dante had always thought it was a stupid saying, but right now he couldn't get the words out of his head. After flopping onto his stomach, he rose to his knees, then to his feet. He stared with resignation at the steep, rocky incline and rubbed his hands against his thighs before he began the slow climb to the top. Slick, sharp shale dug into his palms and tore through the knees of his pants.

Slow and steady. He had to take it slow and steady.

He had to adjust for his injured arm, making sure his feet were set in before he moved upward. Instead of sounding further away, the roar of the river increased the higher he climbed.

Just when Dante began to establish a steady pace, the rock he was using for leverage crumbled away under his palm.

Dante skidded down the rock face, clawing desperately for a handhold. Something caught him at the waist, and ripped a gash through the skin all the way to the top of his ribs. He gasped, making a gurgling cry of pain while he scrambled for something to hold on to.

Dante hooked his hand around a root. His body swung hard into the rock face of the cliff, banging his injured shoulder into the wall. A bright red splash of pain exploded behind his eyes, and for a moment Dante could see nothing. He dangled helplessly for a second before he found a crack to jam his boot into.

He glanced down at the raging river below, glanced down at his battered body. Blood soaked through his shirt and dripped down his pant leg from the cut on his torturously stinging side. The scrape hurt worse than the bullet hole.

His good arm began to tremble when he reached for the next hold and Dante was forced to rest. He crouched on a narrow ledge and laid his face against a smooth, cold rock and gasped for breath.

Again, the moonlight-filled river drew his eyes. It was some eighty feet below, and although he'd never feared heights, he couldn't help but feel insignificant when he stared into its vastness.

For an instant, Dante was almost hypnotized by the dull roar and the sheer beauty of it, the white, frothy caps atop the swirling blackness. He was so exhausted. It would be so easy to just close his eyes . . . but then he remembered Nadia's bruised face. Her stunned, elated expression when he'd burst through that bedroom door.

Gritting his teeth, Dante resumed the climb. Sweat trickled down his face, down his chest. He had to pause sporadically to wipe damp palms on his pants.

Then, suddenly, he was at the top. He peered over the rock overhang and saw a gray ribbon of highway a few yards away.

With a grunt, Dante shoved off with his boot and

launched his upper body over the top. For a few seconds, he simply hung there, lacking enough energy to pull the rest of his body over. Then Dante dug his fingers into the soft earth and clawed his way out.

He might've passed out. He wasn't sure. One minute he was pressing his face into the cool, soft grass, and the next someone was nudging him over with their boot.

Lights shone in his face, blinding him. Pushing off on his elbows, Dante sat up and shielded his eyes.

Had Vandergriff's men somehow found him already?

His tension melted away when a familiar face shoved its way into the light.

"Ronnie!" he said.

The punch caught him in the jaw, knocking him back onto the grass.

Everything went black.

● ● ●

August 7
1:55 a.m.

"He's dead." The gunman shoved his weapon back into the holster and turned to his boss.

"Are you sure?" Vandergriff peered over the balcony. "Because I couldn't tell where you hit him. I thought I saw him bobbing in the water, but I can't see anything now."

"I'm sure. I hit him in the chest."

Nadia couldn't move.

Shock froze her feet, stilled her heart as she pictured Dante sinking lifelessly to the bottom of the river.

Hatred dropped over her like a blanket and she considered rushing Vandergriff, taking them both over the railing. Even if she died with him, it would be worth it to rid the world of that monster.

He was barking instructions at a man he called Peterson and neither of them seemed to be paying any attention to her. A redheaded man stood outside the doorway, blocking her way, but he turned his back to her and quietly spoke into his walkie talkie.

She gauged the distance between them and wondered if she could knock Vandergriff over the balcony before the redhead could put a bullet in her back. Maybe the fall wouldn't kill them. She might even escape him in the water. It was a chance she was willing to take. She tensed, ready to charge.

Then she saw the phone.

It lay on the gray carpet, at the edge of the flowery bedspread. It had to belong to Dante. He'd probably knocked it off its clip when he'd tried to free her.

She edged toward it, her heart pounding like a jackhammer in her chest. In her peripheral vision, she saw Vandergriff start to turn.

Nadia fell to her knees, palming the little phone when her hand brushed the plush carpet. She was counting on the bed to block Vandergriff's line of sight. There was nothing she could do about the redhead at the door except pray that he wouldn't turn around in time to see her. In one smooth motion, Nadia grasped the cell phone, shoved it into her boot, and began to wail.

"Dante!" she sobbed. "You killed him!"

Nadia didn't look up when Vandergriff strode around the bed. She kept howling, remembering what Ronnie had taught her.

Use being a female to your advantage. Make them underestimate you, then kick their ass.

Vandergriff seized a fistful of her hair and yanked her to her feet.

"Will you shut up?" he yelled, and threw her backward onto the bed. He wanted to sound annoyed, but Nadia saw the gleam in his eye. He was enjoying her pain, thriving on it.

That was okay. She planned on enjoying his too.

Real tears wet her cheeks, but they were strong tears. Tears of rage, not tears of defeat. Too bad Vandergriff wouldn't know the difference until it was too late. She would bide her time, wait for an opportunity ...

Then she would take him out.

"You see what happens to people who cross me, little girl?" Vandergriff said, looking pretty puffed up and self-important for someone who hadn't even pulled the trigger.

Wait till you see what happens to people who cross me, Nadia thought, and almost smiled.

Payback was a bitch.

● ● ●

Dante groaned and opened his eyes.

He found himself staring down the barrel of a .44.

"Give me one reason why I shouldn't blow your brains out," Ronnie said. "Tell me you didn't take Nadia to Gary Vandergriff."

"I did," Dante said. "But you have to believe me. I didn't know—"

"Aahh." With a strangled cry of rage, Ronnie smacked the gun against his own forehead, then jabbed it in Dante's face. "I trusted you, you miserable son of a bitch. *She* trusted you."

Dante held out his palms. "Please . . . give me a chance to explain."

"Explain what?" Nick Branson demanded, stepping out of the shadows.

The change in him shocked Dante. He looked like he'd aged twenty years in a matter of hours.

"Explain how you seduced my daughter into believing your lies? How your employer Vandergriff shot you when you were trying to collect your blood money?"

"No! It wasn't like that. When I figured out what was going on, I went back for her. I never meant to hurt her."

A pair of headlights came around the curve and swerved in behind the Humvee. A door slammed and Nick cursed when his wife hurtled out of the passenger side.

"Waynie, I thought I told you to keep her home."

"I tried, boss, but she wouldn't listen—"

"What happened?" Maria asked, her eyes wild. She blanched when she looked at Dante. "Where's Nadia?"

When no one said anything, she hammered Nick's chest with the heel of her hand. "Nick, where is our daughter?"

Nick caught her wrists. He looked so crestfallen, so devastated, that Dante's heart clenched.

What had he done? What was happening to Nadia?

Maria searched her husband's face and what she found there made her crumple right before Dante's eyes.

"No, no, no," she moaned. She cupped her hands over her face and slowly shook her head. "*He* has her? He has my baby?"

Branson reached to touch her and she glanced over his shoulder at Dante. If he hadn't understood the full implications of his actions before, the sheer terror on her face hammered it home.

"What happened? Did he ambush them?"

Branson pointed at Dante, his face a mask of hatred. "He did it. He took her to Vandergriff."

"What?" Maria whirled to face him and Dante wished it were darker. Wished that he couldn't see the pain on her face so clearly in the moonlight.

"How could you?" she gasped, tears streaking down her face. "How could you deliver Nadia into the hands of that monster?"

"I thought he was her father. I thought he would protect her."

There was a moment of utter silence as they all gaped at him. Nick found his voice first.

"Protect her from what?" he exploded. "In all her life, there's been one threat. One horror. And you took her straight to him."

Maria doubled over, clutching her sides. "Oh God, Nick. What will he do to her?"

Her husband shot her a pained look, but didn't say anything. His silence seemed to agitate her, and she grew increasingly hysterical while she paced. Walking over to the Hummer she banged her tiny fists on the hood, then buried her face in her hands and made a strange, keening sound that made the hair on Dante's arms prickle.

Whipping her head up violently, she stalked over to Dante and stopped in front of him. Leaning down, she yanked back her hair to show him her scars. "He did this to me. In the hospital, when I had Nadia. The nurse had just taken her back to the nursery or he would've gotten her too. A man dressed like an orderly walked in and threw acid in my face."

Sickened, Dante looked at Nick. "He lied to me . . . about everything. He told me you did that to her."

"Are you that stupid?" Nick sputtered, throwing his arms wide in frustration. "Does a man in your business not take the time to check out his clients? Especially when an innocent life is involved?"

"I *did* check him out. My research man confirmed Vandergriff's story. He said that Vandergriff was her father—"

Nick spun around, so enraged that he was nearly frothing at the mouth. "*I'm* her father! *I* am. That first time was all a setup, wasn't it? When you rescued Nadia outside that diner. Those men weren't gunning for her. Not really. It was all a show designed to get you inside. You rushed in and saved her, then you gained our trust. How he must've laughed at me for falling for that!"

"Mr. Branson, I didn't know—"

Nick stalked over to Ronnie and seized the gun from his hand. Pressing the tip of the barrel to Dante's forehead, he said coldly, "I believe Ronnie asked you a question, Mr. Giovanni, and I'm interested in the answer. Give me one reason why I shouldn't blow your brains all over these rocks."

Dante swallowed hard and forced himself to meet Nick's glare. "You need me for the same reason Vandergriff needed me. I'm good at what I do. I can get her back."

● ● ●

Nadia could barely move. She felt like a competitor in the Ironman on the day after.

Stupid stun guns. What was it Ronnie had said? They changed the sugar in a person's body to lactic acid or something. The muscles on top of her thighs felt like they were a couple of inches too short, and she was limping. To make matters worse, the cretin behind her kept poking her in the back, urging her to go faster even though she was doing the best she could do.

"Oh, come on!" he exclaimed, and pointed at the bright yellow plane in front of them. "They expect us to fly this piece of crap all the way to California? You've got to be kidding me."

The other man didn't answer. The cretin shoved her again, and Nadia nearly went sprawling onto the dusty airfield. A sliver of panic raced down her spine when the cell phone in her bra shifted. Afraid that it would fall out of her low boot, she'd managed to transfer the phone to her bra while Vandergriff barked orders to the two men who were escorting her. A good thing too, because they'd tied her hands again. Now she wished she'd left it in the boot.

"Leave the girl alone, Cahill," the other man said mildly. "She's going as fast as she can."

Use being a female to your advantage, Nadia thought, and smiled up at her captor.

Peterson.

The corners of his mouth twitched and he almost returned her smile before he caught himself. She judged him to be in his mid-forties, with salt and pepper hair. The hazel eyes that met hers were intelligent and kind.

Good. Maybe she could work on him.

Peterson gripped her elbow and tried to steady her while she struggled to climb the steps of the plane. Apparently, the three of them were going to be the small aircraft's only passengers.

My luck is changing for the better, Nadia thought when Cahill climbed into the cockpit. At least she wouldn't have to sit with him during the trip. He had a #2 pencil stuck behind his ear, and he struck her as the kind of guy who'd sit beside her and poke her with it for the duration of the flight, just for kicks.

"Hey, Peterson, you want to sit up here with me?" Cahill shouted when the plane started to move. "No parachutes back there. The girl's not going anywhere."

"No, thanks," Peterson said with a yawn. "I think I'll stay back here. Maybe catch a nap."

Nadia had gotten the distinct impression that Peterson didn't like Cahill any better than she did.

Use being a female to your advantage, Nadia reminded herself, and began to cry. She had a knack for it, could cry on cue. Her crocodile tears had served her well in the past. Maybe they would this time too.

She sniffled a time or two—quietly, like she didn't want him to realize that she was crying. Peterson shifted uncomfortably in his seat.

Nadia let a sob squeak out, and he glanced at her with a frown. She allowed her eyes to meet his and started crying harder.

"Ah, shoot, miss. Don't do that." Peterson took a crumpled handkerchief out of his pocket and dabbed at her eyes.

"Everything's going to be all right."

"I'm so s-scared," she sobbed. "And my shoulder hurts where Vandergriff used that stun gun on me."

"He shot you with a stun gun?" Peterson sounded disgusted. He grabbed Nadia's arm and gently pulled her forward.

"Which one?" he asked, peering at her shoulder blades. "Never mind. I see the mark."

He mumbled something under his breath, then reached under one of the seats to pull out a little metal box. Peterson popped the latch and grabbed a bottle of aspirin. Nadia watched him twist off the top and fish a wad of cotton out. He shook four tablets into his palm and gave her an apologetic shrug. "I'm sorry. I don't have any water."

"That's okay. I appreciate it," Nadia said.

She opened her mouth, and Peterson placed the pills on her tongue. As she crunched them, she shrugged off the bitter taste. She was already planning ahead. There was a weird little door to her left.

A bathroom?

Nadia toned down the waterworks a bit. She didn't see any point in overplaying her hand.

"So, what did you do to get on Vandergriff's bad side?" Peterson asked.

Nadia fought back an amused smile. Maybe he'd decided talking to her was better than listening to her cry.

"I was born."

Peterson lifted a bushy eyebrow.

"Really," Nadia said, shifting. "That's when Vandergriff started coming after me. My mother is his ex-wife."

"Ah." Peterson nodded. "I was wondering . . . I'm fairly new here. Didn't know what his beef with Andreakos was."

Andreakos. The name still sounded funny to her ears.

Nadia decided to gloss over the story a bit. No one would believe the horrors Vandergriff had revealed to her back at the main house, but she needed to work on Peterson with something. "Vandergriff married my mother when she was fifteen. He beat the crap out of her on a regular basis, but she was too scared of him to get out of there. She lived in that hell for four years. Then Vandergriff hired Nick Branson as head of security at the main house. Nick and my mother fell in love and ran away together. She divorced Vandergriff to marry him."

Peterson leaned back in his seat and squinted at her. "If he was so hung up on her, why didn't Vandergriff fight the divorce? I know from experience that one can be pretty hard to get if the other party holds out."

Nadia shrugged. "He tried. But what can you do when your ex-wife has videotapes of you beating her with a fireplace poker?"

"Not much, I suppose," Peterson admitted.

"Of course, Vandergriff—egomaniac that he is—couldn't handle the fact that they'd embarrassed him. That his wife had left him for another man."

"Ah, I don't know . . . that seems pretty thin." Peterson

wrinkled his nose. "Why obsess about one woman for, what—twenty odd years? Even a psycho like Vandergriff can get women when the money's right."

"Other than the fact that she looks like me?" Nadia joked, and Peterson's face creased in a grin.

"Oh, sure. Other than that," he conceded. "But I have to say, I've seen him come and go with some pretty hot-looking women."

"More going than coming, right?" Nadia said, and Peterson laughed again.

"Stop that. I drank a gallon of coffee this evening and hate the thought of trying to squeeze myself into that crapper over there."

"Oh, man!" Nadia breathed. "You mean this thing's got a restroom? I'm about to bust a kidney here."

Peterson snorted and scratched his ear. "Restroom is too grand of a word. It implies you could actually get comfortable in the thing. Santa Claus couldn't squeeze in there." He winked at Nadia. "But I can see where it might work for you. You are kind of elf-sized, aren't you?"

"Watch it!" Nadia reprimanded, but a smile tugged at the corners of her mouth. "Can I go? Please? You know, it's my time of the month, and—"

"Yeah, yeah," Peterson interrupted, clearly not wanting to hear anything about female bodily functions. Nadia restrained a giggle. It was another trick she'd learned. If a woman ever wanted to run a guy off, that was one subject that worked like a charm. She stood and presented her back to him.

"Well?" she said a moment later, when he still hadn't moved. "Are you going to untie me or what? I'm good, but I'm not that good." She glanced over her shoulder at Peterson, who looked uncertain.

"Come on." She gave him her most winning smile. "What am I gonna do, flush myself? *Drown* myself?"

Peterson snickered. "Not in that john, you won't. I assure you." He rolled his eyes. "Okay, okay."

He rummaged through his pocket and pulled out a knife. Flipping it open, he cut the plastic zip ties that bound her wrists.

"Oh, thank you, thank you, thank you!" She threw her arms around his neck and gave him a quick hug.

Peterson grunted in surprise, then gave her a patient smile. "Okay, but hurry up in there."

"Will do," she promised with a wink. "I'll give you the rest of my Vandergriff theories when I get back."

Nadia limped to the door, opened it, and looked back at Peterson in astonishment.

"I told you so," he called.

Even for a person as small as she was, using the potty would require a tactical maneuver. She could only imagine Dante trying to squeeze in there. He couldn't have gotten those broad shoulders inside.

The thought of him sobered her. Focused her. She wasn't

planning on using the thing anyway.

Standing on the sides of the toilet was preferable to leaning over it, so Nadia climbed on top of it and dug the phone out of her bra.

With a feverish prayer, she punched in her father's cell phone number.

● ● ●

Dante told them everything, from his first contact with Vandergriff to the point where they'd found him on the side of the road. He even thought they believed him. At least they had holstered their guns.

"A drug dealer . . ." Nick snorted. "You seriously thought *I* was a drug dealer? That's rich."

"Yeah, well, so are you. How was I supposed to know where the money came from?" Dante said, but he knew how he was supposed to know, and he hoped Sanders had a good explanation.

Harry Sanders had been his researcher for nearly five years, and a good friend for nearly twice as long. Dante didn't like to think someone he had trusted so completely would betray him like that.

Nick waved his hand toward Dante. "Ronnie, check out his gunshot wound. Looks like he and Waynie got hit in nearly the same spot. How do you suppose they managed that?"

Nick's cell phone chirped a song Dante didn't recognize,

and he flipped it open to answer it.

● ● ●

"Branson."

Nadia's breath caught at the sound of her father's voice and she squeezed her eyes shut. She thought of all the times she'd scared him, all the times she must have hurt him. Nick had only wanted to protect her, and she'd punished him with all the stupid, rebellious things she'd done.

"Hello?"

"Daddy?" she whispered.

She had called him and Maria by their given names since she was twelve, but right now she wanted her daddy, the man who had chased away her nightmares and doctored her scrapes. He would know how to fix this mess she was in.

"Nadia! Nadia, is that you?"

The anxiety and hope in his voice nearly destroyed her. She swallowed hard over the lump in her throat. "Yeah. Look, I don't have much time. I wanted to tell you and Mom that I love you and I'm sorry. Vandergriff has me. He tricked Dante into bringing me to him, but then Dante tried to save me. They killed him, Daddy."

The dam that held back her tears broke. Somehow saying it made it feel final. Nadia sniffled quietly into the phone.

"Honey, Dante's right here. He's somewhat banged up, but he's alive. We found him by the river. Where are you?"

"He's . . . alive?"

She couldn't have heard him right. "Did you say Dante's alive?"

"Yes, he'll be fine," Nick said impatiently. "I'll let you speak to him in a moment, but first you have to tell me where you are."

"Uh, I'm on a plane. We left Rock Island . . ." She paused to look at her watch. ". . . sixteen minutes ago. They're taking me to California."

"How are you talking to me?"

"I managed to grab Dante's cell phone. He dropped it when he was trying to rescue me. I'm wedged in this little toilet, so Vandergriff's men can't hear me."

Her father repeated what she'd said.

Dante was alive!

She closed her eyes and smiled.

"Hey, you fall in?" Peterson yelled.

Nadia jumped and fumbled the phone. She managed to snag it before it dropped into the circular bowl.

"Daddy," she whispered. "I have to go before they figure out what I'm doing. I'll try to call back in a little while."

"No! Don't hang up—"

"Daddy, I have to."

"I love you."

"I love you too. Bye."

Nadia shoved the phone back into her bra and flushed the potty. Throwing open the door, she plastered on a smile and swiped her hand across her forehead. "Whew, that was a close one. There for a minute, I thought I was stuck."

She sauntered back to Peterson and plopped down in the seat beside him. Maybe if she kept him talking, he'd forget to retie her hands.

"Now, where were we? Oh, yeah, about that psychotic boss of yours—"

● ● ●

Dante stared into space, running the numbers in his head.

"Do you have any contacts at the FAA?" he asked, turning to Nick. "We need to get a copy of that plane's flight plan."

Nick's eyes lit. He jumped to his feet. "Of course! If it's a small plane, they'll have to stop for fuel. We can intercept them before they get to California. Ronnie, call Carson James. He'll help us."

Ronnie immediately began pressing numbers into his cell phone.

Nick gnawed his lower lip, mulling it over. "Yes, we have to get her before they make it to California. Our chances will be much better. Vandergriff's estate is more secure than Fort Knox."

Dante leaned forward, resting his elbows on his knees. "Did Nadia say how many people are on board with her?"

"No. I didn't have a chance to ask."

Dante was already formulating a plan, one he was positive

Branson wasn't going to like.

The rescue he had in mind wouldn't happen on the ground. It would happen in the air.

CHAPTER 7

"Are you out of your mind?" Nick demanded. "What you're suggesting is crazy. It's suicide!"

Dante sat in the back of the Humvee with Nadia's father. Ronnie was driving and Maria rode shotgun. Nick had begged her to go home, but Maria had refused to leave, proving which parent Nadia had inherited her stubborn streak from.

"No, I'm telling you . . . it's a good plan," Dante replied. "They'll never see it coming. But there's no use arguing about it until we talk to Nadia again. For all I know, it may not even be an option. We need to know what kind of plane it is, where they are . . . and a big part of this plan depends on Nadia herself. She can't do anything if she's heavily guarded."

"But we can intercept them when they stop for fuel. We can take them on the ground—" Nick said desperately.

Dante shook his head. "You think that will be easy? Storming the plane when they stop for fuel? It would be like buying a front row seat for Nadia's execution."

Maria Branson gave him a sharp look, but Dante had to make his case. "And you said yourself . . . we won't have a chance if he gets her home and locks the place down. Where does that leave us?" Dante leaned forward and asked, "Mrs. Branson, do you have something I can write on?"

Opening her purse, Maria extracted a pen and drew out a small memo book. Dante took them from her and began making a list.

"Do me a favor. Just humor me, okay? Have someone get this stuff together and get it on the plane. We may not need it, but we'll have it on hand if we do."

Dante ripped off the sheet and held it out to him. Nick chewed at his thumbnail and stared out the window. Impatiently, Dante shoved it at him.

"Please, Mr. Branson. I'm qualified to do this. I'm a jumpmaster. I've made over 500 jumps, and I know what I'm doing. I'd never suggest this if I didn't think it was the best option for Nadia."

Nick sighed and took the list. Glancing it over, he exhaled again and picked up the phone. He held a terse conversation with someone on the other end and read off the contents of Dante's list.

Clicking the phone shut, he said, "Okay. You'll have everything you requested at your disposal. I only hope it doesn't come to that. We're going to go with my plan first, but if we can't catch up to them by the time they make a fuel stop, we'll consider yours. Agreed?"

Dante nodded. "Now, let's get the details straight."

They went to work, hammering out the details of Nick's plan and the contingency plan. In a shorter time than Dante would have thought possible, they were in the air, chasing after Nadia.

There was even a set of dry clothing waiting on Dante in the airplane, something he was eternally grateful for. Maria Branson discreetly excused herself to the cockpit so Dante could change.

"Are these Waynie's pants?" he joked, and hooked his fingers in the belt loops to tug them up. They were about three sizes too baggy, loose in the waist and a couple of inches too short.

"Sue me," Ronnie retorted, and tossed Dante a belt. "Do a favor for a guy and what do you get? Smart remarks. While you were plotting to save the world, I had to guesstimate your size."

Saving the world.

That's exactly what it felt like.

"Get over here and let me check out that shoulder again," Ronnie commanded, patting the seat next to him.

Dante wandered over beside him and lifted his shirt. Ronnie nodded a moment later, satisfied with his handiwork. Shrugging the shirt back down, Dante said, "Mr. Branson, there's one thing I don't understand. This . . . *thing* with Vandergriff . . . it's a war. He's moving all out to destroy you. Has it always been like this, ever since you and Mrs. Branson ran away?"

"No," Nick said with a bitter smile. "For nearly three years we did pretty well, but then he found us at the hospital. You know what happened there."

Dante watched Maria emerge from the cockpit. She walked over and took a seat beside her husband.

Nick continued, "So, we ran. We moved a lot, never kept the same identities long, but somehow he found us again when Nadia started first grade . . ."

Maria made a strangled sound in her throat and Nick paused to look at her. She shook her head violently and clamped her hands over her ears.

"Uggh!" She jumped to her feet and fluttered her hands like she'd touched something repulsive. Nick stood and reached for her, but she pushed him away. "No, I'm okay. Stay with them. But I can't . . . I can't listen to anymore about him. I can't bear to think about him with her."

She ran to the cockpit.

Nick stared after her with glistening eyes. Dante had to look away from the pain he saw on the man's face. Ronnie stared out the window.

"If something happens to Nadia, Maria will never survive it," Nick said hoarsely.

Dante doubted either of them would.

"She's been so strong, for so many years, but how much can one person withstand?" Nick murmured.

No one answered, and he cleared his throat. "When Nadia was small, I finally got a man inside Vandergriff's operation.

He gave me some information that protected us for the next eighteen years . . . until now."

"What information, and why just until now?" Dante asked.

"There was only one man Vandergriff feared, and that was his father. Franklin Vandergriff was a monster, just like his son, but he hid it better. He slaughtered Maria's family in a fit of rage, but to the world, he was a respected diplomat and businessman. A man of religion. My spy discovered Vandergriff was funneling money from his father's business into his own pocket. He collected copies of ledgers, dummy invoices Gary Vandergriff had made up for nonexistent accounts payables . . . it was quite an enterprise. I called Vandergriff myself and demanded he back off, or I'd make sure his father and all the board received copies. He was frothing mad, but he knew his father, who spared little patience for him anyway, would surely kill him. It worked for a long time . . ."

"Then his father died," Dante said slowly.

"Yes." Nick glanced at him over steepled hands. "How did you know?"

"The first time I met with Vandergriff was the day of his father's wake. I wondered at the time what was so important he had to meet me on the day he buried his father." Dante scrubbed a hand over his face. "He sure didn't waste any time, did he?"

Nick exhaled. "That may be my fault. I'm afraid I provoked him to a new level of fury, if he had access to his father's mail. I heard the old man was dying. Pancreatic cancer. So,

I decided to take a chance. I sent him copies of the entire file, but . . ." Nick swept his hands wide. ". . . apparently, he didn't get it in time, or Vandergriff would've been disinherited. Back in the day, the old man threatened him with it all the time. I was hoping he would, so Vandergriff wouldn't have the resources to come after us like he has. I should've done it years ago, but I hated to interrupt this reprieve. I knew this day . . . this battle . . . was inevitable, but God help me, I wish there was a way to keep my wife and daughter out of it. Because of Gary Vandergriff, I gave up my name and any ties I still held with my family in Greece, because I knew anyone I loved would be in danger. A million years ago, I was Nicolai Andreakos. I was proud of that man. I'm not proud of the one I've become."

"You saved Mrs. Branson's life," Dante said quietly. "You kept her and Nadia safe for years."

Nick grimaced. "But none of that matters anymore, because I couldn't keep them safe this time. My name isn't all I lost. I lost my self-respect. I lost my courage. I lost my security—another victory I handed to Vandergriff, because since the moment I met him, I've thought of little else."

The cabin of the plane fell silent. Dante wanted to reassure him, but feared anything he said would sound hollow. He was scared too. He thought of the stun gun. What else had Vandergriff done to Nadia?

"Hey, Ronnie, can I use your phone?" Dante asked.

Ronnie handed it to him. Dante sat back in the chair

and called Sanders. He had to know what had happened.

"Do you know what time it is?" a sleepy voice demanded. "This better not be a telemarketer."

"It's confession time, Sanders."

"Giovanni, that you?" His voice changed. The surliness was abruptly replaced by hesitation.

"You nearly got me killed, Sanders. You nearly got someone I care about killed and we aren't out of the woods yet."

"I don't know what you're talking about—"

"Save it," Dante said. "Why did you lie to me about Gary Vandergriff?"

Ronnie shifted in his seat, as did Nick. Both were pretending not to listen, but Dante knew they were. He didn't blame them. He'd lost their trust and now he would have to earn it back again.

There was silence on the other end of the line.

"What happened?" Sanders asked finally.

"Oh, not much. I got shot off a cliff. Had to fish myself out of a river. An innocent girl got kidnapped . . ."

Sanders swore under his breath. "Dante, I swear to you I didn't know it was anything major. Gary Vandergriff told me he knew that Branson was a drug dealer, but he couldn't prove anything. He knew what a stickler you were for details and simply asked me to back up his story."

"And you did this out of the goodness of your heart? Didn't think it was fishy, him asking you to lie about all those things?"

Silence.

Dante felt his temper spike. "You didn't think it was odd, him wanting me to bring him his ex-wife's daughter?" he persisted.

"Vandergriff said the girl was his daughter, that Maria Branson was pregnant when she left him."

"That was some pregnancy. She was almost two years overdue." Dante frowned down at his hands and said, "You didn't check any of it out, did you?"

Sanders sighed. "No."

"Why? We go way back, Sanders. I thought I could count on you to be straight with me."

"Vandergriff gave me a lot of money, Dante. A lot of it. He'd heard about you . . . everybody's heard about you. He wanted you for the job and was afraid you wouldn't take it. He swore to me that you wouldn't get hurt. And the girl—"

"To hell with her, right?" Dante replied and rubbed his forehead.

"You don't understand," Sanders pleaded. "I was thinking of Frannie. You know she's in her first semester of law school. It's put a real drain on our savings. She was working all night and trying to keep up with her studies during the day . . . the money came in handy."

"Oh, I understand all right. I understand that you were willing to sacrifice a girl about the same age as Frannie for money."

"Vandergriff said he wasn't going to hurt her. He wasn't going to hurt anyone. I thought she was his daughter—"

"You're not the man I thought you were, Sanders. Collect your last check and pray you never see me again."

Dante clicked the phone shut and rubbed his face with his hands. The throb of his headache had grown steadily worse as he talked to Sanders. Nobody had principles anymore.

"Dante," Ronnie said hesitantly. "I'm sorry. I shouldn't have hit you. And called you all those names."

Dante shot him a rueful grin. "Yeah, you should've. Hit me, I mean. And you only called me one name."

"You were unconscious when he got to the really good ones." Nick leaned back and gave him a tired smile, leaving Dante surprised by the first glimmer of humor he'd seen in the man.

"Oh."

Ronnie gave Dante a sheepish look. "So, you didn't hear that about your mama and a billy goat?"

"No." Dante slung a big arm across Ronnie's shoulders. "But I'm listening now if you care to repeat it."

"Did I say that?" Ronnie gave him a nervous grin. "I think maybe it was Waynie. So, don't shoot me or bench press me or anything."

Dante cracked his knuckles. "If this plan doesn't work, you have permission to shoot *me*."

The cabin fell silent, each man lost in his own thoughts and worries. Nick's phone sat in the seat beside him. They all stared at it, willing it to ring.

● ● ●

Nadia glanced at Peterson when he came back from the cockpit. He smiled and resumed his seat beside her.

"We're going to be landing soon. Have to make a fuel stop."

"Stretch our legs?" Nadia asked hopefully.

"Sorry, hon. We aren't allowed to let you off the plane. I need to do a few things in the hanger—talk to a couple of guys—but I was thinking maybe I could sneak you something back in."

"An Uzi? A grenade?"

Peterson's smile faltered, and he ruffled her hair. She could tell the situation was beginning to bother him.

"Well, I was thinking more along the lines of a candy bar, a soft drink—something like that."

Nadia forced a smile. "That would be great."

"Any kind in particular?"

"Nah." She stretched her arms over her head and winced at the ache in her shoulder. "I'm not hard to get along with."

Peterson studied her, his eyes serious. "No, you're not." He chewed on his thumbnail and studied her. "Nadia, what do you think Vandergriff has in mind? What's he going to do with you?"

"Who knows?" She shrugged and blew a piece of hair out of her eyes. "Last count I had, he was threatening to make me bear him an heir."

"What?" Peterson looked at her in disbelief. "He said

actually said that? It's like a line in a bad movie."

Nadia rubbed the back of her neck and yawned. "You're telling me. Hapless heroine forced to bear the child of Satan. It's been done already."

Peterson chuckled.

She shook her head, wishing dearly for a cigarette. "All joking aside, he'll do anything to hurt my mother and father. The easiest way to get to them is through me. I think it's like a challenge to him now. He ruined my mother's face and that didn't do it. Then—"

"He did what?" Peterson interrupted. "What did you say about your mother? You haven't told me about any of this."

Nadia stretched out her legs. "She was in the hospital, right after she gave birth to me. Some goon dressed like an orderly walked into her room and threw acid in her face. She has all these scars, on one side of her face . . ."

Peterson blanched.

"But it didn't work. He thought if he destroyed her beauty, he could destroy their love, but what they have isn't just physical. It's deeper, and my father is a better man than that. He doesn't seem to see the scars and my mother loves him all the more for it. Vandergriff may have forced them to live their lives behind gates and security systems, but he's never been able to tear them apart."

Peterson sighed and sat back in the chair, lacing his hands behind his head. "I really have to find a new line of work. I thought security would be exciting, but not as cutthroat as my old job."

"Which was what?"

"IRS auditor."

"Good grief, I'm in worse shape than I thought," Nadia said, and rolled her eyes.

Peterson smiled and patted her hand. "You know I can't help you. Vandergriff would only kill us both."

"It's okay," Nadia said, and meant it. Hopefully, she wouldn't need his help. She didn't want him harmed because of her.

Peterson looked troubled. He shot a glance at the cockpit. "But that doesn't mean I don't want to help you."

"I know. But you do need to find a new employer. You're too good of a guy to work for a sociopath like Vandergriff. Your buddy, Cahill, on the other hand . . ." She nodded toward the cockpit.

"He is *not* my buddy," Peterson declared, and she smiled.

"Whatever. Don't leave me alone with him too long, okay?"

"You don't have to worry about him. I've already told him what I'd do with that #2 pencil of his if he messed with you."

"My hero," Nadia said and closed her eyes. She found herself thinking of Dante. Wondering where he was and if he was anywhere close to her.

How was it possible that she'd just met him?

Time felt eerily skewed, drawn out. A lifetime since she'd approached him in that diner. A lifetime since the night in the garden. She glanced at her watch.

Oops. Slipping into day three. Time had somehow divided itself into two distinct sectors. The time before Dante and the time after.

"Get a grip," she muttered.

Nadia Branson had never mooned over anyone and it was a little disconcerting to be doing so now.

"What?" Peterson asked.

He clutched the armrest while they bumped along the runway. Apparently Cahill's landing abilities were as questionable as his personality.

"Nothing. Talking to myself. It's a sign of caffeine depravation. Chocolate, man. Bring me something chocolate."

"Will do. In the meantime, why don't you try to get some rest?"

"What, and turn my back on an IRS auditor and a pencil wielding sadist?" Nadia teased. Her eyes widened and she slapped her forehead. "Oh, wait. Isn't that the same thing?"

Peterson snorted and opened his palm to reveal a handful of shiny silver quarters. "Not very smart, my girl. You really shouldn't be so rude to the man with the vending machine plan."

"I'm sorry." Nadia struggled to look contrite. "That kind of thing just slips out. It's a short circuit in my brain, I swear."

She glanced out the window. The terrain outside looked almost deserted in the dusky shadows. No lights in the distance. No buildings that she could see. Just her luck. It was probably a private airstrip.

"Hey, Peterson . . ." She nudged him with her foot. "Where are we, anyhow? I don't think we're in Kansas anymore."

"Actually, Dorothy, that's exactly where we are." Peterson unfastened his belt. He stretched and stood when the plane stopped coasting.

Nadia glanced over her shoulder when Cahill came out of the cockpit. Peterson mistook the look on her face for fear.

"I'll be back soon," he said quietly. "He knows better than to hurt you. That's not only my order, it's Vandergriff's too."

Nadia nodded, but she wasn't afraid of Cahill. In fact, she would almost welcome the chance to be alone with him.

She could take him out.

Peterson disembarked after sharing a few hushed words with Cahill. Nadia watched Cahill slide the door to the cockpit shut and lock it, then he turned his flat reptilian gaze on her.

"I've got to step off for a few minutes too," he said. "I thought I'd better warn you, though . . . don't try anything cute. There are armed men all over this hanger, and we all have the same signature on our paychecks."

Nadia bit off a smart remark, realizing that it would cause her more trouble than it was worth. Instead, she pasted on a smile. "No problem here. I think I'm going to try to catch a nap."

She curled up on the seat without waiting for a reply and heard Cahill grunt. Closing her eyes, she waited until she heard his footsteps echo down the ramp before she dared to take out the phone.

Still curled on the seat, she pressed in the number and tucked the phone behind the ear she was resting on. Her hair fell over her face, hopefully providing some camouflage should Cahill decide to check on her.

Her father answered on the first ring.

● ● ●

Nick Branson covered the mouthpiece and cursed. He looked at Dante. "They're in Kansas already. How close are we?"

"Not close enough," he replied. "But we're gaining on them. Let me talk to her."

Resignation shone in Nick's eyes when he handed Dante the phone. They both knew that Dante's plan was the only shot they had.

"Hey, princess," Dante said.

"Hey, yourself, Superman. That was some exit back there. You sure know how to impress a girl."

Dante laughed. It was so good to hear her voice.

"I try," he said. "Do you know what kind of plane you're on?"

"Some little piece of junk DeHaviland. A Super Otter. You can't miss us. The thing is school bus yellow."

Dante's hopes surged. "How many people are on the plane?"

"Two guys. The pilot and a guard."

"Can you take the guard out?"

After a brief pause, she said, "Yes."

He didn't like that hesitation. "You have to be absolutely sure, Nadia. Can you do it or not?"

"Yes, but the pilot said Vandergriff's men are all over the ground here."

"We're not going to move on you there. We're not close enough yet. Do you see the emergency door?"

"Hmmm, the one with the big red E-X-I-T over it?"

"That's the one." Dante grinned. "Now, do you see the locking handle?"

"Yes."

"Think you can open that?"

"Yes."

"Can you jump out of an airplane?"

"I've done it before, but Dante, there are no parachutes in here. Cahill made sure to tell me that."

"You're not going to need one."

She paused. Then, in a funny, squeaky voice she asked, "Did you land on your head when you fell off that balcony?"

"I'll catch you."

"You'll catch me," Nadia repeated slowly. "Are you out of your ever lovin' mind?"

Dante glanced at Nick and snickered. Covering the mouthpiece, he said, "Oh, yeah. She is definitely your daughter."

Nick made a face and Dante smiled into the phone. "We can do it, Nadia. I'm a jumpmaster. You didn't have a problem jumping from that bridge, and you said you've jumped from a plane before, right?"

"At 12,000 feet with an instructor strapped to me. I think there's somewhat of a difference there."

"Do you trust me?"

"Yes," she said instantly.

"Then what's the problem . . . are you chicken?"

Dante winced at the obscenities that remark inspired, but it had its desired effect.

"Okay. But how will I know when it's time to jump?"

"Set the phone on vibrating mode. When we're close enough, I'll call you."

"Oh, no. Now, that's real smart, Dante. What if your mother calls, or some floozy you run with, wanting to know when you'll be back in town? I'd be like Wile E. Coyote flapping around out there."

"You didn't let me finish. We'll have a code. I'll let it ring twice, three different times. How's that?"

"Better."

"Okay. On the signal. As soon as you clear the plane, slow down your freefall by going spread-eagle."

"I have to go. I think they're coming back," she whispered.

"Okay. It's all clear?"

"Clear. And Dante . . ."

"Yeah?" He held his breath. Her voice sounded so soft and vulnerable, and he fought the urge to tell her about all the crazy stuff he felt for her, because he didn't want her to think he doubted they'd make it out of this. Maybe she wanted to tell him the same thing. Maybe—

"If you drop me, I'm going to come back from the dead to haunt your ass."

● ● ●

Where was it? Man, she was clueless. Nadia couldn't believe she hadn't thought of the ringer before now.

It would be hard to explain a ringing bra.

Noise? What noise? That's only my underwear. It rings when I'm supposed to change it.

Looking for the button, Nadia nearly panicked before she figured out the phone was already switched to vibrating mode.

Cahill was back. She could feel his eyes boring into her while he climbed back onto the plane.

God, she hoped he hadn't heard her talking. She feigned sleep, tucking the phone under her thigh. He'd see her if she tried to transfer it now.

Then she heard Peterson's voice as he climbed the steps. Cahill spoke to him. Nadia sat up in the seat and made sure their attention was diverted.

She pretended to stretch, and shoved the phone down the back of her jeans as she rubbed her lower back.

Just wait until Dante heard all the places his phone had been.

The thought made her grin. The man was crazy.

'Trust me,' he said.

'I'll catch you', he said.

She shook her head. Heck, maybe she was the crazy one because 'okay' was what she'd said.

It's going work out, Nadia thought, because she was a big believer in 'what goes around comes around' and she had been a good girl.

Well, most of the time.

Surely fate wouldn't be so cruel as to let her meet a man like Dante and then let her die before she had a chance to ravish him.

"What are you grinning about?" Peterson asked, ducking to keep from banging his head in the doorway.

"What do you mean, what am I grinning about? Is that a candy bar in your pocket or are you just happy to see me?"

"Girl, you're crazy." Peterson chuckled. He fished a chocolate bar out of his shirt pocket and tossed it to her.

"Why does everyone keep saying that?" Nadia demanded, snagging it with one hand.

Peterson had a can of soda in each pocket of his windbreaker. He popped the top and handed her one of those as well.

Nadia had no idea of how thirsty she was until the first gulp of the sweet cola hit her throat. She drank it too fast and paid for it with hiccups. And one burp.

"Excuse me," she said, and hiccupped loudly.

"If you don't stop that, I'm going to sit with Cahill," Peterson threatened.

"You think—" hiccup "—I'm enjoying this?" Nadia managed, but she wished he *would* go sit with Cahill. She didn't want to hurt him.

That was an idea. Maybe he would go to the cockpit if she pretended to go to sleep. But first she'd have to get rid of these stupid hiccups.

Cahill's takeoffs weren't much better than his landings, but soon they were on their way again.

Nadia sucked in a deep breath and held it. She stared at Peterson and started counting off the seconds in her head. He laughed and Nadia was forced to release her breath. She glared at him and tried again. Again, he started cackling. His face reddened and he pinched the end of his nose as he laughed.

"Will you *stop* it?" she demanded, making her eyes wide. "Can't you see I'm trying to concentrate here?"

"I can't help it!" He wiped tears from his eyes. "I wish I had a mirror so you could see your face. You look like a demonic chipmunk."

"Gee, thanks a lot."

"Look, I don't have any water, but you can have the rest of my soft drink if you think it would help."

"No—" hiccup "—thanks. I might explode."

Nadia looked at Peterson, judging him. She liked him; she really did. And she even thought he might help her now. But she didn't know for sure and she couldn't risk it. Too much was at stake.

Over half an hour later, her hiccups stopped.

Nadia knew the exact moment it happened. Her heart had leapt into her throat when she felt the soft vibration of the phone against her skin.

Once. Twice. Then it was gone.

There was so long between the first and second calls that she was afraid she'd imagined it.

One. Two.

By the time the third call started, Nadia's nerves were singing. Her mouth went dry and her heart thundered in her ears.

"Hey, your hiccups stopped." Peterson opened an eye and squinted at her. "Thank God. You were driving me nuts."

Peterson had relaxed around her, was half asleep. He wasn't expecting her move when it came.

Nadia sprang.

She had his gun out of his shoulder holster before he knew what was happening. With a shaking hand, she pointed it at him.

"What are you doing?" he asked, with the dazed expression of a man who's been told a joke he doesn't understand.

"I'm sorry. Please don't move. I don't want to hurt you."

She backed to the emergency door. Cahill still hadn't noticed.

"What are you doing?" Peterson asked again, when she grabbed the thick grip of the locking handle.

"He's going to catch me," she said, because she could think of nothing else to say.

The door yawned open.

The rushing wind dried her lips and threatened to yank her legs out from underneath her. She ejected the clip and sent the gun spinning to the earth.

Cahill had finally realized what was happening. He came out of the cockpit with his gun drawn.

Nadia licked her lips and questioned her sanity.

Then she dove.

CHAPTER**8**

Sunday, August 7
5:45 a.m.

She was free.

Bound by nothing, burdened by nothing.

She was free . . . and it was exhilarating.

The roar of the wind deafened Nadia and her entire vision filled with a view of patchwork earth. It hardly looked real.

The sun was rising and the eastern skyline was a masterpiece of riotous color. Red, gold, and orange exploded against the backdrop of dark gray clouds. It was more than beautiful. It was heaven.

Distracted by the beauty, Nadia almost forgot to follow Dante's instructions. With some effort, she righted her body, then splayed her arms and legs wide in an open jumping jack position.

She wanted to look behind her, to see if he was coming,

but the force of the wind was too great. Nadia couldn't turn her head.

Oddly, she wasn't afraid. Something inside her knew Dante wouldn't let her down again. It was a strange feeling for someone who had always been taught to be on guard, but she trusted him.

Sure, you can trust him—to do his job, the wary, suspicious voice in her head mocked. *That doesn't mean he loves you.*

Nadia felt a little sick inside when she wondered how much of what they'd shared was real and how much had been designed to get close to her.

But Dante had told Vandergriff he didn't want the money. He'd come back for her. Didn't that have to mean something?

It meant he was trying to do the right thing, the cynical voice argued. *It had nothing to do with you.*

Nadia pushed the thoughts away and again lost herself in the rushing wind. As it had on her previous jump, it struck her that she didn't really *feel* like she was falling. It was more a sensation of wind and pressure. Even though she knew she was hurtling toward the earth at a speed somewhere around 110-120 miles per hour, it hardly felt like it.

She saw a flash of movement to her right.

Dante was here.

Nadia caught another glimpse of him in her peripheral vision an instant before he grabbed her. His hands grasped her ankle and worked their way up to her waist. Dante pulled her upright, against him, and attached himself to her with some sort of harness. Nadia shivered at the feel of his big body wrapped around hers.

Nadia wanted to see him, to touch his face, but she had to be content with being held in those arms. Dante hugged himself around her and buried his face in her hair.

Neither of them tried to speak. Not only because it would've been impossible against the roar of the wind, but because a human voice would've been almost sacrilegious in such a setting.

Dante started to play, guiding her with his arms and legs. They flipped and twisted in the air. Nadia felt her soul drift beyond the clouds, beyond the sun as she reveled in being young and alive and in love with the man who held her. He flipped over onto his back and Nadia found herself staring straight up into the dark gray clouds. It was calm, tranquil, almost like floating on water.

Then he pivoted.

Suddenly, they plummeted headfirst toward the ground at breakneck speed. Nadia couldn't restrain the squeal that escaped her lips, part exhilaration and part pure terror.

The patchwork expanded beneath them, coming into sharper focus. Nadia wondered if her heart was going to tear its way out of her chest.

Then she gave into the pressure Dante was exerting and they were upright once again. He pulled her arms toward her and Nadia nodded, understanding he was about to pull the cord. She crossed her arms over her chest and waited. The chute deployed with a loud whoosh and they were yanked upward.

Abruptly, the roar around them ceased, bathing them in a sudden quietness that was almost eerie.

Dante's body created a delicious friction against hers when he began to steer.

The desert.

They were going to land in the desert.

Nadia took in her surroundings in awe. The gray, jagged hills, the rocky terrain interspersed with yellow grass and gray clumps of sagebrush. It stretched out endlessly before them.

She was a country girl, used to wide open spaces, but she had never seen anything like this. It looked like another planet, barren as Mars.

There was absolutely nothing around. No people, no buildings. Nadia had been out in the Pacific Ocean once. All around, as far as the eye could see, there had been nothing but water. She felt the same sense of isolation now that she had then.

Nadia's racing heart, which had finally begun to slow, speeded up again as they prepared to land.

Too fast. They were going too fast.

"Get ready to flare," Dante said, his breath tickling her ear.

"What?" She was disconcerted, couldn't remember what that meant.

"Lift your knees."

She watched Dante's fingers grip the loops. All at once, they slowed. Nadia's feet brushed the ground and nearly tangled with Dante's as they did an awkward sprint and nearly fell.

They were safe. He had done it.

Adrenaline rushed through her veins, stealing her breath, stealing her voice. Almost stealing her legs.

Dante unhooked her and Nadia spun around to face him. Her mouth opened and closed like a fish's, but she couldn't say a word.

● ● ●

"You okay, princess?" Dante asked. He unhooked himself from the parachute and shrugged out of the big backpack he wore beneath.

When she didn't respond, he glanced up at her.

She literally took his breath away.

Nadia's wild eyes sparkled like no jewel he'd ever seen, and her cheeks were flushed with excitement. In that instant, Dante saw something in her face that he'd never seen in another's.

He saw a kindred spirit, and his soul responded to her.

Dante seized her waist and pulled her to him, crushing his mouth to hers. Nadia was more than ready for him. The desire between them was something hot, something tangible. And spiked by the adrenaline rush they both were experiencing, it was almost violent.

Nadia's nails dug through his shirt. One of his hands

twisted in her hair. Dante sank to his knees in the dirt, pulling her with him and then pushed her backward onto the hard, pebbly ground.

● ● ●

Vandergriff whistled while he walked the perimeter of his estate, cheered by his last call from Cahill. He'd felt a rush of relief when Cahill confirmed they were safely back in the air. The fuel stop had been his only worry, the only weakness in his plan. He wasn't worried in the least about California. He had enough men in place there to rout Andreakos' pitiful crew, but Kansas was different. He'd barely had time to assemble a skeleton crew on the ground, but it turned out to be unnecessary. Andreakos simply hadn't had time to react.

Vandergriff barked orders into a walkie talkie. Tonight, Andreakos would hit, and hit hard. He had to be ready to take advantage of it.

Despite the battle he knew was coming, Vandergriff felt jovial. His bounty hunter had blindsided Andreakos. How delicious to imagine the agony and frustration his enemy suffered at this moment.

His cell phone rang. Vandergriff lifted it and stared in puzzlement at the number glowing in the green LCD light. What was Cahill doing calling again? He answered the call.

"Surely you're not in California yet," he said, glancing at his watch.

"No, sir. We're still in the air. Uh, Mr. Vandergriff . . . we have a problem."

"Problem?" he demanded. "What, with the plane?"

On the other end of the line, Cahill fell silent.

"What is the problem?" Vandergriff asked.

Cahill cleared his throat, then cleared it again. "The girl is gone."

Vandergriff heard the words, but he couldn't comprehend them. "Gone? *Gone?* Are you trying to tell me she's dead?"

Cahill didn't respond.

Vandergriff's last strand of patience snapped. "Cahill, if you don't answer me, so help me, I'll—"

"She jumped out of the airplane, sir," Cahill blurted. "She took Peterson's gun away from him and jumped out of the airplane. I've never seen anything like it. She, uh, she wasn't wearing a parachute."

Vandergriff's mind whirled and he leaned against an oak tree. He scrubbed his eyes with his fist. "Okay, so she's dead," he mumbled, more to himself than Cahill. "It's still okay. It will still work."

This wasn't what he'd planned, not yet anyway, but regardless, it would be a swift, crippling blow to Andreakos. Now, he only had to capitalize—

"No, sir," Cahill said quietly, snapping Vandergriff' attention back to the conversation.

"No what?" he asked, confused.

"She's not dead. She jumped. The bounty hunter jumped

from another plane and . . . he caught her. They parachuted to the desert floor."

For a moment, Vandergriff stood there, utterly stunned. Utterly frozen.

This wasn't happening. This couldn't be happening.

"What?" he screamed, and was shocked by the madness he heard in his own voice. "What?" he squawked again, like a deranged parrot, but he couldn't seem to force anything else out.

"I've got a parachute in the cockpit," Cahill offered. "Do you want me to go after her? We're circling the landing area."

"Of course I want you to go after her, you idiot! I'm calling in reinforcements. Don't even think of coming back without that girl."

"Sir—"

"Cahill, dead or alive. Find the girl and the bounty hunter and bring them to me."

❀ ❀ ❀

Nadia gasped his name as Dante's lips found the hollow of her throat. His hand stole beneath her shirt.

Slowly, Dante became conscious of another sound, a distant roar that wasn't quite drowned out by the pounding pulse in his ears. He looked up to see the yellow plane circling the sky above them.

A few yards away, the ground exploded into a plume of orange smoke.

"What is that?" Nadia shouted.

"A marker," he said, already scrambling to his feet.

He reached for Nadia, and another one exploded on the other side of them. More orange smoke. But it wasn't just smoke. It was a thick, paint-like substance that coated the surface around it. He'd only seen them used in military training.

"Is it gas?" Nadia asked when Dante hauled her to her feet and grabbed the backpack.

"No. It acts like a flare, to show them where we are. Like a big, orange bullseye. They're coming after us."

Grabbing her hand, he began to run, heading for the rocky hills on their left. He looked at his wrist, at the tracking device Nick had given him.

It would all come down to which group found them first, because there was nowhere to hide. The place was wide open.

They scrambled up a red-streaked hill, and Dante scanned the area below. A narrow, rocky valley lay between the surrounding hills. Then he saw the aging structures built into the sides of those hills.

Maybe. Just maybe there was something to work with.

Dante started down the hill. The loose rocks rolled underneath his boots and he lost his footing. He let go of Nadia's hand to keep from dragging her along with him when his feet skidded out from underneath him, and he began to slip down the steep incline on his back.

Another orange cloud exploded to his left. Trying to right himself, he couldn't slow his mad descent as he went skating along the rough surface on his behind. He landed with a thump on the valley floor, slapping his injured shoulder against the rock.

The pain was bright and sharp and he clutched his wound, emitting an agonized groan. He blinked through the dust in his eyes, looking for Nadia.

A red cloud of dust rocketed toward him. Nadia was sliding too.

There was no way to catch her. No way to cushion her fall. Dante winced at the sound of her body smacking against the desert floor.

He scrambled over to her, clutching his shoulder as he ran. "Are you okay?"

He was relieved to hear her muttered curse.

Nadia lay flat on her back, blinking up at him. Then she held out her hand. Dante hauled her up. Her arm was scraped, bleeding, but she didn't seem to notice. She was too busy laughing.

"What's the matter with you?" he asked, grinning despite his pain. "That *hurt!*"

She snickered. "You got a seat left in those pants, Slick?"

"I doubt I've got a butt left in these pants," he replied, rubbing his hip. "And you weren't exactly Ms. Grace and Finesse, you know."

"Yeah, yeah. It was your fault. I was doing fine until

you tripped me. Hey, what's this?" she asked, finally noticing their find.

The shadowy spots he'd seen from above were exactly what he'd hoped they were. Mine shafts. Old, abandoned mine shafts.

Perfect hiding places.

A couple of weathered boards covered the entrance of the nearest shaft. Planting his boot on the doorframe, Dante grasped one of them and pulled with all his might, even though it made his shoulder scream.

He had overestimated the rotting wood and the rusty nails that held it. The board gave way easily and he tumbled backward on his rear.

"Don't know your own strength?" she smirked.

Nadia stepped around him and was about to walk inside when Dante grabbed her ankle.

"Wait, babe. We need to check it before we go in there. Rattlesnakes like it in these things."

"Rattlesnakes?" Nadia asked, and took a step backward.

Her eyes looked greener than ever in contrast with her dirt-smudged face. Dante found it amusing that, even covered in dust, Nadia was still the most beautiful, breathtaking thing he'd ever seen. He managed to tear his gaze away from her long enough to dig one of the flashlights out of the backpack, along with a revolver.

"And scorpions. And bats," he said. "You'd better let me go first."

"Hey, be my guest," Nadia muttered, stooping to peer into the dark space. Then she jerked backward, covering her nose with her hand. "Oh, man . . . it stinks in there!"

When Dante touched her elbow, she jumped.

"Easy there," he joked. "I'll protect you."

Smoky eyes shot daggers through him. Dante winked at her and played the light on the gray-brown floor of the shaft.

"Watch that rock pile you're standing by," he said, pointing at her feet. "Snakes like those too."

Nadia moved instantly, coming to stand behind him.

After a cursory examination, Dante gingerly walked inside. Nadia was right. Something did stink in there. The shaft smelled musty, but there was another smell beneath that. Something foul.

Dead.

Dante backed out of there in a hurry, nearly tripping over Nadia in his haste to get back outside.

"Did I mention mountain lions?" he asked.

She frowned and crossed her arms over her chest. "You're lying.

"If I'm lion, I'm dyin'," he replied, before he thought better of it.

Nadia punched him in the stomach and stuck her head back inside the shaft. This time they both heard it. A low, feline growl. She raised her head abruptly and rapped it on the rotting gray board above her.

"Ow, ow, ow!" she moaned. Her hand clutched at the

injury that Ronnie had so recently patched for her. "Let's get out of here."

"Get over there," Dante said. "I have an idea."

After mashing around a small sagebrush with the toe of his boot, he grasped the prickly thing and pulled it out of the ground. Stepping carefully over to Nadia, he used it to brush away the footprints leading from the shaft.

Now all Vandergriff's men would see would be their tracks leading into the shaft. With any luck, they'd barrel in after them.

Nadia laughed. "You're good."

"The best."

"We'll see about that." Nadia gave him a bawdy wink that made him want to prove himself to her right here, right now. He wanted her more than he'd ever wanted anything in his life.

She wanted him too. It was in her touch, her smile. In those wild green eyes.

Did she have any idea how crazy she made him feel?

The roar of the plane faded in the distance and Dante looked up in surprise. Where were they going?

Even though they'd marked the landing area, he couldn't believe they wouldn't circle around, watching them.

Then Dante saw him. A tiny dot in the sky.

They had company. The plane was simply going back for reinforcements.

"Come on," he said, anxious to hide somewhere before

their visitor landed.

They hurried to the next cluster of shafts, with Dante scrubbing away their tracks as they went. This shaft had no barriers nailed up. Dante inspected it carefully, his ears tuned for the soft whir of a rattlesnake or the growl of a cougar. He took Nadia's hand. She gazed across the way at the first shaft they'd entered.

"Aren't all these things connected?"

"Not necessarily."

"What if the cat finds us?"

"What if Vandergriff finds us?" he replied. "Don't tell me the fearless Nadia Branson is chicken."

"I am not. And if you say that one more time, I'm going to smack you," she said, and grabbed the flashlight out of his hand. "Well, what are you waiting for? Let's go."

Dante smiled behind her back and followed her through the entryway.

They moved silently through the shaft, alert for the warning sound of any predator. Dante had his revolver in his hand, but he wasn't sure he could use it in here. Any shot could ricochet off the rock walls. He dug through the backpack and pulled out another light, curious about his surroundings.

They turned the first corner and the sunlight from the entryway disappeared completely. The darkness was thick, oppressive, and Dante felt a little claustrophobic. The beams from the flashlights stopped dead a few feet in front of them, swallowed up by the inky blackness beyond.

Dante played his light on the thick slabs of wood that acted as support beams and wondered how old they were, how stable. Even the air in the place smelled old. He was suddenly very conscious of the weight above them. Cracks snaked across the rock ceiling and Dante wondered how much movement it would take to bring the whole place down on top of them.

His heartbeat picked up when the shaft abruptly narrowed. Dante extended his arms and his fingertips brushed both sides. He had to duck to keep from hitting the low ceiling. Wondering how Nadia was doing, he played the light over her left shoulder to illuminate her face.

She was smiling.

Dante chuckled and shook his head. Everything about this girl surprised him.

"What?" she whispered.

"You like this, don't you?"

"Being alone with a totally hot, although somewhat clumsy guy in the dark. What's not to—whoa!"

Nadia stopped and reached behind her to place her palm against his chest. She shone her light down at the floor in front of her, at the deep fissure in the earth. It was narrow enough to cross over, but several feet deep. Deep enough to hurt a person if he stumbled into it.

He was really going to have to start paying attention to more than Nadia.

"Maybe we could set a trap," Nadia suggested.

Dante shook his head. "I'm afraid we'll trap the wrong ones. Your father is tracking us too. With this." He held up the GPS device on his wrist for her inspection. "I'm not high on his list of favorite people right now. I'm pretty sure a broken leg wouldn't help my case any."

"I bet he and Maria are going insane," Nadia said ruefully, and leapt over the fissure before Dante could help her.

"You should've seen his face when I told him I wanted you to jump out of that plane without a parachute. I thought he was going to shoot me." He hesitated and said, "Nadia . . . I meant to tell you before . . . I'm so sorry for everything . . . for all the trouble I've caused you."

The narrow tunnel emptied into a wide room. Nadia turned and stuck her flashlight under her chin, making a face at him.

"What are you talking about?" she said lightly. "This is the most excitement I've had in ages."

Dante's stomach knotted and he worked up the nerve to ask her what he really needed to know.

"Did he hurt you, Nadia? Other than the stun gun. Did Vandergriff touch you? Because if he laid a hand on you, I'll—"

"No, shhh." She placed a finger on his lips to silence him, then lowered her light and trailed her fingers along his jaw. "He didn't have time. Some maniac was running around the place, setting everything on fire."

"Are you telling me the truth?"

203

"If I'm lion, I'm dyin'," she said, and he could hear the smile on her face, even though he couldn't see it. "And besides, I—"

"—never lie," he finished.

"Well, except for that one time, but I wasn't keen on getting hit with Vandergriff's bug zapper again. That thing hurt." She punched his arm. "Hey, you remembered!" she said, sounding pleased.

Dante smiled. "I think I remember everything you've ever said to me, starting with R 20—"

"You must've thought that was real funny when I flirted with you like that at the diner." Nadia sounded embarrassed and Dante wished he could see her face, see her blush.

He laughed. "I didn't think it was funny at all. You threw me for a loop. I was supposed to be the one who did the flirting. The one in control. I even had this big plan to get your attention. You were supposed to be some bored little rich girl, but you turned out to be . . . you. When you bit my ear . . . oh, man!"

Nadia fell silent, and Dante wondered if he'd said something wrong.

She slid in closer to him. Her breath warmed his chest through the thin material of his shirt when she said, "Dante, I want to talk to you about something, and be honest, even if you think it will hurt me. All the things that happened between us, in the bathroom, in the garden . . . were they only pretend, part of your plan? It's okay if it was. I can get past it, but I need you to be straight with me now."

"Nadia, please don't think that," he said, and ran his hands down her arms to circle her wrists. "I admit, that first part, in the diner . . . I wanted to make an impression—and no, before you ask—I didn't know those guys were going to attack you. Vandergriff set that up for me as much as he did you. He fed me this big story about some drug dealer being after you because of Nick."

"What?" Nadia asked with a surprised laugh. "Why on earth would a drug dealer be after Nick?"

Dante rubbed the back of his neck, embarrassed. "It's a long story and I'll explain it all to you later, but for now I want you to know that every time I touched you, or kissed you, it wasn't part of some plan. I did it because I wanted to, because I wanted you. This thing between you and me . . . it didn't make my job easier. It made it harder. I felt like a dog when I took you to Vandergriff, but I believed I was doing what I needed to do to protect you. Do you believe me?"

"Yes."

Dante leaned toward her. They laughed when their foreheads bumped, then he kissed her. For a moment, Dante lost himself in her touch, in the sweetness of her kiss.

He could've stayed like that with her forever, but he realized they had things to take care of first. Reluctantly, he untangled himself from her and pulled away.

"We need to secure this place."

They found two other entrances into the room, one of

which was partially blocked by fallen rock. Dante contemplated the other one, trying to decide whether to block it off or leave it open as an alternate escape route. A few big, loose rocks were piled beside the entrance and he decided to move some of them there, not to completely block it, but to make sure they would know it if someone was coming through.

"I'm going to move these. You stand back and shine the flashlight on them and tell me if you see anything move. I doubt we see any rattlers this far back, especially in the summertime, but you never know."

Nadia didn't respond. She simply shone the beam where he'd asked, and Dante knew better than to comment on the way it twitched.

Dante shoved the rock over with his boot, not wanting to expose his bare fingers. When nothing scurried, hissed, or rattled at him, he rolled it over to the entrance. Pushing over the third rock, he detected movement.

"Scorpion," Nadia said, directing her beam at it. The wicked-looking little creature scuttled through a crack in the wall.

While Dante set a similar alarm near the opening they'd entered through, Nadia walked the perimeter of the room, kicking rocks and sometimes piling them against crevices in the wall.

"Hey!" she hissed, and he looked up. She stood near the tunnel opening, her head cocked. She motioned for him and he crossed the cave to her.

"Did you hear that?" she whispered.

Dante listened for a long moment. Finally, he said, "Hear what?"

"I thought I heard a shot . . . maybe somebody yelling."

They remained silent for a few minutes, then Dante chuckled. "I think you're imagining things."

Nadia scowled, but didn't comment. He clicked off his flashlight.

"What now?" she asked.

"Now we wait for the cavalry. Maybe they'll catch up soon. Cut off your flashlight so we can conserve batteries."

She shone her light under her face, making sure he saw her frown. "You don't have any more with you?"

"Another set for each of us, but we shouldn't use them right now. We may need them all."

"You have anything to build a fire with?"

"We can't build a fire. I don't know what kinds of gasses could be trapped under here, and it would use too much of our oxygen."

Dante sat on the cold rock floor and laid his revolver beside him. There was a challenge in his voice when he said, "Besides, I thought you liked it in the dark. Are you afraid, princess?"

● ● ●

He's going to pay for that, Nadia decided. *But maybe not right this minute.*

She clicked off her flashlight and sat in his lap, grinning when she heard his sharp intake of breath.

The blackness around them was solid. Nadia literally could not see her hand in front of her face. All she could hear was the labored sound of Dante's breathing.

Then he touched her.

His rough fingers trailed across her bare shoulders. His left hand stilled as he skimmed over the two little burn marks. Then he retraced them.

"Is that where Vandergriff got you with the stun gun?" Dante asked, his voice tight.

"Yes, how did you—"

"That's what finally tipped me off. The smell of ozone. And the look in your eyes. You're a rotten liar, you know."

Nadia chuckled. "So, that was a test, with the paper and pen? I was trying so hard not to blow it. He told me he'd kill you . . ."

"Bastard," Dante muttered. One big hand reached underneath her hair and started massaging the nape of her neck. "I bet you're pretty sore."

"Not too bad." Nadia craned her head and pushed back her hair to give him better access to her neck. "I'm tough."

"I know you are.

She sighed when his big, warm hands kneaded the aching muscles in her back and neck. And shivered when he brushed his lips against the burn.

"What, kiss it and make it all better?" she joked, but

her mouth was dry. "Because in that case, I have a few more places you might want to check out—" She broke off, gasping when he untied the straps of her halter top and pushed it down to her waist.

Her flimsy little strapless bra followed suit.

"Your phone," she said idiotically, reaching to pat the waistband of her jeans. "I think I lost—"

Dante cupped her breasts in his rough hands and Nadia forgot whatever she was babbling about. His arousal pressed against her blue-jeaned bottom, and she very nearly forgot her own name when he began to stroke her nipples with the pads of his thumbs. She leaned her head against his chest and groaned.

"Turn around," he whispered.

The urgency in his voice made her face flush hot in the dark. She twisted around in his lap and he groaned at her movement. Nadia straddled him and tugged his shirt over his head, gently untangling his necklace when it caught. She brushed her breasts against his chest, and was electrified by the feel of Dante's bare, hot skin pressed against hers.

Dante cupped her breasts in his hands and lowered his head. He raked his tongue across one taut nipple, then took it in his mouth.

The quick flicks of his tongue, at first pleasurable, became maddening as the tension built inside her. Unconsciously, Nadia rocked against him, trying to satisfy a thirst she couldn't quench, a desire that wouldn't be fulfilled until she had him inside of her. He pressed his face between her breasts and she stroked his head, enjoying the rasp of rough stubble against her palm.

"I wish I could see you," he rasped. "I hate this darkness."

But she didn't. It was exciting, erotic, sending her other senses into overdrive. Every touch, every sound seemed amplified.

She supposed that was why she was the first one who heard the rocks move.

CHAPTER 9

L isten," she hissed.

Dante tensed beneath her. His breath seemed to stop, and his fingers brushed hers when he fumbled for his gun.

There it was again.

A scraping sound came from the entrance they hadn't used. Then a crash echoed when one of the rocks bounced against the shaft floor.

Even though Dante pressed his mouth against her ear, he spoke so quietly that Nadia had to strain to hear his instructions.

"Get against the wall. Take the backpack with you and stay down. Don't move or make a sound until I tell you."

Nadia nodded and slowly climbed off him. Clutching the backpack and her flashlight, she realized for the first time how heavy it was.

What on earth did he have in there?

She started backing up and kept backing until she felt

the cool rock wall press against her skin.

A shiver of déjà vu raced through her, but she wouldn't let that memory intrude. Things were different this time. She wasn't alone.

Retrieving the blouse and bra that was shoved down around her waist, she was eternally grateful Dante hadn't discarded them on the rock floor. Nadia didn't relish the idea of being found topless by either group.

Vandergriff might not kill her right away, but her father definitely would.

She no longer heard Dante and had no sense of where he was in the darkness. It was amazing how such a big man could move so silently.

The crash of the rocks jarred the silence as whatever was on the other side of that tunnel broke through. The clattering seemed to go on forever, and Nadia was sure she heard a human moan. She saw a flash of light and caught a glimpse of a human, bloodied face when Dante clicked his flashlight on, then off again.

Was that Cahill?

Then she heard another sound. One that made the hair on the back of her neck stand to attention.

A low, feline growl.

"Nadia." Dante's voice was casual, calm. "Bring your flashlight and come to me. Stay close to the walls and move slowly."

Dropping the backpack, she moved toward him in the pitch black. Her pulse roared in her ears. The darkness was disorienting, almost suffocating. Holding out one hand, she felt for the wall.

She opened her mouth to speak to him, to attempt to pinpoint his location again when she tripped over a rock. Her feet flew out from beneath her and Nadia sprawled face first onto the dusty floor. The flashlight flew from her hand and crashed against the rock. It made an eerie, clattering sound when it rolled away.

The big cat growled again.

"Dammit!" she cried, frustrated by her clumsiness and tasting blood.

"Are you okay?"

"I dropped my flashlight."

"It's okay. Come toward my voice."

In another situation, Nadia might have laughed. Dante's voice was as calm and controlled as a TV weatherman's. He wasn't trying to be quiet, but he wasn't being too loud, either.

Finally, her outstretched hands grazed his bare back. He grasped her arm and felt along it until he found her hand. He pressed his flashlight into it.

"Shine the light on me," he commanded.

"Dante—"

"Do it."

She shone the light on him. Dante held his arms wide at his sides and spread his legs like a man caught in the middle of a jumping jack. He slowly waved his arms. Nadia noticed the big bandage on his left shoulder, his limited range of motion. His gunshot wound.

"What do you think you're doing?" she demanded.

"Making myself look as big as possible. The worst thing you can do with a mountain lion is make yourself look like a small target."

Nadia had been so intent on Dante and following his instructions that she hadn't even looked for the cat. She glanced past Dante to the opening and nearly dropped the other flashlight.

Yellow eyes glowed at her from inside the yawning black hole.

With her heart stuttering in her chest, she jerked her gaze down to the man lying on the floor. It was Cahill, or what was left of him. He still had the pencil shoved behind his ear. One blue eye stared at the ceiling and the other one—

With a cry of revulsion, Nadia took a stumbling step backward.

"Nadia! Nadia, you have to stay calm. The cat's injured and that will make it more aggressive."

Swallowing hard, Nadia stared at Dante's back and tried to hold the flashlight beam steady.

Calm down, she told herself. *Quit acting like a baby.*

"Why don't you shoot it?" she asked, hating the trembling she heard in her voice.

"For one thing, a bullet could ricochet in here and hit one of us. For another, we're the intruders here. I'd say that's a mother protecting her cubs and—shine your light on her—

see the blood on her shoulder? This idiot's shot her. Doesn't look like it's a mortal wound, but more than enough to make her want to tear us apart."

Dante continued waving his arms and, to Nadia's amazement, the glowing eyes retreated back into the tunnel.

"Come on." He turned to Nadia. "Let's get out of here."

"Don't . . . leave me," Cahill gasped.

Nadia nearly screamed, yanking her light back to his body. She'd thought for sure he was dead. His chest—oh, God, his chest was ripped wide open.

Dante took the flashlight from her hands and squatted beside the dying man.

"Are you Catholic?" Cahill wheezed, looking up at Dante with glassy eyes. "Last rites . . . I need . . ."

"Aw, man. I'm no priest. You know that."

"Don't leave me," he pleaded again. Each breath he took made a wet, sucking sound in his chest and Nadia had to turn her face away. Even a man as cold as Cahill didn't deserve such a death.

"Are you Catholic?" he asked again.

"No." Dante sighed. "My grandma was, but, much to her dismay, my father married a Methodist. That's the church I went to when I was a kid. Look, I remember a little prayer my mother taught me. Would you like to hear it?"

"Yes. Please."

Dante cleared his throat. "Heavenly Father, I have erred and strayed from Thy ways. Instead of following You, I have followed desires of my own heart. I have left undone things which I ought to have done, and I have done things which I ought not to have done, and there is no peace within me. Spare thou them, O Father, which confess their faults. Restore thou them that are penitent. By Your grace I ask for forgiveness. Amen."

Nadia was touched by the soft, simple prayer Dante recited for the man.

"One more . . . time," Cahill said.

Dante repeated it, this time pausing between lines to allow Cahill to echo each verse. Moments later, he gave a deep, shuddering breath, and died.

Dante grimaced. He stood and retrieved his T-shirt.

"Are you okay?" Nadia grasped his hand. It was cold as ice.

"Yeah. I was thinking about my grandma. She gave me this when I joined the Marines." He tugged the silver medal from underneath his shirt and held it up for her inspection. "St. Michael. He's the patron saint of soldiers. I remember how she used to beg me to go to mass with her. And my ma, she still teaches Sunday school. She has four kids and as soon as any of us were old enough to balk, we quit going with her. I was wishing I'd gone more with either one of them, just so I'd have known what to say to that guy."

"I think you did a wonderful job." Nadia squeezed his fingers.

He pulled his hand away and slung his arm around her waist. Caressing her hip, he said, "Maybe when we get out of this, I'll take you to the old neighborhood. Show you around New York."

"Take me to meet the folks?" Nadia said with a smile.

"Yeah. I don't know so much about introducing you to my little brothers, though. I'd have to beat them away from you with a baseball bat."

"Are they as handsome as you?"

"I suppose," he said with a chuckle. "But I got all the charm."

"Ah, well. That's seals it, then. I'm picky. I want the whole package." Nadia wrapped her arm around his waist, both nervous and excited at the thought of meeting Dante's family.

They retrieved the backpack and headed out of the shaft.

"I was hoping we'd get to stay in there for awhile, but now we're going to have to move in the heat of day."

"Do you have water in there?" Nadia asked, pointing at the backpack.

"Some. I hope it's enough to do us until your father gets here. I have a water purifier, too, in case we find a water source."

They ventured out into the sunlight and Nadia winced from both the sudden brightness and the oppressive heat. The wind blew, but it was scorching and felt more like a slap than a breeze.

When she could open her eyes, she surveyed the terrain.

Where did Dante think they were going? And on foot, no less. It all looked the same to her, an endless expanse of rocky hills and sagebrush.

"Hey, what's that?" She pointed over Dante's shoulder at the golden cloud in the east. It hovered a few inches above the ground and seemed to be moving toward them. Dante glanced around, his brown eyes widening.

"Get back to the shaft."

She hesitated, watching it approach.

He grabbed her arm. "Run!"

● ● ●

When Vandergriff saw the small plane descending onto the airstrip, he pitched the radio receiver he held against the wall. It bounced off the dingy yellowed wall with a thwack, taking another chip out of the peeling paint.

What was Peterson doing back here, and where was Cahill, and why in the hell couldn't he raise either one of them on the radio?

He ran outside to meet the plane.

Impatiently, he waited for the doors to open, then boarded before a sheepish-looking Peterson could climb off the plane.

"What are you doing back here?" Vandergriff demanded. "You're supposed to be circling the target area!"

Peterson wiped a hand down his face. "We've got a leak in the hydraulics, or the gauge is screwing up or something. I tried to radio you, but I couldn't get through. Cahill marked the area, though. You shouldn't have any trouble seeing it."

"From the air," Vandergriff snapped. "It'll be more difficult from land. And where is Cahill? I can't get him to answer me either."

Peterson shook his head and shoved his hands in his pockets. "I haven't been in contact with him at all since he jumped."

Vandergriff fell heavily onto one of the seats. "What happened? *How* did this happen?" His eyes narrowed. "Why wasn't the girl tied, anyway?"

Peterson sighed. "I let her go to the bathroom, and never bothered to retie her. She's such a little thing . . . I'll be honest, I never saw her as much of a threat. I never saw any of this coming."

Frustration made Vandergriff's eye twitch. He was blinking like he had Tourette's, but he couldn't make it stop. "Did she say anything? Anything at all?"

"She said, 'He's going to catch me.' Then she jumped."

"How did she *know* he was going to catch her?"

The cell phone in Vandergriff's pocket chirped noisily and he snatched it out. "Cahill, is that you?"

"No, boss. It's Nelan. We've almost reached the coordinates you mapped us, but I don't see a plane."

"The plane had to come back to the airstrip. You're going to have to locate the markers and find them yourselves. Cahill is supposed to be down there too. Maybe he'll update us soon. They couldn't have gone far on foot. Find them." Vandergriff gripped the phone, hatred surging through him like an electric current. "And when you do, I want you to gut that bounty hunter like a deer. Save the girl for me."

He snapped the phone shut and turned to Peterson. "It's okay. They're almost there anyway." More for himself than Peterson, he mumbled, "We can still pull this off. I have a spy in Andreakos' camp. He says they're tracking the girl by GPS. Do you know anything about GPS, Peterson?"

"I'm afraid not, sir," Peterson replied, sitting beside him.

"My man can't get close to it. Andreakos and that Mc-Namara fellow are monitoring it at all times. I told him to do whatever he has to do to slow them down. You need to call Baxter. We'll be joining him shortly. He's in charge of the second group, and we're coordinating an ambush for Andreakos. We have to head them off long enough for Nelan to find that girl." Vandergriff pinched the bridge of his nose. "How did they pull this off?"

He said he'd catch me.

The girl hadn't known where he was taking her until the last moment. She had to get in touch with the bounty hunter from the plane. How?

Underwood indicated that the GPS unit was with the bodyguard. There was no way the girl could've gotten to the radio, no way that Andreakos had turned both Peterson and Cahill.

Vandergriff buried his face in his hands and leaned over, pulling the skin around his eyes taut to try to stop that damnable twitching so he could think.

He spotted a little silver phone lying on the floor beside Peterson's shoe.

Vandergriff dove to pick it up, startling Peterson. He grabbed it and waved it in Peterson's face.

"Is this yours?" he asked.

"Uh, no, sir."

"Is it Cahill's?"

Peterson frowned, then shook his head. "Cahill didn't have a cell phone with him. He borrowed mine to call you when we stopped for fuel."

Vandergriff flipped open the phone and stared at the numbers. Then he squeezed his eyes shut like he was trying to get a premonition from touching it.

"This is how she contacted them. If I press redial, I get Andreakos on the other end of the line." Vandergriff gritted his teeth. "Maybe I should call him and tell him what I'm going to do with his precious little girl when I get my hands on her again."

When his thumb moved for the button, Peterson grabbed his wrist.

"Wait! I think I know how we can use this to our advantage."

Vandergriff stared at him. "What do you mean?"

Peterson shot him a crooked grin. "Why, I think I should be the one to call Andreakos. I talked to his daughter on the plane. I was nice to her. We have a connection."

"What are you getting at?" Vandergriff asked irritably, pressing his fingers against the sides of his eyes.

Peterson shrugged and leaned back in the seat. "Your

man on the inside . . . suppose he isn't your only contact with Andreakos? I could tell Andreakos that I liked Nadia, and I'm sorry for what happened . . . and that I'll do everything I can to help him get her back. I'll agree to spy on you. I could be his new best friend."

Vandergriff gave an incredulous laugh. "Peterson, that's amazing. Really, it is." He frowned and shook his head. "But Andreakos is no fool. Why should he believe you?"

Peterson pressed his hands together in front of his face like he was praying, then he dropped them and smiled. "We give up your spy."

"What? Are you crazy?" Vandergriff demanded, jumping to his feet. "I can't give him Underwood . . . a bird in the hand is worth two in the bush. Andreakos may never trust you, and I will have lost my only edge."

"Let me do it right before the attack! Your spy is useless after he leads them into the ambush. And you said yourself, they won't let him anywhere near the GPS. What good is he to you?"

Vandergriff stared at the phone. Peterson was right. Maybe there was something he could use here. Although he hoped for the best, he didn't really think he could kill Andreakos in the fray. Too many men around him. This might be his next best shot.

"Okay," he said slowly. "But not until we're ready for the attack."

"When will that be?" Peterson asked, and Vandergriff

shook his head.

"I like you, Peterson. You show great initiative, but I learned early from my father to never reveal all my plans to any one man." He squinted at him. "Now that I think about it, you seem awfully eager to help me. Why is that?"

Peterson snorted and rubbed the back of his neck. "I'm awfully eager to help *me*. That girl embarrassed me. She escaped under my watch, so I feel like it's my responsibility to get her back."

Vandergriff pocketed the phone and clamped a hand on Peterson's shoulder. "Come on then. We've got a lot to decide before you make that call."

● ● ●

They sprinted toward the shaft and Dante wrenched her back inside an instant before the sand and pebbles began striking the outside of the shaft.

"Dust devil," he explained, folding her against his chest. "That stuff's a bitch if you get it in your eyes."

Nadia listened to the rocks beat against the wall for a moment, then yawned and rested her face against Dante's T-shirt. Some of her adrenaline had melted away and now she simply felt tired. It was nice, leaning there against him. She closed her eyes and listened to the gentle thump of his heart.

"It's over," Dante announced, and gently smacked her rear. "Let's move."

Nadia groaned and reluctantly pushed away from him. She was moving through the entryway when he grabbed her arm.

"Do you hear that?" he whispered.

Nadia immediately glanced back into the mine shaft. "Hear what? Is the cat back?"

"No. Out there."

For a long moment, she heard nothing. Then there it was. A faraway buzzing sound.

"Motorcycles," she said.

"Maybe it's your father."

"Maybe not," Nadia replied, watching Dante pull a two-by-four away from the entryway.

"You have a gun," she pointed out.

He grinned. "Gee, you're a violent little thing, aren't you?"

She made a face. "Yeah, I tend to get that way when I'm dirty, sleepy, and hungry."

"If it's your father, they should come straight to us." Dante tapped the device on his wrist.

Nadia peered out the entryway. "Let's check it out," she said, and moved into the sunlight.

The heat beat down on her bare shoulders and her clothing stuck to her. The hill they'd slid down blocked their view of the motorcyclists. With Dante on her heels, Nadia scrambled up the rocky surface.

"We can't let them see us," Dante whispered as they neared the top.

"Gee, you think?" Nadia rolled her eyes. She was near

the top now. Crawling on her stomach on the rough red rocks, she peeked over the top of the hill.

And found herself straight in the path of an incoming motorcycle.

She could see the grooves of the treads as the front tire of the motorcycle spun toward her head.

Rolling to the right, Nadia felt a blast of hot exhaust when the motorcycle sliced through the air inches from her face. The machine was airborne, hanging in the air above the hillside and Nadia could only gape at it. It came down gracefully at the bottom of the hill. Its blond rider kept going.

He hadn't even seen them.

While she was processing that fact, another motorcycle topped the hill, spraying her with a fine mist of sand and pebbles. She heard the rumble of an engine. Another one was coming and it sounded too close—

Dante seized her and they tumbled backward, down the steep incline.

Movement. Dust. The pain of the rocks scraping against her skin. That was all Nadia was conscious of during their breakneck slide. The thump at the bottom stunned her, stole her breath, but she caught movement out of the corner of her eye.

Dante was up and running.

Nadia shook her head. How was he still moving? Even her teeth hurt.

She was beginning to wonder if he was some sort of

robot. If he was, she was going to order herself two of them.

While she watched, Dante scrambled for the two-by-four he'd left at the foot of the hill. One of the motorcycles had turned. It was heading right for him. Dante waited on it, poised like a crazed matador.

The other rider. He had to have seen them. Where had he gone?

He came roaring around the side of the hill, also heading straight at Dante. Nadia saw the gun in his hand. She recognized his face through the open helmet.

It was one of the thugs from the diner.

Nadia scanned the ground, searching for any kind of weapon. In her desperation, she seized a rock about the size of her fist and chunked it at him. It caught him square in the back.

The cyclist bobbled and turned to glance at her. Scraping her knuckles against the ground, Nadia grabbed another one, not daring to take her eyes off the rider. She hurled another missile at him. This time she missed by a foot, but at least she had diverted his attention from Dante. He changed directions, heading toward her, but he stuck his gun back in the holster. Nadia got the message.

Vandergriff wanted her alive.

You've got one more shot, she told herself. *Make it solid, make it true.*

Closing her fist around the smooth, hot stone, Nadia let it fly. The rock caught the man in the center of his throat.

Stunned, she watched him topple off the bike. His handgun went flying in one direction and the unmanned motorcycle veered off in another.

"Dante!" she shouted.

Nadia retrieved the gun and chased after the wildly careening motorcycle. It crashed against the bank and lay on its side, wheels spinning. As she ran, Nadia heard the other motorcycle bearing down on her. But there was nowhere left for her to go.

"Nadia! Nadia, get on."

Dante slowed beside her and she threw herself on the back of the bike, almost losing the gun in the process.

"Wicked fastball!" he shouted, while she righted herself. "Remind me not to get on your bad side, princess."

Nadia clutched his waist, grinning. Then she saw the crimson stain darkening the back of his shirt.

"Your shoulder is bleeding!"

"Yeah, I think I tore it open again. But it'll be okay."

The first rider had parked his bike and stood waiting for his companions by the mine shafts. His mouth opened in a surprised O when he saw the couple barreling toward him. Nadia opened fire.

He dove for cover and she emptied the clip into the bike. The front tire exploded as she riddled it with bullets.

"Whooo hoo!" she shouted, and tossed the empty gun into a clump of sagebrush.

"You're enjoying this too much!" Dante yelled over the

roar of the bike. "Now I know how Clyde felt when he hooked up with Bonnie."

She was still laughing when they crested the top of the next hill.

• • •

Dante drove at breakneck speed for several miles, twisting and turning through the hills until he felt sure he'd thrown off any pursuers. He had a stupid smile on his face, even though his shoulder was throbbing.

Nadia was crazy. Brave. Fearless.

The image had burned into his brain. The dark-haired beauty hurling rocks at an armed man to save him. Those wild green eyes. He had finally met a woman who shared his adrenaline addiction.

He just wasn't sure whether or not that was a good thing.

"Check out those clouds." He pointed ahead of them. "It looks like we're going to see some rain."

"Rain? In the desert?" she asked, and pressed herself against his back.

"Yeah. I only hope it isn't too much at once. They have flash floods here sometimes. Wouldn't that be something to get caught up in?"

Nadia sighed. "The way this day is going, I wouldn't be surprised at all. I'm an optimist, Dante. I really am, but even I have to wonder if we're going to make it through this damn day."

He grinned. "Oh, yeah. We're going to make it."

Before the words were out of his mouth, the fuel gauge inched from yellow to red. Dante hoped the reserve was full. He was reaching to flip it over when he saw the bulky structures dotting the landscape ahead.

Nadia's going to love this, he thought, and leaned back to tell her what was ahead.

"A ghost town!" she screeched, deafening him. She nearly toppled them in her haste to look over his shoulder. "How cool!"

It wasn't much of a ghost town, just a few haphazard piles of gray rocks and rotting wood that used to be buildings, but Nadia insisted on stopping.

"Watch out for open mine shafts. And rattlesnakes," Dante warned.

Nadia saluted smartly and skipped off to inspect the ruins.

"What was this?" she asked, pointing at the wide, rusting tin roof that rested on the ground in an inverted V. Whatever structure it had once protected was long gone now. A few dilapidated boards still braced it. More lay scattered on the ground.

"I'd say it was once an old hoist house."

"Okay . . . what's a hoist house?"

"Mining operations used them to protect equipment from the elements, store ore. That sort of thing."

"Cool," she said and crawled beneath it.

"Nadia—"

"I know, I know. Be careful." She crawled back out a moment later and said, "Off with that shirt. I want to check out your shoulder."

"It's okay."

"Don't argue with me, I'm in a mood," she warned, and he snickered when he thought of the rock hurling. "And besides, I like ordering you to take off your clothes. Have you got a medical kit in that bag?"

With a sigh, Dante dug it out and handed it to her. He peeled off his shirt and sat cross-legged on the ground in front of her. A hot breeze kicked up the dust around them and Dante shielded his eyes while Nadia gently pulled back the tape to inspect his gunshot wound. She didn't say anything for such a long time that Dante twisted to look at her.

"What?"

"He shot you with a .22?" she asked finally.

"Yeah, what about it?"

"I thought you were *shot* shot. With a real gun. I mean, what sort of weapon is this for a hired thug? You'd think the guy would have a .44 or something that would do some real damage—"

Dante snorted. "I'm sorry you're disappointed by the size of the hole in my shoulder, princess. But if it's any consolation, it really does hurt."

"Ah, you big baby. Here I thought you ex-Marines ate nails for breakfast. And you know what I meant. It was strictly an observation on technique."

He grunted.

Nadia cleaned the wound and changed the bandage. "There!" She smoothed the tape in place. "I think you'll live."

"Thanks for your compassion. It makes the pain so much more bearable," he said.

Nadia winked. "What pain? That's like a paper cut or something . . . and I told you, I get that way when I'm tired, hungry, and dirty."

He winced, and pulled a hand down his face. "I've seriously got to feed you, don't I?"

Nadia laughed. "It would be nice."

Dante rummaged through the backpack and pulled out two brown packets. "MRE's," he explained. "Also known as Mr. E's."

"MR whats?" Nadia asked, then waved her hand. "Never mind. If it's food, I'll eat it. I don't care what it is."

"Okay, so do you want possum a la `orange or rattlesnake teriyaki?"

"Smart alec." Nadia smacked the back of his head. She plopped down beside him and seized the packets.

"Hmmm . . . turkey with savory vegetables or vegetarian pasta fagioli."

She contemplated it for a moment, then tossed him the turkey. "I don't really know what this is, but I'll try anything once."

Dante watched with amusement as she ripped open the packet and inspected the contents.

"Vegetarian whazzit, crackers, jam—ooh, a chocolate

oatmeal cookie—orange beverage base, Tabasco sauce, accessory pack."

"Army rations. These things have a shelf life of three years."

"Imagine that," Nadia said dryly, tearing open the accessory pack. "Salt, pepper, chewing gum—moist towelettes?" She cocked an eyebrow at Dante.

He shrugged.

She started to tear open her packet and he said, "Wait, hand it here. You've got to cook the thing."

"In what?" she demanded and shoved it into his outstretched hand. "Don't tell me I have to wait for you to build a fire?"

"Cranky, cranky," he chided, shaking his finger at her. "It will only take a minute and we don't have to build a fire."

He detached a small square from the accessory pack and shook it out. "Flameless, self-heating pouch. You have to pour water in here, up to the fill line—it doesn't matter if it's clean water or not—and it causes a chemical reaction, making the water heat, then—"

"Enough with the MacGuyver lesson. Just feed me," she said, clasping her hands together. Dante laughed at her mugging.

He poured the water in the bag, taking care not to waste any, and dropped Nadia's entrée packet inside. He zipped it shut and said, "Five minutes. That's it."

He took her hand and placed it on the outside of the bag. "See, it's already getting hot."

Nadia grunted. Dante fixed his bag and set it beside hers.

"Uhh, that stinks!" she said, fanning herself. "I hope that's not the food I smell."

"It's the chemicals. But don't get your hopes up on the food. It's not much better, but it's protein."

Nadia was getting antsy by the time he proclaimed it ready. Dante took out his pocketknife and carefully slit the heater, letting the steam escape before withdrawing the food pouch.

It wasn't exactly piping hot, but it was warm enough. He tore the edge off his turkey packet and squeezed some into his mouth. A skeptical looking Nadia followed suit. He watched with amusement when she swallowed hard and started coughing.

"You okay, princess?" Dante laughed.

He poured water into her beverage packet and handed it to her. She took a big gulp and grimaced.

"Maybe I misunderstood. They give these to our troops or the enemy?"

"Put some Tabasco on it."

"No way. Then I have to drink more of that orange crap."

For all her complaining, Nadia polished off her MRE. She saved her chocolate cookie for last, and was regarding it with such delight that Dante couldn't help laughing. Then he really laughed at the look of surprise on her face when she popped it in her mouth.

"Bleaaaah," she said. "Tastes like chocolate covered sawdust."

"Gripe, gripe, gripe. You really are a princess. Next time I get stuck in the desert, I think I'll take Waynie with me instead."

Nadia snorted. "Yeah, you just do that. You think *I'm* a whiner . . . he'd have never survived that first slide down the hill."

"Yeah, you're a whiner." Dante tossed a small, foil wrapped packet to her. "Here you go, whiner. Just for you. Freeze dried chocolate."

After a hesitant nibble, Nadia popped the square into her mouth and moaned with exaggerated ecstasy. "Oh, man. That's more like it."

Dante leaned back on his elbows to watch her, and she frowned.

"What's the matter with you? Why are you all the way over there? Afraid I'll bite?"

"I'm thinking I'm pretty safe, since I'm not made out of chocolate or anything."

Dante gazed up at the rolling black thunder clouds. They were going to get rained on soon. He was grateful for the cloud cover anyway. Without those clouds, the heat would be pretty miserable at this time of day. It was still hot, but not unbearably so. He cleared his throat.

"Nadia, there's something I need to get off my chest."

She lifted her eyebrows. "Hmmm, like that shirt, maybe? Because it's a shame to cover that chest up. I'm getting kind of fond of it."

Dante laughed. "Cut it out. I'm trying to be serious here. I feel like I owe you an explanation, for taking you to Vander-griff."

Nadia took his hand and he stared at her. She was so beautiful, so dazzling . . . Dante wondered if he would ever be able to look at her without feeling a little spark. He tucked a lock of her dark hair behind her ear and she smiled.

"It's okay, Dante. You already told me. I know he tricked you. He lied to you."

"I made it easy for him. I should've been more careful. But the truth is . . ." He paused. "I wanted this case."

"Why?" Nadia's voice was quiet. Dante thought he saw a flicker of apprehension in her green eyes.

"It reminded me of my own situation. Of my own child."

Nadia blinked and swallowed hard. "You, uh . . . you have a child?"

"Yeah, a little girl. Lara. She's six now." He dug his wallet out of his back pocket and removed a picture from it. Handing it to her, he said, "This is an old one. She was only a baby there."

"She's beautiful." Nadia stared at the picture, then turned her face away. "Do you also have a wife?"

"Not anymore."

She shot him a curious glance. "What happened?"

Dante shrugged. "She decided she could do better."

Nadia traced her finger in the dirt beside her. "Your ex-wife must be the biggest idiot walking the planet," she said.

"Waking up with you every morning doesn't sound too traumatic to me."

Dante laughed. "She never woke up with me. We were married about three hours. Well, technically, it was a little longer, with the paperwork and all, but it was pretty much over instantly."

"Whoa! Worse than Britney Spears." Nadia lifted her eyebrows. "What happened?"

"Her father. I got a job driving for him right out of high school. The first thing he said to me was, 'Boy, stay away from my daughter.' But you know how it is when you're eighteen. Forbidden fruit and all that. Plus, Sharon started hanging around the garage all the time. One thing led to another . . ." He shrugged and Nadia nodded.

"She came to me one day and told me she was pregnant. We were both scared, but I told her everything would be all right. Her mother was out of town and Sharon wanted to wait until she came back before we told them, but it all blew up before then. Her old man caught us kissing. He ranted and raved and fired me on the spot. He and Sharon had a big fight and she told him about the baby. He went ballistic, and had me escorted off the premises. We ran away that night."

Shame burned his face. It still hurt to talk about that night, but somehow it didn't feel awkward with Nadia.

"We were married in this cheesy all-night wedding chapel. We both had a little money saved up and decided to just take off, hoping some of it would blow over by the time we got back. We'd stopped to spend the night at a motel off the interstate when her father caught up with us. He had a couple guys with him and they held me down while he talked to her. He told her what a miserable life she'd have, married to a working class guy like me, how we'd have to scrape to get by. He was begging her to go with him, I was begging her to stay. In the end, she decided to go with him."

"Oh, Dante!" Nadia sighed. "I'm sorry. What about Lara? Do you get to see her at all?"

"Sharon kept in touch for a few months, without her father's knowledge, but I think we both knew whatever we'd had between us was over when she walked out that night. I tried to call her, tried to see her to find out how she was, but I could never get past Martin's people. Then one night, out of the blue, Sharon calls and asks if I could meet her at the park near my mom's house. She had Lara with her. She'd been born two weeks earlier and I hadn't even known it."

Dante smiled, remembering how small she'd been, how soft and beautiful. "That was the only time I've ever held my daughter. But Martin somehow found out about it. He had some guys come visit me. They threatened my family, my mother and my brothers, if I didn't stay away. He was a powerful guy. Next thing I knew, I was fired from my new job, and nobody seemed to be hiring. I was only a kid myself; I didn't really know what to do. The next time Sharon called, I told her I was joining the Marines. I was going to save up my paychecks and get us a house someplace far away from her father, where we could be a family."

"What did she say?" Nadia asked quietly.

"She went along with it. She'd write me, I'd write her and send the letters to one of my brothers and Sharon would pick them up from him. A few times, she even sent me pictures of her and Lara. Then, the letters stopped. I was going crazy, afraid something had happened to them, but I was in a foreign country and couldn't get home. About seven months later, I got a letter from her. She said she was marrying someone else, a senator's son, and he wanted to adopt Lara."

"Oh, no."

"That's what I said. Oh, no, he's not adopting my kid. I was mad, threatened to sue Sharon for custody, but we both knew I was stuck in the service for another year. Plus, I wouldn't have had a snowball's chance, but that didn't stop me. As soon as I got back, I went looking for them."

"Did you find them?"

"Yeah. They'd moved to Alabama—that's where his family was from. They live in a mansion outside of Scottsboro. I figured they wouldn't be too happy to see me, so I parked on the street and walked up the driveway. I saw them playing in the yard. Sharon's husband was rolling around in the grass with Lara. She was giggling and screeching 'Dada' and it just kind of stopped my heart. Sharon was sitting in a lawn chair, watching them with this content smile on her face. I think it scared her to death when she looked up and saw me.

"She and I talked for a long time. I even talked to her

husband, but in the end I walked away. This guy loved Lara, and he could give her all the things I never could. That's all I want for my daughter, to be happy, but I think about her all the time. She should be in first grade now and I don't know anything about her. Not a day goes by when I don't wish I'd done things differently, but so much time has passed."

"I'm sorry." Nadia's voice was soft, sincere.

Dante gave her a rueful smile. "I am too. But I know she's being taken care of and that will have to be good enough. That's why I took Vandergriff's case. Here he was, giving me this situation that was so much like my own and I was thinking, 'What if it was Lara?' If she were in danger, I'd do anything to protect her. In a way, returning his daughter to him felt a little like getting mine back, you know?" He shook his head. "Man, I can't believe I fell for it. The story he fed me was so close to mine. I should've known it was fishy. He really played me."

Nadia squeezed his hand. "Vandergriff is like that. He's a master manipulator, and he has no boundaries. I wonder sometimes how different my parents would be, how different *I* would be, if we'd never heard of Gary Vandergriff."

Dante shot her a sympathetic look. "I bet it wasn't easy growing up in your house. Did your parents even let you out to go to school?"

"No. I was always home schooled." She paused and gave him a funny smile. "Well, that's what they tell me, anyway. But I remember things . . . the green and blue plaid uniforms we wore, a little girl I used to play with named Kim."

"I don't understand," Dante said softly.

"Vandergriff kidnapped me once," she said in a 'no big deal' kind of voice. "I was probably five or six years old. About the same age as Lara."

Dante's breath left him. He reached for her, but Nadia held out a hand to stop him. Her face flushed and she wouldn't meet his eyes. "No. I'm okay, really. It's only . . ." She swiped at her eyes. "You're the first person I've ever told about this. Please don't tell my parents."

"Your parents?"

"I act like I don't remember. It's easier on them like that. Now they act like they don't remember either." She frowned and scratched her head. "And I really *don't* remember much, so it's not like I'm lying. Only little flashes of stuff. I remember a root cellar, one of the old kind that was dug into the earth. I was a kid, right, so it was just this faded gray door built into the ground. I didn't know what it was, or where I was. That's my first memory of Gary Vandergriff . . . of him yanking open that door and lowering me into the hole. He told me there were snakes in there, and that they would find me if I moved or screamed for help. Then he locked me inside."

Dante swore. He reached for her again, but Nadia pulled away. A choked sound rose from her throat and Dante couldn't tell if it was a laugh or a sob. Maybe it was both.

"Please don't touch me yet. I want to tell you this and

I think if I let you hold me, I'll cry and never be able to get it out."

She suddenly looked much younger than her twenty-four years. Dante could see that scared little girl. The pain in her eyes made him want to take her in his arms, to stop her from reliving this, but he realized she needed to tell someone.

"I won't touch you until you tell me to," he said.

"It was so dark in there. Cool. Sort of like the mine shaft. Probably the only reason I didn't freak out back there was you. I got a flash of it when I was backing against that wall, but I thought, no, I'm okay. Dante's with me." She winked at him, and Dante's heart twisted.

She was so strong.

"It smelled damp and kind of funky, like rotting vegetables. My legs were tired, but I was afraid to sit down. I kept away from the dirt walls because I figured that the snakes were probably there too. My legs finally gave out, so I sat there in the dirt and listened for snakes. I guess that's why I hate the damned things today."

She smiled at Dante, but he didn't know if he returned it or not. He was frozen. Hurt because she had been hurt. Angry that someone could do that to a child.

He wanted to tear Gary Vandergriff limb from limb.

"I remember someone throwing open the door, and I didn't care who it was. Didn't care if it was the bad man. It didn't matter as long as I got away from the snakes. But it was my daddy." She didn't look up, simply kept tracing circles in

241

the dirt with her finger. "It was the only time I've ever seen my father cry."

"It's okay for you to cry too, princess."

She shook her head and lay on the ground. Dante stretched out beside her. He blinked when the first drops of rain hit his face.

"Nope, not yet. I don't have any tears to waste on Gary Vandergriff at the moment." She wrinkled her nose and smiled. "Now, what was I saying? Oh, yeah. Nick and Maria sent me to all these shrinks who wanted me to talk about it. To draw it. To act it out. And I'd always notice how upset they would both get afterward, even though they couldn't go in with me. I figured the doctors were telling them everything I said. So, I quit talking about it and drawing it and whatever. They'd say, 'Nadia, tell me about the root cellar' and I'd say, 'What root cellar?' or 'Nadia, tell me about the snakes' and I'd say, 'What snakes?' Then it was over. They told my parents I'd repressed it, and that was about the finest news they'd heard, I'm sure."

She studied her fingernails and said, "The guy on the plane asked me why Vandergriff never gave up. Never moved on. I think it's because he's used to crushing anyone who opposes him. Vandergriff could hurt my father, but he couldn't destroy him." Nadia shrugged and raked a hand through her hair. "But anyway, I stayed home after that. My father brought in tutors. Ronnie says that's why I'm such a social reject."

"You are not a social reject." Dante smiled and squeezed

her fingers.

"Maybe not, but I'm different. I know that. I don't have real friends, other than Ronnie and Waynie and the rest of my bodyguards. The people at college think I'm crazy and fun, but they don't understand me. I listen to them complain about their parents and boyfriends and curfews and think, is this all you've got to worry about?"

She laughed, a sad laugh that made Dante want to hold her, chase away her insecurities.

"I'm glad you're different," he said. "Because I'm different too."

Nadia chuckled and closed her eyes against the misting rain. Dante closed his too. "You are, aren't you? That's what I like about you, Dante. When I'm with you . . . I don't feel weird."

"Thanks . . . I think."

"You know what I mean. It's like I've finally found someone like me—"

"Kindred spirits," he supplied.

The rain came harder, and Dante sensed Nadia stand.

"Kindred spirits," she said. "Hey, I like that."

Dante opened an eye to squint at her through the sheets of rain. Nadia was shimmying out of her blue jeans. She stood over him, wearing nothing but a skimpy black bra and panties.

"Let's play in the rain," she said with a grin.

CHAPTER **10**

Nadia tilted her head back, letting the rain beat the dust from her face and cool her parched skin. The looming thunderhead blotted out the sun, and the thick, sweet smell of sagebrush perfumed the air around them. The desert, so arid and dead moments before, now smelled earthy and alive.

She sensed Dante move away from her and dared a peek as she massaged the dirt from her scalp. Nadia froze and simply stared when Dante tugged off his boots and socks.

His brown eyes met hers, and he unbelted his jeans and slid them over his narrow hips. Nadia's breath caught in her throat as her gaze raked over the tan, chiseled body that was now clothed only in a pair of tight black boxers.

Just looking at him made her weak with sexual hunger.

Dante scooped up their clothes and tossed them underneath the old roof. Not an ounce of fat betrayed that body. He was magnificent. He was perfect.

And he was headed straight for her.

"Here," he said huskily. "Let me help you with that."

He ran his big hands into her hair and worked the strands between his fingers. Nadia found herself staring at his chest, at the sunburst tattoo that surrounded one nipple.

Impulsively, she raked her tongue across it.

Dante groaned and tugged at her hair, pulling her face up to meet his. She expected a violent kiss, a demanding thrust of his tongue, but he fooled her. His lips were gentle on hers, tasting, exploring, as the rain streamed off their faces. The hardness of his arousal pressed against her stomach.

Reaching behind her, he unhooked her bra. Nadia watched it fall to the ground, watched his hands cup her breasts. The sight of his rough, tan fingers against her flesh made her breath quicken.

Then one of his hands dropped lower. It caressed her hip, and then stole inside the edge of her lacy panties. Nadia gasped, staring up into his dark eyes. Those eyes widened and his hand faltered when he found her hot and wet. Ready.

"I've been ready for this since the day I met you," she whispered.

Dante dropped to his knees in front of her, as if her words robbed him of his power. Cupping her buttocks in his hands, he pulled her closer and kissed her abdomen. His fingers found the edge of her panties and tugged them an inch lower. His tongue traced the streak of white skin just below her tan line.

Dante pressed his face against the lacy material. Nadia

groaned and ran her hands over his head. Two days' worth of dark stubble tickled her palms, scratched the soft skin on her thigh. It made him look dangerous, even sexier.

Hooking his thumbs underneath the edge of the panties, Dante slid them off her hips, down her legs. Her thoughts were a jumble and Nadia didn't even remember stepping out of them, but there she was, naked in front of him. He nudged her feet apart and pressed his face between her thighs.

A strange, throaty voice crying out in the rain.

It's me, Nadia realized, but she didn't even know what she was saying.

His tongue moved faster and faster, driving her to the brink of madness. Her legs quivered, threatened to give out on her, and Nadia clutched at his shoulder to keep from falling. Heat built within her, seared her. Nadia found herself thinking crazily about a term paper she'd once done on spontaneous combustion.

Was this what it was like, she wondered, to burn from the inside?

Like a crazed woman, she shoved him backward onto the desert floor. Dante looked at her in surprise, but she didn't care. She was beyond caring. She straddled him, heedless of the rain, heedless of the rocks that bit into her knees.

Nadia yanked down his briefs and lowered herself onto his shaft. Dante cried out as she took him inside her.

He was so big that Nadia was almost afraid she couldn't handle him, but the fit was perfect. Tight. He filled her and

Nadia shrieked when he began to move.

He clutched her hips, pushing himself deeper, urging her faster. Faster. Nadia rode him hard as sheets of warm, gray rain beat against her back.

Lightning streaked the sky and thunder shook the ground, but Nadia scarcely noticed. Their coupling was as wild and passionate as the storm that swirled around them.

Nadia screamed when the climax rocked through her body. Spots danced before her eyes and she was sure she was going to pass out. Her muscles tightened helplessly around him and Dante roared. His fingers dug into her hips, and he gave one last powerful thrust.

Neither moved. Neither tried to talk. Suddenly, everything was quiet around them except for the rain pounding on the hoist roof and the sound of their own breathing.

A little shocked by her ragged gasps, Nadia stared down at Dante. He looked as shell-shocked as she felt. Pushing a handful of dripping hair out of her face, she laughed.

Dante smiled and cupped her face in his hand. She pressed her mouth against his palm.

"That was . . ." Nadia shook her head, unable to find a word that seemed adequate. "That was . . ."

"Not bad," Dante said blandly, then held up his hands to ward off Nadia's blows. He caught her wrists and pulled her face to his.

"That was . . ." He paused, kissing her. ". . . the most amazing experience . . ." Another kiss. ". . . of my entire life."

There was so much she wanted to say to him—I love you, I need you—but somehow the words wouldn't come. She'd never said them to anyone. Had never felt them before now. It scared her to death.

Laughing, the lovers stood and tried to clean the mud from their bodies before they ran for the shelter of the hoist house. Dante removed a thin blanket from his backpack and spread it out in the narrow space. They made love again while the rain beat against the aging tin roof.

"We'd better put on our clothes," Dante said reluctantly. "Your old man could be here any time, and he'll shoot me for sure if he catches us like this."

"Yeah, I guess you're right." Nadia sat up and reached for her shirt. "And *he* carries a .44."

"I know. I've already been on the business end of his .44."

She frowned. "What?"

He told her about the climb out of the river and what he'd found waiting for him at the top.

Nadia laughed and covered her face in her hands.

"Sorry," she said. "They're a little . . . protective."

"Hey, I deserved it. But they did give me a chance to explain. Ronnie even fixed up my shoulder for me."

She fingered the rolling tape on his shoulder. "Speaking of which, I have to fix your bandage again, and I'd better check out that side too. You're covered in scratches. You look like you've been tangling with a wildcat."

"I have." Dante grinned at her and gently slapped her

behind when she reached over him for the backpack.

Nadia doctored his scrapes, then rubbed the dark stubble on his head.

"I like that. Stubble on your head, stubble on your face. You look downright *dangerous*."

"Baby, I *am* dangerous."

She giggled when he pushed her back on the blanket. He raked his face against her bare stomach.

"Ow, ow! Stop it! That hurts."

Dante took the antibiotic salve from her hand and began dotting it on her various injuries. "Maybe if you're nice, I'll let you shave my head when we get back home."

Nadia snorted. "Ha! Maybe if you're nice, I'll let you shave my legs."

He smoothed his big palm down her bare thigh, making her shiver. "I think I can handle it."

"Oh, really?"

"Quit looking at me like that," he admonished, his brown eyes wary.

"Like what?" Nadia took his hand and pulled it to her mouth. Dante groaned when she traced his finger over her bottom lip and started sucking on it.

"You insatiable brat. You've nearly killed me already. I'm just a fragile shell of the man I was before I met you," Dante said, closing his eyes. He leaned his head back and Nadia crawled into his lap.

"I bet Superman would be up for it," she whispered, then

caught his earlobe between her teeth. He groaned again.

"Superman wears his underwear on the outside of his pants. Besides, he never had to deal with the likes of you."

It was nearly an hour before they got back into their clothes. Nadia rested her head on Dante's chest and drifted into a deep, dreamless slumber.

❋ ❋ ❋

Whup-whup-whup

The sound invaded her sleep.

What was that?

Nadia stirred against Dante. Even in sleep, his arm tightened around her and pulled her up close.

Whup-whup-whup

Nadia blinked and tried to make her bleary eyes focus. It was dark outside. Really dark. Nighttime. How long had they been asleep?

Whup-whup-whup

"Dante!"

He sat up immediately, his eyes wild in the moonlight.

He didn't have the same trouble she did shaking off his sleep. His revolver was already in his hand.

"You've got to hide. You see that ore bin over there?" He pointed at the boxy wooden structure across from them. "Get over there when I tell you and don't come out until I come get you."

"I'm not leaving you."

"You have to. I'm hiding too, but there's not room in that thing for the both of us."

"Dante—"

"Please." He kissed her forehead. "Trust me."

"But—"

"Please."

"Okay." She crouched at the edge of the shelter and waited on his signal.

"Go!" He slapped her bottom and she took off, scrambling into the tiny wooden box, praying the whole thing didn't collapse with her.

Praying she wouldn't disturb any resting creatures.

The whup-whup-whup sound was getting louder. The helicopter was close now. A spotlight danced across the ground in front of her, illuminating the motorcycle they'd had no way to conceal.

A sick feeling rolled through her stomach as she scanned for Dante. He had nowhere to go. Nowhere to hide.

Peering through the cracks in the weathered old boards, Nadia watched the helicopter land. Three men emptied out of it. She recognized one of them.

Peterson.

Then she saw the cold blue eyes of the devil himself. Vandergriff had come out to settle this one personally.

Watching in horror, she saw the men storm toward the hoist house. Dante walked out, holding his hands high.

The helicopter blades stopped turning and Nadia could hear Vandergriff's voice raised in anger.

"Where is she?"

"She's gone!" Dante shouted. "She's probably halfway out of the state by now. I'm a decoy and you were stupid enough to fall for it."

She winced when Vandergriff struck Dante across the face with the butt of his gun. Dante sank to his knees.

"Check it out!" Vandergriff yelled to his men. "Find that girl."

"I'll check over here," Peterson said, and Nadia ducked back, afraid he would see her in the darkness. She wondered if she could reason with him. If—

Peterson stuck his head in the opening and stared at her.

"Your father's on his way," he whispered, then yanked his head back outside.

"Nothing in there," he called out, and proceeded to walk around the ore bin, making a show of checking underneath it.

Nadia sat in stunned silence.

Vandergriff screamed, an incoherent cry of rage.

He jerked his rifle up and pressed the barrel against Dante's forehead. Nadia squeezed her eyes shut, terrified she was about to witness her lover's execution.

● ● ●

"Wait!"

Dante jerked his gaze to Vandergriff's hit man.

"Mr. Vandergriff . . . if I might say something."

"Go ahead, Peterson."

"Sir, the Andreakos girl is in love with this guy. She told me herself. I think we can use him, maybe get another shot at her."

What was this? And where was Nadia?

Dante had to force his gaze back to the ground, not wanting to tip them off. When the man had checked the ore bin, he had been holding his breath.

Stay back, babe, he thought fervently. *Stay hidden.*

"What do you suggest?"

"I think we should take him back to Tennessee. Get word to Andreakos that we have his daughter's boyfriend. We can set them up. They come after him, we attack the home front while they're chasing their tails. If we're lucky, you might score more than one Andreakos from the deal."

Vandergriff was silent for a long moment, then he lowered the barrel of the gun.

"I like it." He grinned and slapped Peterson on the back. "But I say we just kill him now. They'll never know the difference."

Peterson shook his head. "Andreakos is too smart for that. He'll demand proof. What harm is there in carrying this guy back to Tennessee? Once the plan is in motion, you can kill him then."

"Okay, Peterson. You continue to impress. I like a man

who can think quickly on his feet." Vandergriff grinned at Dante. "Secure his hands and load him on the helicopter."

"Hands behind your back," the other man commanded.

Dante complied. When the plastic tie tightened around his wrist, he remembered the GPS.

The man yanked him to his feet and Dante fumbled at the bracelet on his wrist. He couldn't get the snap open. His pulse thudded in his ears. He had to get it off. The only thought more horrifying than Vandergriff getting his hands on Nadia was the thought of his leaving her in the desert to starve to death.

At least if she had the bracelet, her father could still track her. He snagged the snap and surreptitiously shook it loose, letting it fall to the ground. Dante hurriedly stepped away from it, toward the helicopter. He hoped Nadia would find it and not wander off on her own.

Dante glanced back at the ghost town as the aircraft lifted off, searching for some sign of her. He saw no movement, no evidence of life. Squeezing his eyes shut, he silently began reciting his mother's prayer.

Praying Nadia home.

❂ ❂ ❂

Nadia waited until she could no longer hear the helicopter before she stepped out of her hiding place. Hugging herself, she walked back to the hoist house and stared up at the inky sky.

She had never felt so completely, utterly alone.

Peterson was a mystery. He had saved her and had saved Dante too. At least for the time being.

Your father's coming.

Had he really said that?

Nadia could no longer be sure. All her brain could process was the fact that Gary Vandergriff had Dante. She sank to her knees in the dirt next to the spot where they'd made love and tried not to cry.

Stop it, she commanded herself.

It could be worse. It could be much worse. And Peterson got him to take Dante to Tennessee. That was better than California.

It was home turf.

Her father would find her. Her father would know what to do.

A bolt of pure, blind panic shot through her.

How would her father find her? They were miles from the landing spot, miles from anything. She didn't even know if Vandergriff had left the backpack.

A coyote howled in the distance, its forlorn cry sounding as bleak as she felt. Nadia scrambled to her feet and was running toward the hoist house when she saw it. The moonlight glinted off the piece of silver.

The tracking device.

She choked back the sob rising in her throat. Even when his own life was being decided, Dante had been thinking of her.

"I'll get you back," she said aloud, turning her face up to the sky. "I won't let you die, I swear it."

She crawled back into the shelter. The blanket was still there, but Dante's backpack was not. Nadia lay on the blanket and pressed her face to it, trying to catch a hint of Dante's scent.

"Hurry, Daddy," she whispered. "Find me. We have to save him. I can't let Vandergriff kill him."

Somehow she must've dozed off, although she didn't know how. Nadia jerked upright, her heart thumping wildly in her chest until she figured out what had jarred her from her sleep.

Four-wheelers. She heard four-wheelers.

Her father!

Her father had come for her.

Nadia started out of the shelter, then hesitated.

What if it was a trick? What if it was more of Vandergriff's men?

"Nadia! Nadia, are you here?" Nick Branson's voice shattered the silence around her.

Scrambling out of the shelter, Nadia waved her arms as the bright headlights approached. She saw her father. She saw Ronnie and Waynie. Their faces lit when they saw her running toward them.

"Daddy! Daddy, I'm here."

Her father bounded off the four-wheeler and seized her in his arms. "Nadia, my darling. I was so afraid I'd never see you again. Are you okay? Did he hurt you?"

Nadia was so relieved to see him that she couldn't say anything. She clutched him tighter.

There was still time. Time to find Dante.

"Daddy, they have him. We've got to get back to Tennessee. Vandergriff took Dante with him, but he didn't find me."

Nadia knew she was babbling, but she couldn't help it. She was nearly weak with relief at seeing her father and Ronnie. There was still time. "We've got time to figure out a plan, go in there and get him—"

"Nadia—"

"One of his men helped me. Peterson. Maybe he'll help us again."

"Honey—"

Nadia turned away from him, already formulating her plan. Ronnie and Waynie stood beside their four-wheelers, strangely silent.

"Ronnie, do you still have those surveillance scramblers? We can knock out his cameras—"

"Nadia!"

Her father's voice was sharp this time and Nadia spun to look at him. His handsome face was grim.

"What?"

"We're not going after him. This time, there will be no rescue."

CHAPTER 11

Monday, August 8
1:55 a.m.

"What? What are you saying?" Nadia asked, rubbing her forehead. Her father reached for her, but she backed away from him, confused by the resignation she saw on his face.

"We can't go after Dante. Vandergriff will be waiting on us. He'll slaughter us all."

"No! I won't accept that. Dante saved my life. Doesn't that count for something?"

"Dante's also the one who put your life in jeopardy in the first place. Let's not forget that."

"It was a mistake. He thought he was protecting me."

"Nadia, I can't risk anyone else's life." Nick paused. "Eddie Franks is dead. So is Hal Jacobi."

"What?" Nadia blanched, then hugged her arms across her chest. Eddie Franks wasn't that much older than her.

He'd been employed by her father two or three months be-fore Dante arrived on the scene. Hal Jacobi had been there almost a year. He was a quiet, friendly bear of a man with two small children.

"That's what took us so long to get to you. We had a spy in our midst. Dan Underwood. He sabotaged our vehicles, stole supplies, then he led us into an ambush."

"Dan Underwood . . . are you sure?" Although Nadia didn't know him as well as some of the other guards, she had never seen anything that would make her suspicious of the man. Then she recalled Vandergriff saying that name back at the house. She'd been too shaken to notice at the time.

"Yes, I'm sure." Nick Branson's voice was bitter. He glanced at his watch. "Come on. If we leave now, we can make it back to the plane before daybreak. Your mother is in hiding, but I won't rest until I'm sure the both of you safe again. Maybe we'll leave the country, go back to Greece—"

"No! Can't you see? If you let Vandergriff kill Dante, he wins again. We'll never be free of him. We'll never be able to stop looking over our shoulders."

"We'll talk about it on the plane."

She planted her feet and glared at him. "We'll talk about it now."

"Nadia, we really need to get moving."

"He's right," Ronnie said softly.

"Fine," she said, clenching her teeth.

Nick climbed on his four-wheeler and scooted up to give

her room on the back. Nadia ignored him, climbing on back of Ronnie's instead. Not another word was said until they reached the plane.

● ● ●

With a smirk, Vandergriff leaned back in his seat and studied Dante while the plane lifted off the runway.

"I thought you were a professional, Giovanni. Don't tell me you let yourself get distracted over a piece of tail."

Dante said nothing. He sat still, mentally gauging the distance between them.

"She's a hot little thing, don't get me wrong. I just can't see risking your life for a girl like that. Especially when you aren't even sleeping with her."

Vandergriff watched Dante's face for a reaction, then he smiled.

"You *are* sleeping with her! Wow, our little Miss Andreakos moves fast. A whore like her mother. Probably puts out for all her bodyguards, though. What's that dark-haired fellow's name? Reggie, Ronnie?" He waved his hand dismissively. "I always had a notion about those two. Tell me, Dante, is she good in the sack? Her mother sure was. Wait—" He held up a hand as if to ward off Dante's comment and grinned. "Never mind, don't spoil my surprise. I can hardly wait to find out for myself."

Even though his hands were tied, Dante lunged at him.

Vandergriff wasn't expecting the attack. Apparently, neither were his bodyguards because they made no move to block it.

Dante heard a satisfying crack when the top of his skull met Vandergriff's nose. While Vandergriff howled and clutched at his spurting nose, Dante smiled and sat back in his seat.

Vandergriff grabbed Peterson's gun and rammed it under Dante's chin.

"I should blow your brains all over this cabin," he raged.

"Go ahead. Then I won't have to listen to any more of this adolescent bull—"

"Hey!" Peterson interjected, handing Vandergriff a wad of paper towels. "Don't let him get to you, Mr. Vandergriff. Stay focused on the big picture. Don't let some two-bit bounty hunter mess up your plans."

Somewhat mollified, Vandergriff handed Peterson the gun. Dante saw the fist coming, but he couldn't do anything to stop it. Vandergriff's blow caught him square in the jaw, sending a bolt of pain racing to his brain.

"It's going to be a pleasure killing you, Giovanni. Who knows? Maybe you'll even get to see Nadia again. With me. Maybe I'll let you watch."

● ● ●

Her mother must've been watching for their approach, because before Nadia could climb off the four-wheeler, she heard a commotion. Her mother vaulted out of the plane and raced down the steps so rapidly that Nadia feared she'd fall and break her neck.

"Nadia!" she shouted.

She pushed though the wall of guards spread across the tarmac and seized Nadia in her arms. Maria hugged her so tightly she nearly lifted her off her feet, then pulled back to clutch Nadia's face with both hands.

Tears streaked her mother's cheeks and fear darkened the eyes that scanned Nadia's face. "Did he hurt you?" Maria demanded. "Did that monster touch you?"

"No, Mama," Nadia choked out.

Maria's eyes were wide and glassy. "The truth, Nadia," she said sharply. "Don't try to protect me. I need to know."

"He didn't touch me, Mama. He didn't have time. Dante busted in there—" Nadia covered her face with her hand. "He . . . he . . ." she squeaked, and sobbed on her mother's shoulder.

Maria's hand smoothed Nadia's hair. "What about Dante, honey?" When Nadia couldn't answer, she said, "Nick, where's Dante?"

"Vandergriff," her father replied heavily. "Vandergriff has him."

"Oh, baby," Maria whispered into her hair. "Let's get on the plane, and you can tell me what happened."

"No!" Nadia pulled away. "I'm not leaving here until we figure out how to rescue Dante."

Nick stepped forward. "Darling, be reasonable. You said yourself that Dante's headed back to Tennessee. We're accomplishing nothing by standing around here. Get on the plane and we'll talk."

Nadia glared at him, then ran up the steps to board the plane. She took a seat and stared out the window, tears of anger and frustration stinging her eyes.

Her father wasn't going to help her. He was really going to let Dante die.

Nick reached for her hand, and she said, "Don't. Don't touch me."

"Nadia, honey, put yourself in my shoes. Try to understand—"

"You're a coward. That's what I understand," she said bitterly. "I never knew that about you. I always thought I could count on you."

"I won't have you talking to me like that," Nick said, hurt shining in his brown eyes. "I'm still your father. And you *can* count on me. That's why we can't go in there. I have to look out for you—for my family—not some bounty hunter who got us in this mess in the first place."

"I love him!" Nadia blurted.

The words probably shocked her as much as they did her father, but they were true. Her mother glanced at Nick.

"You love him?" Nick threw up his hands. "Oh, that's just wonderful. How is that possible, Nadia? You barely know him."

263

Nadia wiped away an angry tear. "I know enough. I know if the situation was reversed, he'd help me get you."

"That only proves he's a fool. If Vandergriff ever gets his hands on me, I don't want a any of you to attempt to rescue me. I want you and your mother to get as far away as possible."

"So, you'll be content to let him pick us off one by one and never have to worry about retaliation?"

"Dante isn't one of us. He isn't part of our family. He's a stranger—"

"He's part of me!" Hot tears scalded Nadia's face. "I love him, and if you let him die, I'll never be able to look you in the eye again."

Nick's voice softened. "Honey, you're young. There will be other men. You'll find someone—"

She struck the armrest with her fist. "Don't you say that to me! Don't you dare. All my life, I've felt like something was wrong with me. Like I didn't belong anywhere. But now I know where I belong, and it's with Dante."

Nick covered his mouth in exasperation. "Nadia, honey . . . you don't know anything about him. Everything he's told you could be lies—"

"It seems a lot of things you've told me have been lies. What's the difference?"

Nick stiffened. "I've never lied to you."

"Oh, really . . . Nick *Andreakos*?"

Her father blanched, but Nadia couldn't halt the words pouring out of her mouth. "All that stuff about the people you love being the most important things—what if it was Maria? You'd go after her."

"That's different." Nick squeezed his eyes shut and rubbed the bridge of his nose. "She's my wife. Your mother. Not some woman I barely know."

"She was once. And you saved her then." Nadia stuck out her chin, challenging him. "How long did you know my mother before you fell in love with her? How long did you know her before you were willing to risk your life for her?"

"More than three days."

"Not much more. I've heard you talking. I've heard you tell her how you fell in love with her the first time you talked to her. Why does love at first sight apply to the two of you and not the two of us?"

Maria looked away, but Nick met Nadia's stare. He pointed his finger at her. "Dante *used* you. He knew you were attracted to him and he used that against you. Can't you see that? Yes, I admit . . . he did make up for it. He got you away from that man. I will be eternally grateful to him for that, and I really wish there was some other way . . . but I can't risk getting my men killed to go in after him."

Nadia stared stonily out the window. "Then I'll go by myself."

"The hell you will."

Nadia glanced at Maria, who she instinctively felt was her only hope of swaying her father. "Mama," she said. "Vandergriff told me . . . he told me the things he did to you."

265

Maria flinched like she'd been slapped. She crossed over to sit beside Nadia and stared down at her hands, her fingers nervously working her engagement ring. "Do you think less of me?" she asked quietly. "Do you think I'm a coward too?"

Nadia took her hand. "No. I think you're the strongest person I've ever met, but now we both know what he's capable of. I know about your father and brothers. I know what he did to them."

"Nadia, stop this right now!" her father said, his face ashen. "Your mother has suffered enough because of this bastard . . . I won't let you hurt her further."

Nadia ignored him, twisting to face her mother. "Mama, I love Dante. I'm not trying to hurt you, but you have to help me. You know what he'll do to Dante."

"That is not our concern—" Nick began.

"The hell it isn't!" she snapped. "He sacrificed himself to protect me. If not for him, I'd be in Vandergriff's bed by now."

Maria shuddered and glanced at Nick. "Maybe we could—"

"No!" he yelled, throwing his arms wide. His voice softened when her mother flinched. "No, Maria. Can't you see? This is exactly what Vandergriff wants us to do. It's a trap."

"But Nadia—"

"She may be angry now, but in time—"

"What?" Nadia demanded. "I'll forget? That's your fix for everything, isn't it? What if I can't forget? I didn't forget the first time he kidnapped me, so what makes you think I'll forget this?"

Maria's head snapped around violently. Nick froze in his tracks.

"You—you remember that?" her mother stammered, lurching to her feet. She crossed over to Nick, who woodenly wrapped an arm around her shoulders.

Some of Nadia's anger deflated when she looked at their pale faces, but her desperation had reached a fever pitch. "I remember," she said softly. "I remember the root cellar, and how scared I was. I remember how glad I was to see Daddy when he threw open that door. You saved me then, Daddy. Save me now."

Nick's eyes shone with tears. The sight of them rocked Nadia as much as it had the first time she'd seen them, when he'd thrown open that root cellar door and found her alive.

"That's what I'm doing," he said hoarsely. "I didn't want to say this in front of you, but you leave me no choice. Dante's probably dead already. He probably never even made it out of the desert. Gary Vandergriff knows me like I know him. He knows I would never risk you, or your mother, for anyone. He's planned this for years, and now his plan has failed. We, more than you, know his fury. He will lash out at anyone around him, and Dante is his easiest target."

Maria fingered the crucifix around her neck. Tears rolled down her cheeks and her voice was halting when she whispered, "For the devil is come down unto you, having great wrath, because he knoweth that he hath but a short time."

Nadia turned away.

They were terrified of Vandergriff. So terrified that they were willing to let an innocent man die in the middle of a fight that wasn't his.

It was going to be hard to get him back on her own, but she'd be damned if she didn't try. Silence fell and the pilot asked everyone to take their seats and buckle up.

Nadia stared out the window and tried to formulate a plan. Distracted by her thoughts, she jumped when Ronnie plopped down in the seat next to her.

"Seems you made a friend on that plane, huh?" Ronnie nudged her with his shoulder and the concern on his handsome face was nearly her undoing. She quickly looked back out the window. It was a moment before she trusted herself to speak.

"I was going to ask about that. He scared me to death when they got Dante. He stuck his head in right where I was hiding and said, 'Your father's on his way.'"

"Yeah. He contacted us after you jumped. Said he wanted to do what he could to help you."

"Peterson's all right," Nadia said, allowing herself a smile.

"We didn't believe him at first—thought it was some kind of trick—but then he outed Underwood." Ronnie gave her a wan smile. "He said you were the bravest person he'd ever met. Assuming brave and crazy are interchangeable, I'd say he's right. I would've loved to had a picture of your face when you jumped out of that plane."

"I wasn't afraid. I knew Dante would catch me." She shot an accusing glance at her father, but Nick looked away.

"Peterson was supposed to circle the landing site until Vandergriff got there, to monitor your movements, but he radioed in some phony plane malfunction and turned the thing around. He tried his best to slow them down."

"Maybe he can help me get to Dante! He'll at least know if Dante's still alive." Nadia sat up straight in the seat. "Vandergriff was going to execute Dante in the desert, but Peterson stopped him. He bought me some time."

Nick groaned. "Now you've got her started again, Ronnie."

Nadia ignored him. She was going to rescue Dante and there was nothing her father could do to stop her. Already she was compiling a mental list of the supplies she would need.

And by the time the plane touched down in Tennessee, she had a plan.

● ● ●

"They're not . . ." Vandergriff grunted as he swung the golf club, striking Dante in the back. ". . . coming."

Sweat rolled off Dante's face and he clenched his teeth against the pain, determined not to make a sound. Determined not to give Vandergriff the satisfaction.

He hung from a beam in Vandergriff's garage. His wrists had burned for awhile, abraded by the ropes that bound them, but now he couldn't feel his arms at all.

"Nobody's coming to rescue you. You're dispensable to them. You are nothing but . . . hired help."

Dante hoped he was right. He hoped Branson had Nadia on a plane somewhere, getting her as far away from this bastard as possible. But he had a sick feeling in the pit of his stomach.

Nadia wouldn't give up easily.

Dante knew enough about her to realize Nadia wouldn't go down without a fight and it scared him to death. He could accept the fact that he was going to die, but he couldn't accept the thought of her dying on his behalf.

Another blow caught him in the kneecap. This time Dante couldn't stop the grunt of pain that escaped his lips.

"You mean nothing to them," Vandergriff continued. "You mean nothing to her."

Dante squeezed his eyes shut and gritted his teeth as Vandergriff flailed at him. He'd once had a girlfriend who was into meditation. After a couple of weeks, he'd realized *medication* might've been more appropriate in her case, but she had taught him one thing. How to turn his thoughts inward. How to block out the present.

Dante focused on his breathing. He visualized the light and walked into it. Passing through the light would take him to his sanctuary. He liked that word. Much better than his "happy place", as she'd liked to call it.

Looking around, Dante was hardly surprised to see his sanctuary had changed. It was no longer the little island on the South Pacific, where blue-green waves beat against white sand in hypnotic rhythm.

It was the desert, in the middle of a rainstorm.

He could almost smell the rain. The heavy, sweet scent of sagebrush. Turning slowly, he spotted her. It was the first time anyone else had ever been in his sanctuary, but Nadia was a welcome guest. She had her head tilted back, letting the rain stream off her face. Then she looked at him. Those vibrant green eyes widened and she smiled. He smiled back and started walking toward her.

● ● ●

A Fed-Ex van waited at the gate. Nick reached for the window button, but Ronnie's hand shot out to stop him.

"Hang on a sec, Mr. B," he said, and scrambled out of the car. He and Anderson talked to the driver. They followed him to the van, then walked him over to the car. He held an envelope and clipboard.

The deliveryman smiled as Nick rolled down the rear window.

"Are you Nick Branson?

"Yes," he said.

"I have a delivery for you, sir."

Nadia looked from Ronnie, who stood by on full alert, to the small envelope the messenger held in his hand. She knew who had sent it even before she saw the return address. Gary Vandergriff's name was scrawled the top left corner in bold capital letters.

Nick signed for it and thanked the delivery man, who held the letter out to him.

Ronnie intercepted it, ignoring the startled look the messenger shot him. The man touched the brim of his cap and climbed back into his truck. Ronnie waited until the truck was out of sight before he returned to the car. He crawled in beside Nadia. The gate swung open and they started up the driveway.

"Mr. B, may I?" Ronnie asked, and Nick nodded.

Ronnie turned it over in his hands, then shook it by his ear. After a few moments of inspection, he slit it open, peered inside and passed it back to her father. Nick didn't move. He simply stared at the envelope in his lap.

"Well?" she said, and he hesitantly picked it up.

As he emptied the contents into his lap, Nadia realized she was holding her breath. She choked back a sob when Dante's silver St. Michael medallion fell out.

In agonizing slow motion, her father shook open the letter. He grimaced and refolded it quickly. When he tried to tuck it into his shirt pocket, Nadia jerked it out of his hand.

One typewritten line jumped out at her from the middle of the page.

Just the first piece, more to follow.

With a cry of rage, Nadia ripped up the letter. Before

they could react, she flung open the car door and threw herself out. She hit the ground running.

The car screeched to a stop, and Nadia heard the commotion behind her as she raced down the driveway.

"Somebody grab her!" Nick yelled.

One of the guards stationed at the gate came at her like a linebacker. Nadia tried to dart around him, but while she was trying to get past him, one of the other guards took out her legs.

Nadia went down hard, smacking her face against the ground. Her lips mashed against her teeth, and her mouth filled with the coppery taste of blood.

"Dammit, Hargis, are you trying to kill her?" Ronnie said as he sprinted over to help her.

Nadia accepted the hand he offered and let him haul her upright.

Her father ran up to them, out of breath. "Nadia, are you all right?"

Deliberately, Nadia spit a mouthful of blood inches from Nick's shiny black shoes. She pointed at him. "If you do this to me, you are no better than Vandergriff. You can't keep me here forever. When I get out—and I will get out eventually—I will leave and never come back."

Nick held his hands out beseechingly. "You can't mean that."

Nadia spat again and wiped her mouth. "Watch me."

Ronnie stepped between them. "Mr. B, I'll go. Let me

go help Dante."

"No," Nick said. "I can't do it. I won't risk any more lives. Nadia, I love you and one day you'll see that I'm doing this for your own good. Ronnie, take her to her room."

Nadia glanced at Ronnie, and a tear slipped down her cheek at the resignation on his face

Ronnie shoved his hands in his pockets. "I'm sorry, Mr. B, I can't do it. This is wrong and I won't be a part of it."

"Oh, for heaven's sake!" Nick threw up his hands and stalked away. He pivoted and said, "Ronnie, I'm telling you, I can't risk it."

Ronnie shot a pointed glance at Nadia. "Seems to me you're risking a lot more, Mr. B. On the plane, you were talking about all the things you've lost because of Vandergriff. Don't let your daughter be one of them."

Nick paled, and for a moment Nadia thought he was going to listen to Ronnie, but instead, he shook his head. "Look, Ronnie . . . just go to the house. Once everyone calms down, we'll talk things over."

"We don't have *time* to talk things over!" Nadia cried. "Don't you get it? Dante could be hurt right now."

Or dying, she thought, but couldn't say out loud.

She shot Ronnie a pleading glance. "He needs us."

It'll be okay, he mouthed, and she wished she could believe him.

Nick motioned to the guard who tackled her. "Jim, take Nadia to her room and lock her inside. I want you stationed

274

outside her door until further notice. Brent, I want you outside under her window. Under no circumstances is Nadia allowed to leave this house."

The bodyguard picked her up and threw her over his shoulder like a sack of potatoes. Fury ripped through Nadia. She kicked and flailed at the guard, but he was too strong.

She was so enraged she couldn't speak as the bodyguard carried her inside the house and up the stairs. He tossed her on the bed and quickly shut the bedroom door behind him. She bounced back up and ran to try the knob. He held it firm.

Nadia picked up a glass music box her father had bought her when she was thirteen and hurled it at the window, taking vicious satisfaction in the shattering glass. She collapsed on the bed, trying to figure out how to get out of here. Restless, Nadia jumped to her feet and ran to the window. The top of Brent's blond head was already visible though the branches of the oak tree. He waved up at her.

Wild thoughts raced through Nadia's head. Maybe she could climb onto the roof. Or maybe—

Nadia's gaze fell on the wastebasket by her bed.

She'd set the place on fire, that's what she'd do. They'd have to let her out then. She'd have to be ready when they opened the door.

First, she needed to gather her things. To ensure that her father couldn't walk in on her before she was ready, Nadia wedged a chair under the doorknob. Striding over to her closet, she yanked open the door and pawed around the top shelf. She removed the battered Nike box from beneath a stack of photo albums. She kept her "emergency fund" stashed inside—a roll of cash and three credit cards she seldom used.

She stuffed them all inside a canvas bag, along with a set of black clothing, and tossed it on the bed. Making a face, she stripped off her soiled red halter top, jeans, and underwear and put on clean clothes. She wished she could take a shower, but there was no time. She had to get moving.

Something nagged at her, some bit of memory teased her subconscious.

Her thoughts kept turning to the closet.

What was it about the closet?

After she pulled a black T-shirt over her head, Nadia's gaze returned to the rack of clothes. The memory hit her so hard that she took a step backward. The memory of being sixteen years old and grounded. Of sneaking out of the house to go to a rock concert with her friends.

Of course! She knew how to get out.

Impatiently pushing the clothes hangers aside, she pressed along the back wall of the closet until she felt a crack. Inserting her fingers in the tiny gap along the top seam of the paneling, Nadia tugged. One of her fingernails snapped, but she ignored the pain. With a little effort, the center panel came away in her hands, revealing the small boxlike structure behind it.

Nadia gave a triumphant squeal. The old laundry chute.

How could she have forgotten that?

She hadn't had to use it in years and didn't think her parents had ever known of its existence. Long abandoned, it deposited into the basement, a room seldom used by any of the Bransons.

One of the first additions to the house had been a new, modern laundry room on the first floor, and as far as she knew no one entered the basement except an occasional maintenance man.

She zipped the bag shut and shoved it through the opening. Craning her head, she listened for the muffled thump a moment later as it hit the basement floor. Her route, she soon learned, wouldn't be nearly so quick or so easy.

Even though she was small, the narrow passageway looked like it would barely accommodate the width of her hips. Nadia pushed aside the racks of clothes and grabbed the rod they hung from. Pulling herself up with her arms, she shoved her legs inside. Somehow, she managed to twist around in the tight space. It felt awkward going in backward, but Nadia knew from past experience that she didn't want to land on the concrete floor headfirst.

The passage was constricted, coffin-like, and Nadia had to fight a sense of claustrophobia as she used her arms and feet to scoot down the sloping tunnel on her belly. The metal creaked and groaned, causing the hair to prickle on her arms.

She didn't remember it doing that when she was sixteen.

Horrific images of the shaft breaking away, visions of herself trapped within the walls like a dying rat filled her head, but she impatiently pushed them away. Dante was the one in danger. Dante was the one she had to worry about.

The air in the shaft was thick and musty, and it tickled Nadia's nose. She had to stop once when a fit of sneezing caught her. It echoed inside the chute. The weird, tinny sound unnerved her, and she prayed her parents couldn't hear her from inside the house.

Finally, her feet had nothing to push off against. Tired and sweaty, she twisted around again for leverage, and with one hard shove she landed with a thump on the cool basement floor.

Now all she had to do was get past the fence. She considered trying to recruit Ronnie, but she didn't want to risk being seen by any of the other guards.

Hefting the bag over her shoulder, she whispered, "I'm coming, Dante."

CHAPTER 12

Monday August 8
7:45 p.m.

Warm air blew in his face and cool concrete pressed against his cheek. Dante tried to blink, but his lids refused to close over his dry eyes.

Where was he?

The last thing he remembered was Nadia, the desert. Slowly, he realized he was lying in front of a fan. It irritated his eyes and he tried to push himself away from it. His muscles screamed when he attempted to shift.

He couldn't move his arms.

"There you are," a man's voice said. "I was beginning to wonder about you."

The man grasped his shoulder and pulled him upright. Any part of Dante's body that wasn't numb felt like it was on fire as the man tugged him to a sitting position against the side of the building.

Dante's eyes felt grainy and raw, like they were full of sand, but he tried to focus on the man in front of him. Suddenly, he knew exactly where he was and exactly how much trouble he was in.

"Vandergriff," he rasped, and tried to look around.

He couldn't turn his head either.

"He got bored after you zoned out on him. But I'd say he'll be back pretty soon to check on you. Would you like a drink of water?"

Dante nodded, and tried to recall the man's name.

Pierce? Peterson. That was it.

He glanced around the room when Peterson disappeared out the door. The garage was nearly bare, indicating Vandergriff probably didn't spend a lot of time here. The shelves across from him were empty, save for a can of paint thinner.

Peterson reappeared and squatted beside Dante to hold the glass to his mouth. The cold water stung his lips, but Dante gulped it down gratefully. His throat was as dry and raw as his eyes.

"I was on the plane with Nadia," Peterson said. "I have to say, I'm impressed. That was a pretty gutsy rescue. I didn't know what was going on." He paused, and smiled at Dante. "She sure is something, huh?"

Dante looked at the man. Was this another of Vandergriff's games? Get someone to chat him up, to find out—what? What could he possibly know that would be any value to Vandergriff?

He wished he could think more clearly.

"Yeah, she is," he said finally.

The door behind Peterson burst open.

"Good morning!" Vandergriff said. Two dark half moons dipped underneath his eyes and his nose was taped and swollen. If it wouldn't have hurt so much, Dante might have laughed.

"Did you sleep well, Mr. Giovanni?" Vandergriff asked.

He was so excited he was nearly bouncing, and Dante's stomach lurched. What was going on?

"Peterson, I owe you, buddy," he said. "Your plan is working perfectly! I can't believe Andreakos actually fell for it, but I think he's going to play right into our hands."

Dante cast a sharp glance at the man beside him, but Peterson's face was unreadable.

Dear God, what was Nadia planning?

Peterson slowly stood and leaned against the wall. "What's going on, sir?"

"There's a lot of activity at the Andreakos estate this morning. They're getting ready to move on us. And when they do—Bam!" Vandergriff smacked his hands together. "We'll hit them where it hurts, right in their own backyard. While Andreakos is trying to bust down my door to get some lowlife bounty hunter, my men will be busting down his own door and there won't be anyone around to stop them."

No, Dante thought. No. Surely Nick Branson was smarter than that.

Vandergriff clapped his hands together. "I love this! Just like chess. Tonight I capture Andreakos' queen."

"What happens now, sir?" Peterson asked.

Vandergriff chuckled and removed a hunting knife from the sheaf on his belt. He began cleaning underneath his nails with the tip of it.

"Now, I think it's time for you to give your buddy Andreakos another call."

● ● ●

A faint mist hit Nadia in the face while she maneuvered the rental boat through the water. She'd begun to wonder if the idiot at the marina was even going to turn her loose with it, once he realized that there was no big, strong man waiting for her at the dock to drive her around. Especially since it was getting dark.

She drove aimlessly for awhile, killing time until the faint purple shadows of twilight turned to black. Her mind turned the plan over and over, looking for flaws.

She figured she and Dante had a 50/50 chance of survival. Those were odds she could live with. If she did nothing, Dante had no chance, and *that* she couldn't live with.

Nadia had dressed entirely in black. Thin black jacket, black turtleneck, black pants, black boots. She had a black ski mask in her bag, along with an assortment of other goodies it had taken the better part of the day to acquire. All she could do was pray that Vandergriff hadn't killed Dante already.

The river was quiet. Nadia cut the motor and scanned the area. A houseboat, complete with Christmas lights and blaring rock music drifted lazily by on her right. To her left, tucked in a little cove, two fishermen skimmed spinner baits across the silvery water. No one seemed pay any particular attention to her.

Using the smaller, quieter trolling motor, Nadia pulled to the dock. She tied her boat next to Vandergriff's boats. It looked much the same and she hoped it wouldn't attract any attention if it was docked next to the other ones.

Deep breath, girl, she told herself. *Here we go.*

Even though she went through the motions of a mental pep talk, Nadia felt calm. In control.

Love conquers all. Good triumphs over evil. Karma.

Nadia wasn't sure if she believed in any of those things, or all of them. All she knew was that she was through letting Gary Vandergriff dictate her life.

One way or another, it ended tonight.

She pulled the mask over her face and reached into the bag strapped around her waist to extract a gun and a small black object that looked like a walkie talkie. Moving in a crouch, she climbed the snaking wooden steps. When she was near the top, she turned the receiver on.

The red LCD light glowed strong and solid. A camera was nearby.

But what she held was no walkie talkie. With one touch,

Nadia used the video blocker to scramble every camera within 800 square yards.

She moved quickly through the night, keeping an eye out for the guards who monitored the perimeter. She wouldn't have a lot of time.

The grounds were quiet. Nadia didn't see the first guard until she had nearly reached the house. His back was to her. He stood motionlessly on the front deck, staring out at the water.

A sudden clatter sounded inside the house, followed by a muffled shout. Nadia scrambled underneath the deck an instant before the front door banged open.

"What's going on?" the guard asked.

"Cameras are down. Secure the premises."

Crouching low, Nadia took off, darting around the side of the house. It took her a moment to find what she was looking for in the darkness. Using both hands, she yanked the electric meter off the side of the house and tossed it as far as she could. She hadn't expected it to be so lightweight.

The house plunged into darkness and the amber security lights winked out. It took Nadia's eyes a moment to adjust to the sudden blackness. Inky, rolling clouds obscured the full moon above while Nadia moved stealthily around the house, trying to find the best entry point.

An orange glow in front of the garage stopped her in her tracks.

A cigarette.

The light moved back and forth as the man paced.

Dante wasn't in the house. He was in this building and this man was guarding him. Even as that dawned on her, Nadia realized how much her hesitation had cost her. Voices came around the side of the house.

She could barely make out the bulky outline of a gazebo ahead. Nadia's hand flew to her chest, seeking the outline of Dante's medallion through her jacket before she darted inside the structure. She crouched beneath the low wooden bench and watched the yellow flashlight beams approach.

One of the men was close now. So close that she was afraid he would hear her ragged breathing.

If I get out of this mess, she thought, *I swear I'll never touch another damn cigarette.*

Nadia held her breath when he took a hesitant step inside the gazebo.

I'm going to have to shoot him, she realized grimly.

But he casually played his beam over the surface and stepped back outside, obviously expecting bigger quarry. Once again, her small stature had saved the day.

The wait was excruciating. A cramp twisted Nadia's calf while she craned to hear the men's muffled conversation. Wincing, she shifted position, trying to exert enough pressure to straighten the aching muscle.

Finally, the men moved back around the side of the house and Nadia crept out of the gazebo. She hugged the side of it, watching the telltale glow of the guard's cigarette drift back and forth.

Honeysuckle grew rampant on the grounds and the sweet smell was making her queasy. When she backed away from the gazebo, her foot caught on one of the cobblestones surrounding it. She caught herself and stared down at it, grasping an idea.

She hefted the smooth rock in her hand and eased closer to the garage. With one fluid motion, she sent the rock crashing against the side of the gazebo.

The cigarette dropped to the ground and the man bellowed, "Who is that? Show yourself!"

He hurried to the gazebo with his gun drawn, and moved right past her. Nadia slipped up behind him and pressed the barrel of her gun against his back.

"On your knees," she said.

He hesitated and she poked him with the gun. "I said, on your knees. Now!"

He dropped to his knees and she crashed the butt of the gun against his base of his skull. He crumpled noiselessly to the ground.

Nadia moved stealthily toward the garage, terrified of what she would find waiting for her inside.

She eased open the door, unsure if Dante was alone. Slipping inside, she shut it behind her and edged along the wall, unable to see anything. She stood in the pitch black, listening for any movement.

The garage was utterly quiet.

Her heart thumped painfully against her ribcage. Was

Dante dead? Was he even here, or was this simply another of Vandergriff's traps?

Reaching into her pocket, Nadia extracted a flashlight and hesitantly flipped it on. She scanned the light around the room, and her hand jerked when the beam landed on Dante's crumpled form.

Her lungs emptied at the sight of his battered face. She snatched off her mask and ran to him. Dropping to her knees, she pressed her hand to his throat.

"Please, please . . ." she whispered. Tears stung her eyes when she caught the faint thread of his pulse beneath her fingertips.

● ● ●

"Dante, can you hear me? Talk to me."

Dante frowned, watching the rain stream off Nadia's face and beat against the dry desert floor. Her lips were moving, but what was she saying?

Her voice sounded anxious. Desperate. "Baby, you have to help me. We've got to get out of here now."

Someone was shaking him. The desert scenery around him faded away as Nadia's voice grew more urgent.

"What has he done to you?" she whispered, and he heard the catch in her voice.

Nadia was crying.

The realization was like a slap in the face and Dante tried

to open his eyes. He squinted at the beautiful woman hovering over him and his heartbeat quickened.

She was really here. Oh God, what did she think she was doing?

"Nadia?" he asked, his voice rising in panic. "You have to get out of here before they find you."

Suddenly, the door crashed open. They were bathed in brilliant white light.

"Well, well. What do we have here?" Vandergriff asked, astonishment plain in his voice. "The little birdie got free, then came home to roost!"

Dante felt Nadia stiffen beside him. She shoved her hand in her pocket and slowly stood.

Don't draw down on them, Nadia, Dante tried to say, but he couldn't push out the words.

"I was expecting company, but I wasn't expecting you to come alone. How delightful! What's the matter, Daddy Nick wouldn't help you?"

"I can take care of you on my own," Nadia said.

Dante looked at her in surprise. Her voice was calm. Cold. He could still see the tracks of her tears on her face, but her eyes sparkled like green ice.

Vandergriff dropped the spotlight from their faces and set it on the floor. Its circular base rolled in a small arc, making a funny scraping sound on the cement floor as the light danced.

Vandergriff's shadow loomed high and black against the rafters like some sort of demon's as he advanced toward them.

He clapped his hands together and said, "Peterson! What did I tell you? This must be my lucky day."

Nadia smiled.

She held up her hand and Dante saw she wasn't holding a gun. It wasn't a gun at all. His heart froze as he stared at the little black box.

"See, now that's funny," Nadia said, waggling the remote. "Because I was thinking just the opposite. Today isn't your day."

She slowly unzipped her jacket to reveal the belt of explosives fastened around her waist. "Today just ain't your day at all."

● ● ●

For a long moment, no one said a word. No one moved and maybe no one even breathed. Then Vandergriff broke the silence.

"You're bluffing," he sputtered.

"Try me," Nadia said with more confidence than she felt. "What have I got to lose?"

Vandergriff managed a laugh. "You won't blow us up. You'd kill yourself and your boyfriend too."

She pretended to mull it over. "But, golly gee, I would be taking you with us. It might just be worth it. Besides, look at my alternative. I will never be your slave. I would rather die than let you touch me. And Dante . . . Dante would die anyway."

"She's bluffing," Vandergriff turned and told his men, but he wasn't looking too sure of himself anymore.

With her other hand, Nadia tugged her ski mask the rest of the way off and tossed it on the floor. Shaking her hair free, she said, "You know, there was some truth in all those lies you told Dante. You might not be my father, but you're the one who made me. You stole my childhood. You've made my parents live in fear behind iron gates. And if you don't think I can be as cold and ruthless as you are, why don't you just step up and see? I've got enough explosives here to blow this whole place off the map."

"What do you want?"

"What I want and what I'm demanding are two different things. I want you dead, but I'm demanding safe passage out of here, with Dante. Cut him loose, Vandergriff."

No one moved. Vandergriff's men looked at him uncertainly.

"Do it," Nadia said. Her thumb poised over the red button. "Or so help me, I will."

Vandergriff stared at her for a long moment. Then he nodded. One of the men stepped forward, but Nadia held up her hand and shook her head. Pointing at Vandergriff, she said, "No, I told you, I want *you* to do it."

Glaring at her, Vandergriff advanced toward Dante. He unsheathed the knife on his belt and squatted to cut the rope around Dante's wrists.

Nadia was afraid to look directly at them, afraid one of

Vandergriff's men would try something. Out of the corner of her eye, she watched Dante struggle to stand. His legs wouldn't support him.

"Nadia," Dante said, and the frustration in his voice broke her heart. "I can't do this. I can't walk. Leave me and get out of here."

"Not a chance, babe," she said breezily. "We're a team now. Butch and Sundance. Bonnie and Clyde—"

"Slick and princess," Dante supplied. She heard the smile in his voice and wanted to look at him, but she didn't dare turn her back on Vandergriff's men.

"There ya go," Nadia said, and nodded at the five men. "All of you, hands against the wall. Spread your feet. We're going to do this slow, one man at a time. You—" She pointed at Peterson. "Empty the clip on your gun and walk slowly toward me."

Peterson glanced at Vandergriff, and Vandergriff nodded. Peterson ejected the clip and walked toward Nadia with his hands raised above his head.

"Are you packing another piece?"

He nodded. "Ankle holster."

"Take it off. Slow." He did as she instructed and she made a show of patting him down, her eyes never leaving Vandergriff's face. He stood braced against the wall, his icy blue eyes tracking her like a snake.

"Take off your shirt," she told Peterson. "I want you to go around and collect all the ammunition in it. Lay the guns beside it."

"No way, that's not happening," Vandergriff said immediately. "My men aren't going to disarm. That would be suicide. You have my word, no one will take a shot at you."

"Your word?" Nadia said, and rolled her eyes. "Oh, yeah, like that means anything to me. Come here, Vandergriff."

"No."

Nadia felt a twisted sense of pleasure at the fear in his voice. It was about time he had a taste of his own medicine.

"I told you, all I want is safe passage to my boat, so you're going to be my shield, should one of your boys here get any ideas."

"That's not necessary—"

"Shut up. That's not negotiable." Nadia glanced at Peterson. "You're going to help Dante. The rest of you, lead the way. I'm a little jumpy, so don't try anything funny unless you want to be a headline in tomorrow's paper."

She grabbed Vandergriff's shoulder and twisted him roughly around. Slipping her fingers through his back belt loop, Nadia jerked him close to her. Sweat dampened his shirt and Nadia could almost smell his fear.

"What's the matter, lover boy?" she whispered in his ear. "I thought you *wanted* to get close to me."

He growled, low in his throat, and she laughed. She gave the place a final glance, then prodded him toward the door.

As Nadia marched them across the yard, she stared at the back of Vandergriff's head and fantasized about his death.

What a macabre little parade we are, she thought, when they began the slow, steep trek down the wooden steps.

The storm clouds were rolling off, allowing a little moonlight to peek through. It wasn't much, however, and the darkness made Nadia nervous. She squinted ahead, trying to watch the armed men in front while hiding behind Vandergriff.

The walk down the narrow steps to the dock was torturously slow. Nadia had to worry not only about the men in front of her but also anyone who might be slipping up behind.

Finally, they stood in front of the boats. Nadia gave Vandergriff a shove that sent him sprawling across the wooden dock. He flipped over on his back and glared at her with murder in his eyes.

"Huh uh." She waved the remote. "Be nice."

She looked at Peterson. "Are you as ready as I am to get out of here? Help Dante onto the boat."

Without looking at Vandergriff, Peterson did as she commanded, struggling under Dante's weight. Nadia carefully climbed in behind them, never taking her eyes off Vandergriff and his companions.

"Now, Peterson!" Vandergriff shouted, when Nadia turned her back to the man.

Nadia smiled when Peterson replied, "Sorry. I forgot to tell you, Mr. Vandergriff. I quit."

Shock dawned on Vandergriff's face.

"Go!" she yelled at Peterson.

When the boat pulled away from the island, Nadia blew

Vandergriff a kiss. She had to laugh at the look of impotent rage she received in return.

"Go, go, go!" she shouted and, as expected, his men were already climbing into their boats by the time Peterson rounded the first bend in the river.

Vandergriff was coming after them. No big surprise.

He knew she wouldn't blow herself up unless she was sure to take him with her. On the water, his gunmen would try to take her out at a safer distance. And he was certainly mad enough to give it a try.

"Are you guys okay?" She dropped the remote on the seat beside her and crawled over to where Dante lay in the bottom of the boat.

"Easy there, princess," he said, staring at the remote.

"What?" She grinned. "Are you worried about this little thing?"

Nadia picked it up and pressed the button.

● ● ●

Dante stared at Nadia in horrified disbelief. Somehow the realization that she'd bluffed her way out of there with nothing at all was more frightening than the thought of actual explosives.

She tossed the remote to him and watched for Vandergriff's men, her dark hair whipping in the wind.

With an impish smile, she said, "I have no idea what that goes to. Some damn thing of Waynie's."

"Nadia!" Peterson yelled. "Here they come, and they're closing fast."

The two pursuing boats ran side by side, cutting through the frothy water. Dante struggled to his elbows to see what was happening.

Peterson took a sharp turn, blowing by two fishermen who trolled near the bank. One of them lifted a walkie talkie and turned to watch them go by.

It was Ronnie.

"There!" Nadia yelled, and pointed at the houseboat.

Peterson cut their speed and idled up beside it, just as Vandergriff's boats closed in.

A man in a straw hat and a bright Hawaiian shirt walked out on deck. In his hand, he held a remote that looked somewhat like the one Nadia had used.

Nick Branson.

Shocked, Dante glanced from Nick to Vandergriff's approaching boat.

Vandergriff had seen him too. He waved his arms and frantically shouted orders to his men. They lifted their guns to fire at Nadia's father.

Nick gave Vandergriff a friendly wave and pressed the button.

The world around them exploded.

CHAPTER **13**

Monday, August 8
11:02 p.m.

The boat pitched violently, and Nadia almost tumbled over the side. While she clawed for a handhold, she felt Dante's hands grasp her waist. He yanked her down on the floor beside him as a piece of metal whizzed by her head. A wall of heat slammed into them and Dante twisted to shield her with his body. Finally, the roar subsided and she heard her father shouting.

"Nadia, are you all right?" he yelled.

She tried to answer him, but her reply was muffled against Dante's chest.

"Nadia!" he cried frantically.

Dante shifted and stared down at her. Nadia touched his face and smiled.

"She's okay, Mr. Branson," Dante called over his shoulder.

He exhaled softly and wrapped her in his arms, planting a kiss on top of her head.

Yes, she thought, burying her face against his chest. *I'm okay now.*

Slowly, they sat upright. Nadia stared at the chaotic scene before them in numb detachment.

It was over. It was really over.

The water was on fire. Bright flames danced across the black water as the gasoline burned off the wreckage. Huge chunks of the debris blazed, filling the air with acrid black smoke that stung her eyes and constricted her throat. Nadia turned her face into Dante's shirt, coughing.

"Well, come on, then," her father said. "We've got to get moving."

Something bumped against their boat and Nadia realized it was a body. It floated face down beside them.

Was it Vandergriff? Nadia craned to see, but she couldn't tell.

From the houseboat, one of the bodyguards reached for her hands and Nadia shook her head. "Help Dante board first. He's hurt."

Brent nodded and Peterson helped Dante to his feet. They struggled to the helm of the boat and Nick joined the men who helped pull him aboard.

"Come on, Nadia." Her father reached down for her. "We need to get out of here."

Covering her face against the smoke with her jacket,

Nadia nodded. She leaned over the edge of the boat and took his hands.

When Nadia stepped up onto the bow, Gary Vandergriff exploded out of the water in front of her.

He seized Nadia's ankles and ripped her from her father's grasp. Her fingers scraped against the side of the houseboat, seeking purchase and finding none on the slick surface. She had just enough time to suck in a breath before Vandergriff dragged her underneath the frigid water.

They shot downward, rocketing away from the surface. Nadia saw the glow from the fire for an instant and then there was nothing. Nothing but blackness.

She grappled with Vandergriff, trying to break his iron grip, but her movements felt slow and ineffective against the weight of the water. The surface was so far away.

Just when she thought he was going to drag her to the very bottom of the river, Nadia wriggled one of her legs free. She kicked viciously at the area where she thought his face might be.

Her boot made contact with something and suddenly she was free. But her relief was short-lived. Before she could kick her way to the surface, one of Vandergriff's arms clamped around her waist.

Her lungs burned, begging for oxygen, and she nearly panicked. Frantically, she fought him—twisting, kicking, flailing.

Nadia couldn't hold on much longer. At any moment her tortured lungs would force her to take a breath that wasn't there.

● ● ●

Dante threw himself over the rail of the houseboat, his injuries forgotten in his terror. Plummeting into the cold water, he glimpsed Peterson splashing in beside him. Nick had already gone under.

Where was Nadia?

Dante opened his eyes and strained to see in the darkness. Already he sensed Peterson moving up beside him. Night diving could be a claustrophobic experience for the uninitiated. The dark water was heavy, oppressive. Smothering.

Propelling his body deeper, Dante groped blindly in the inky blackness. His fear spiked with every second that passed and he had to block the horrible images that threatened to break his will.

He couldn't lose her now. Not now, when they'd made it through so much.

His fear broke his concentration. When Dante started to push to the surface for another gulp of air, his fingers snagged something solid.

Something human.

Fingers clutched at his wrist. Dante grabbed a fistful of cloth and kicked his way to the surface.

This wasn't Nadia. He knew that already.

And if it was Gary Vandergriff, he'd beg to return to his watery grave before Dante was through with him.

Dante broke through the surface and realized he held a sputtering, choking Nick in his grasp.

"I—I can't see her," Nadia's father gasped. "I can't see anything under there."

Dante didn't respond. He simply took another deep breath and dove.

● ● ●

Vandergriff clasped Nadia, pulled her against him like a partner in a grotesque death dance. When she pushed at him, fighting to break his grip, her hand brushed something hard. Her reflexes—even her thoughts—were slowing, but she realized what it was.

Vandergriff's knife. The one he'd used to cut Dante free.

With a burst of hope, Nadia grabbed for the leather sheaf and fumbled with the snap. At the last moment, Vandergriff must've realized what she was doing because he released her waist and tried to twist away from her.

Too late, Nadia thought.

The ivory handle of the knife felt solid in her hand. With a smooth upward motion, she buried it to the hilt in Gary Vandergriff's chest.

Air bubbles hit her face when he gasped. Then he let her go.

Nadia kicked her way toward the surface.

Her lungs gave out just when she broke the surface and

her first breath was a mixture of air and water. Choking, sputtering, she went down again. A pair of strong hands seized her hips and pushed her back up.

"I got you! I got you," Dante said, hoisting her above his shoulder. Nadia sagged against him.

"Here, let me have her."

Nadia recognized Ronnie's voice, but she couldn't see him. Her eyes burned and she couldn't stop coughing.

The next thing Nadia knew, she was lying on one of the narrow beds on the houseboat and a sea of anxious faces hovered over her.

"There she is." Dante tried to smile, but his face was gray. "You okay, princess?"

"A little waterlogged, but I think I'll make it," she said with a weak smile.

Nick Branson cupped his hands over his face, blinking back tears. Nadia reached for his hand.

"Thank you, Daddy. Thank you for helping me," she whispered.

Nick tucked a damp lock of hair behind her ear and said, "I almost blew it. I almost blew the whole thing. You were taking too long, and I was so scared the plan wasn't working—"

"We don't have to be afraid anymore," she said. "I killed him."

Nick stared at the space over her head. "I know. We found his body."

"What about the police?"

Her father gave her a wan smile. "What about the police? Those two fishermen near the bank saw the whole thing. One of the boats was operating without running lights. It was a head-on collision."

Nadia knew without saying that they wouldn't be able to trace the explosives. Nick Branson was a careful man.

"But the knife—"

"Nadia, don't ask questions you don't want the answers to. It was self-defense. No one will be able to prove Vandergriff's death wasn't an unfortunate accident."

"What about him?" Dante jerked his head toward Peterson. "I don't understand . . . I heard him talking to Vandergriff about setting you up."

Nadia cleared her throat. "You mean old double agent Peterson here? He's been spying for us since they picked you up in the desert, feeding Vandergriff false information. He found your phone on the plane and he and Daddy came up with a plan. They let Vandergriff find the phone next, and Peterson spoon fed him the plan. This whole time, Vandergriff thought Peterson was working against us, but it was the other way around. Peterson managed to divert two thirds of Vandergriff's goons tonight."

"The name is Bond, James Bond," Peterson joked.

Nadia rolled her eyes and clutched Dante's hand. "Can you guys give me and Dante a minute alone?"

Her father nodded and they left the cabin. As soon as they shut the door, Dante took her into his arms. Nadia held onto him a little tighter than necessary, a whirlwind of emotions swirling inside her. The boat lurched as they picked up speed and slipped down the river.

"Are you really okay, princess?" Dante asked, brushing his fingers against her cheek.

Nadia squeezed her eyes shut and nodded.

He sat on the narrow bunk beside her and Nadia traced her fingers over his jaw.

"Your poor face," she said miserably. "And your wrists . . ."

They were raw and bleeding and the sight made tears well in her eyes. She lifted his shirt to inspect the ugly black bruises.

"Damn him," she said.

Dante grabbed her wrists and forced her to look up at him. "I'm okay. Really. Thanks to you."

His reassuring smile gave way to a frown and he folded her into his arms. "Baby, you're shaking."

In the safety of his arms, Nadia's composure finally cracked. She clutched his shirt, sobbing. "I was afraid I was going to lose you. So afraid that I'd find you dead and that I'd never get to tell you I love you." She pulled back and stared into his face as tears streamed down her cheeks. "I do. I do love you. And I'm not sure what your plans are from here, or if I'm even a part of them, but I swore that if I ever saw you again, I wasn't going to hold anything back—"

"Nadia—"

She was babbling again. All the things she'd wanted to say to him burst from her mouth. "And you don't have to say anything. I know we haven't known each other long, and I'm not expecting anything—"

"Nadia." He gently placed his finger against her mouth to silence her.

She looked up at him, suddenly more afraid than she'd been in the heat of battle. Her heart wasn't something she shared easily.

"I love you too."

Nadia closed her eyes, his words echoing in her ears as his hand stroked her hair.

"When you went under that water and we couldn't find you . . ." He paused, swiping at his eyes. "I was so scared. I knew—*I knew* from the first day I met you that you were the one I wanted. The first time I saw you, I wanted you. Then you kissed me, and I knew I had to have you. Now I know I don't ever want to let you go."

She finally dared to look at him and was surprised by his vulnerable expression. Nadia saw her own fears reflected on his face and thought about what he'd said, about them being kindred spirits.

He'd been right.

"I don't know where I'm going from here, either. I only know I want you with me, wherever it is," Dante said, then he kissed her.

A long, slow kiss that melted away her fears and assured her that her heart was safe with him.

Nadia laughed and brushed the tears from her face, a little

embarrassed at them. "I'm sorry for acting like such a . . . *girl*."

Dante grinned. "I like girls. And don't worry about proving to me how tough you are. Honey, I'd rather know you had my back than the whole United States Marine Corp."

A rap on the door interrupted them.

"All ashore that's going ashore," Peterson called.

● ● ●

His head felt like it was made of stone. Dante groaned and rubbed his eyes with one hand. Nadia lay across his other arm.

How long had he been asleep?

A glance at the bedside clock told him it was fifteen after six. He'd fallen asleep after Nick's doctor had left around midnight.

Sometime during the night, Nadia had showered and changed. She was wearing the silver nightgown she'd worn that night in the garden. Dante smiled and pressed his face into her still damp hair, breathing deeply of the sweet lilac scent of her shampoo. He slid his hand down one silk clad hip, but she was sleeping so soundly he didn't have the heart to wake her.

A shower. He needed one too. Dante hated to lie here with her like this when he felt so grungy.

Carefully easing his arm from underneath her, he limped down the hall to the bathroom.

Fresh towels and a change of clothes awaited him on

the hamper lid. Turning the hot water on full blast, Dante stripped and climbed into the shower. His muscles screamed in protest. He'd never been so sore in his life. The water stung his many cuts, but it felt wonderful on his aching body. Dante stood there for a long time, scrubbing and letting the hot water beat against his back. By the time he climbed out, he almost felt human again.

He dressed slowly and padded back to the bedroom in his bare feet. Since Nadia was still asleep, he headed downstairs hoping to find something to make a sandwich with. The white, button-down shirt they'd furnished him with was a little too tight across the chest, but he buttoned it anyway as he walked into the kitchen.

Maria Branson sat at the kitchen table, staring out the window with a cup of coffee in her hand.

"Good morning, Mrs. B," Dante said.

She glanced at him, and her lips quirked in a smile. "Hi, there. I think you mean good evening."

Dante looked out the patio doors in shock. He'd mistaken the faint sunlight streaming into the bedroom window for sunrise, when in reality the sun was beginning to sink in the west.

"I've never slept that long in my life." He ran a hand down his face and shook his head. "Do I look as rough as I feel?"

Maria laughed. "I don't think you want me to answer that. Let's just say that you make *me* look pretty."

"Aw, you're like Nadia." He smiled and sat at the table across from her. "It'd take more than a scar to hide your beauty."

"Ooh, I see that you're a sweet talker," Maria said, rising. "No wonder my daughter is so taken with you."

She walked to the refrigerator and peered inside. "Since you thought it was morning, I suppose you want breakfast. Do you like omelets?"

"I love them, but you don't have to go through the trouble—"

She waved off his protest and started pulling things out of the refrigerator. "I'm surprised you could sleep at all with Nadia hovering over you like a worried mother hen. Where is she, anyway?"

"She's upstairs, still asleep. After the doctor left, I crashed. I wouldn't have noticed if she'd brought in a tambourine band."

Soon the kitchen was filled with the mouthwatering aroma of sautéed onions and eggs. Dante was practically salivating by the time Nadia's mother laid a heaping plateful in front of him. He dug into it with relish.

"Oh, um, that's wonderful," he said, closing his eyes and savoring the first bite of food he'd had since the MRE in the desert.

"I'd like to think it's my cooking, but I know you're starving," she said with a smile.

"Ah, no. This is great."

Maria bounced something on the table underneath her palm. A coin, maybe. Dante felt her eyes on him while he ate, hearing the clack-clack-clack as it struck the gleaming oak surface.

She cleared her throat and wrinkled her nose. "I suppose this is the part where I ask you what your intentions are for my daughter."

Dante stopped eating and looked at her. "I love Nadia, Mrs. Branson. I want it all with her, a house, kids. Everything."

Clack-clack-clack.

With a sad smile, she asked, "Will you take her away from here?"

"I'll live wherever Nadia wants to live. I don't care, as long as I'm with her."

The object came to a rest beneath her palm.

"I think you should know that you're not the man I would pick for her," she said softly. "The two of you are too much alike, and that scares me. But maybe that's what Nadia needs. Regardless, I do realize that it wasn't my choice to make. It was hers, and she chose you."

She stood and slid her palm along the table, stopping in front of his plate. Her eyes shone as she lifted her palm. Surprised, Dante stared down at the table, then back up at her.

"Take care of her," Maria said. She leaned to brush a kiss on top of his head as she walked past.

"I will," Dante said, but she was already gone.

After he ate, he wandered out into the garden and sat on the marble bench, staring up at the sky. It was there Nadia found him.

• • •

"Hey, handsome, what are you doing out here?" She hiked up the hem of her gown and crawled into his lap, facing him.

Dante smiled and wrapped his arms around her. "I like this place," he said. "I come here to think."

Nadia returned his smile, recalling their previous conversation here. "Oh, yeah? What are you thinking about?"

"Getting married."

His words shocked her so badly she nearly fell off his lap.

Dante laughed. "Easy there!" He grabbed her hips and pulled her closer.

Nadia's mouth went dry. She licked her lips and rubbed her palms on her thighs. Trying to sound casual, even though she felt dizzy, she asked, "Anybody I know?"

"Some crazy chick I met a few days ago. Do you think I can talk her into it?"

He held up his hand. Nadia gasped when she saw her mother's engagement ring resting on the first knuckle of his little finger.

With all the things she wanted to say to him, the only thing that came out was, "I can't cook."

Dante laughed. "I can cook a little. I don't think we'll starve."

"Are you sure?" she asked anxiously.

"Yeah, and there's always takeout."

Nadia punched his shoulder. "You know what I mean. I'm not sure I know how to be a good wife. What if you regret this later? There are so many things you don't know about me."

"I know all I need to know." He slid the ring on her finger. "I know that you'll be there for me, for better and for worse. I know I love you. I know you love me. That's all that matters."

Dante cupped her face in his hands. The look in those brown eyes stole her breath. "How about it, Nadia? Will you marry me?"

"Yes." She held her hand up and blinked at her mother's ring. This was crazy, but it felt so right.

She kissed him.

They stayed in the garden until the waning sunlight disappeared, talking and planning their future together.

❁ ❁ ❁

Dante laughed when Nadia's stomach rumbled.

"What, you're not hungry?" she asked defensively. "I'm starving. I haven't eaten since you tried to poison me with that stuff in the desert."

Dante kissed her palm. "Your mother cooked an omlet for me. That's when she gave me the ring."

"Does my father know?"

Dante's smile faded. "I don't know. I haven't seen him since I've been up."

"Oh, I can't wait to tell him!" Nadia started to climb from his lap, but Dante caught her hips.

"Stay for just one more minute," he said, and nuzzled her neck.

"Umm." She leaned toward him. "Who needs food anyway?"

"You do. I know how irritable and mean you get, and I'm too beat up to defend myself right now."

"Speaking of defending yourself, just wait until you see what I have planned for you tonight. A real bed. . ." She undid the first two buttons of his shirt and slipped her hand inside. "Maybe a nice, hot bath together."

Dante smiled. "Are you sure your father won't shoot me?"

"Nah, we'll just gang up on him again." Nadia leaned down to kiss him, but Dante pulled back.

"Again?" he asked.

Nadia hesitated. She took his hand in hers and rubbed his fingers. "Nick and I had this huge fight after he found me in the desert. He didn't want to us to come after you at first."

Even though Dante had expected as much, had even hoped for that reaction from Branson while he was being held captive, it still stung.

You're disposable to him, Vandergriff had said.

It looked like he'd been right.

Nadia started talking faster, a sign of her discomfort that Dante had learned to recognize. "It was nothing to do with you personally. He was afraid we would all get killed. Ronnie tried to take up for me, but Nick had me trapped in my room." She gave him a nervous laugh. "I escaped through the laundry chute."

When Dante didn't say anything, she sighed. "Of course, they caught me trying to get out the gate. Ronnie took up for me, my mother took up for me, even Waynie threw in his two cents . . . but I think the clincher was that Nick finally realized how much you meant to me. I told him I loved you, and that I would never forgive him if he didn't let me try to get you back."

Dante shifted. "So, you blackmailed him into helping."

An uneasy feeling settled in the pit of Dante's stomach. He had the feeling that Branson wouldn't be too thrilled about their engagement.

Nadia shrugged. "Well, yeah. But none of that matters now, does it?" Nadia touched his chin, forcing him to look at her. "He did help, and now we're here together, safe and basically sound, right?"

He gave her a grudging nod, and she smiled. Leaning to brush a kiss by his ear, she whispered, "I love you."

"I love you too."

She kissed him again. "I'm going to find Nick and get something to eat. Want to come with me?"

"Maybe in a minute. You go ahead."

Nadia wandered up the path in her bare feet, her silver gown shining in the moonlight. She blew him a kiss, then disappeared behind the rosebushes.

Dante closed his eyes, suddenly feeling cold despite the warm night air.

It wasn't the same.

Nadia wasn't Sharon, and he wasn't some scared kid anymore.

Things would be different this time. They would have to be, because he couldn't stand to lose Nadia.

Taking a deep breath, Dante stood, wincing when his sore muscles protested. Reluctantly, he limped to the house to see what kind of scene awaited him.

He slid open the doors and walked into an empty living room. Muffled voices came from the dining room, and Dante slowly made his way toward them.

When he reached the doorway, he heard Nick Branson's voice. "You're what? Getting married?"

He laughed and Dante froze.

"Do you seriously expect me to let my daughter marry some damn *bounty hunter*?"

Nick's words seared him. Dante turned away and hobbled up the stairs.

He was hurt, and angry that he'd let a man like Nick have the power to hurt him in the first place.

It wasn't fair. No matter what he did, or how much he loved her, he would never be good enough.

Frustrated, he crawled into Nadia's bed and pulled her pillow to his face. Whatever happened next would depend on her.

She opened the door nearly twenty minutes later and slipped inside. She looked like she'd been crying. The sight of her red-rimmed eyes filled him with dread.

"What's wrong?" he asked tersely, and sat up in the bed.

"Nothing." She turned away from him and picked up her brush. Pulling it through her hair, she said, "I thought you were going to join us."

"I didn't think your father would want to eat with the hired help."

Her hand stilled in mid-stroke and she turned to face him. "What's that supposed to mean?"

"What did Nick say when you told him we were getting married? Did he tell you that princesses don't marry losers like me?"

Temper flashed in her green eyes, but Dante had managed to work up a pretty volatile mood himself. "What's the matter, Nadia? Did you come up here to tell me you've changed your mind?"

Nadia set her hairbrush back on the dresser and rubbed her forehead. "I'm trying real hard not to be pissed by that comment, but you know what . . . it's not working. I am not your ex-wife, Dante."

"So, what did Daddy say, after the 'I'm not going to let my daughter marry some damn bounty hunter' part?"

Nadia drew back like she'd been slapped. A strange look passed over her face, and she crossed her arms over her chest. "You want to know what he said? Why don't you go ask him yourself?"

Dante stared at her, but she simply lifted her chin in that stubborn way of hers.

"Fine." He stalked out of the bedroom with Nadia on his heels.

His overnight bag awaited him at the foot of the stairs.

Nick sat in the living room, sipping a glass of tea. He glanced up at Dante, and said, "There you are. I'd like to have a word with you."

Dante grimaced. "Yeah, I can guess what that word is."

"So, Nadia told you what we discussed?"

"She didn't tell me anything, but I want to tell you something . . . I love her. We're meant to be together, and I'm not walking away."

Nick lifted his eyebrows, and shot Nadia a puzzled look over Dante's shoulder. "Yes," he said slowly. "I gathered that from the engagement."

"I may not be some rich lawyer or doctor, but I can make her happy."

"I'm sure you can." Nick's frown deepened and he steepled his hands in front of his face. "I have a feeling . . . am I missing something here?"

Nadia laughed.

Confused, Dante turned to look at her. She walked up beside him and slipped her arm through his. Laying her head against his shoulder, she said, "He heard what you said, about not letting your daughter marry some damn bounty hunter, but apparently that's all he heard."

"Oh!" Nick's face turned red, then he laughed. "I see."

He motioned for Dante to sit on the couch beside him. Reluctantly, Dante did. Branson set his glass on a coaster and said, "Sorry about that. I was teasing Nadia. She's so excitable these days."

"You mean . . ." Dante glanced at Nadia. She winked at him. " . . . you aren't going to stop the wedding?"

"Stop the wedding!" Nick laughed so hard he had to wipe his eyes. "Son, I'm not even sure *you* could stop the wedding, now that Nadia has her mind set on it."

"Damn straight," she said, and perched on the couch arm beside him. "So, don't get any ideas."

"But my clothes—" Dante gestured toward duffle bag at the foot of the stairs.

"If you'll remember, Waynie took them out to the barracks after you accepted my offer of employment. Now that you're family, I thought we should move you back into the main house. I'd hate for Nadia to have to slip out of the house again. It's a wonder she didn't get wedged in that laundry chute. We'd still be looking for her."

Now that you're family . . .

Dante's face flushed hot, and he shot Nadia an embarrassed grin. "You just had to let me flounder around here and make an ass out of myself, didn't you?"

She shrugged. "Well, you needed to hear it from him, not me."

Nick patted his shoulder. "That's women for you, son. Her mother does me the same way."

Nadia snorted and shook her head. "I can't believe you thought I wasn't going to marry you because Daddy said so."

Nick sighed. "She's never listened to me before, and I'm not expecting her to start anytime soon. Besides, I'm not complaining. I think you two are a perfect match if I can keep you out of trouble, which brings me to my next point. I'd like to offer the both of you jobs at Branson Industries— well, Andreakos Industries now. Perhaps I can keep the two you so busy you won't have time to get into mischief. And it's only right that you assume some of the duties at the firm. After all, you and your children will own it one day. What do you say?"

Nadia looked at Dante and Dante laughed, staring at his future father-in-law. "Hey, I don't even know what it is you do. Remember, I was thinking until recently that you were a drug dealer."

Nick rolled his eyes. "Security. My firm provides personal security for people in the form of electronic systems, guards, and whatever other devices we deem necessary. We do some government contracts. Work against hackers, that sort of thing. I assure you, I'm no drug dealer. If you accept my offer, I'll pay for a month long honeymoon anywhere you want to go."

Dante grinned at Nadia. "I hear the desert's nice this time of year. It's the rainy season."

● ● ●

Two weeks later

"Hey in there!" Ronnie called, and rapped on the door. "Is everybody decent?"

"Come in," Nadia yelled as her mother struggled with the tiny row of pearl buttons up the back of her gown.

Ronnie cracked open the door and stuck his head inside, his hand covering his eyes.

"I'm dressed, you goof," Nadia said.

Ronnie peeked through his fingers. "Whoa—oh, my God, she's wearing white!"

Nadia tossed a box of tissues at him. It missed, bouncing off the door frame, and Ronnie cackled.

"Kidding. I'm only kidding. You look beautiful." He slipped inside and closed the door behind him. "Dante's a lucky guy. And he's ready. He sent me in here to make sure you hadn't changed your mind or anything. I told him you'd better not have. I don't wear one of these monkey suits for just anybody."

Nadia smiled and shook her head. "Nope, he won't get off the hook that easy. And you look very handsome. Thank you for being my maid of honor."

Ronnie winced. "Don't call it that. I've already taken enough ribbing from Dante's little brother about walking down the aisle with him. I don't need any more from you. It's not my fault you don't have any girlfriends. And it *will* be your fault if I don't have any girlfriends, after they hear about this."

"Quit your yapping."

Nadia motioned him over so she could straighten his tie. "The thing is, you want your best friend standing up there beside you. Other than Dante, you're it. I can't help it that I like hanging out with losers."

"Back atcha, loser," Ronnie said, and nudged her shoulder with his.

Nadia smiled and kissed his cheek. "Ooh, you smell good too. Hand me that bouquet, loser."

She brought the flowers to her face for a quick sniff, then lifted her eyebrow. "How does Dante look in his tux? Sexy, I bet."

Ronnie threw up his hands. "Yeah, he's adorable. Look, I'm out of here. Are we going to get this show on the road some time today? This collar itches."

"We're done." Maria stood and smoothed out her dress. "Ronnie, will you please tell Waynie I'm ready for my escort?"

"Sure thing, Mrs. B," he said, and headed for the door. Nadia followed. She peeked through the crack and watched as Ronnie whispered something to Waynie. They both laughed.

Men.

She didn't have time to worry about them. Dante was waiting.

● ● ●

The garden was beautiful. Nadia had decided she wanted the ceremony to be held there, and that was fine with Dante. The place held some good memories. Red roses were everywhere, bathing the area with their sweet, heavy scent.

It was a small gathering, just the families, and that was the way they'd wanted it. His family, though shocked at his sudden engagement, had embraced Nadia after he'd made it clear how much he loved her.

This is the best day of my life, Dante thought.

A smile tugged at the corner of his mouth when he watched Ronnie and his brother J.T. walk down the cobble-stone path side by side. J.T. leaned to whisper something to him. Ronnie scowled and stared straight ahead.

"What did you say to Ronnie?" Dante whispered, when J.T. took the best man's spot beside him.

J.T. smirked. "I told him he was the ugliest bridesmaid I'd ever seen and he could forget me dancing with him at the reception."

The brothers snickered, earning a reproving glare from their mother.

"So, are you ready to settle down, bro?" J.T. asked.

Dante glanced toward the back, where Waynie stood at attention in the doorway, fidgeting with his tie. Even though the big man meant to whisper, the sound carried up the aisle when he said, "Oh, my God, she's wearing white!"

Half the assembly turned in time to see his demure little bride make a not so demure little gesture.

Dante laughed and whispered to J.T., "Somehow I don't think 'settling down' is appropriate in this case."

EPILOGUE

Three months later

They weren't coming.

Swallowing hard over her disappointment, Nadia stared out the window at the falling snow. Her breath fogged the window pane, and she traced a heart on the glass with her index finger.

"I tried, babe. I really did," she whispered.

"Hey, Nadia. Could you give me a hand over here?" Waynie called.

She turned to watch the big man struggle with the banner. Whenever he managed to get one end up, the other would fall. Suppressing a smile, she walked over to help.

The conference room at Andreakos/Giovanni Industries had been transformed. Balloons of every color imaginable covered the plain white ceiling. Streamers exploded from the center of the room to the corners.

"It's crooked," Nadia said.

Waynie gave a weary sigh and adjusted his end of the banner. "How's this, your Majesty?"

"Up just a little . . . there!"

HAPPY 26TH BIRTHDAY DANTE

"Perfect!" she said, surveying the room and the conference table that doubled nicely for a buffet table.

"The only thing that's missing is the pony rides," Waynie said. "Or have you got that covered too? Does Dante get to ride a pony?"

Nadia folded her arms over her chest and said testily, "The ponies were all taken. He'll have to make do with a jackass. Your saddle is over there."

"Oooh, good one," Ronnie said. He laughed as Nadia ducked the roll of streamer Waynie tossed at her head, then tugged on Nadia's sleeve.

"Hey, if you're through playing, I thought you might want to know that Dante and your Pops just pulled into the parking lot."

"Still no show on the others?" Nadia asked.

Ronnie shook his head and gave her a sympathetic smile. He knew how much this meant to her.

"Okay. Take your places everyone!" Nadia commanded. "Somebody hit the lights." She glanced at Ronnie. "Could you keep an eye out for me, just for a few more minutes?"

"Sure," he said, an instant before the lights winked out.

● ● ●

"So, what's the big meeting about?" Dante asked his father-in-law.

It must be something major to get Nick out of the house on a Saturday morning. The former workaholic had become a certifiable slacker.

"I'd rather not say until we get inside. Now, where did I put my notes?" He patted his coat pockets absently.

"Okay," Dante said. "Just tell me I haven't screwed up anything. You're giving me that look—"

"What look?"

"That look you gave me when I told you I wanted your daughter to jump out of that airplane."

Nick chuckled. "Oh, no. Nothing like that. As a matter of fact, you and Nadia are doing a wonderful job running things."

"We're a good team." Dante grinned. "I'm the brains, she's the brawn."

"Yes, well, you're doing such a good job that I'm considering stepping out entirely. Maria has always wanted to see Paris, you know."

Dante raised his eyebrows and threw open the door to the conference room.

"Surprise!"

Dante staggered backward into Nick and nearly fell.

Something hit his face and he instinctively threw up a hand before he realized it was only confetti.

Clutching his heart, he grinned at Nadia.

She smiled back and sashayed over to him, singing a breathless rendition of *Happy Birthday, Mr. President.*

He pulled her close and kissed her. Before he released her, he whispered, "You know, my birthday's not for two weeks."

She looked at him like he was crazy. "Well, if I threw a party on your birthday, then it wouldn't be a surprise, would it?"

Dante chuckled. Life with Nadia had proven to be anything but predictable.

"You little sneak," he said. "I ought to have known you wouldn't get up that early to go shopping."

Maria stood behind Nadia, and Dante leaned to brush a kiss across her cheek. "Morning, Maria."

"Good morning, Dante."

Nick came up behind his wife and wrapped an arm around her waist. Dante could hardly believe the transformation in his in-laws. Gary Vandergriff's death had released them. They acted as carefree as newlyweds. He supposed part of that came from Maria's new self-confidence. Even though she had a couple of surgeries yet to go, Maria's most recent one had done more than they'd even hoped for. Along with her freedom, she was regaining her face.

Someone called Nadia away and Dante found himself standing alone with Waynie, who was happily munching a handful of barbeque potato chips.

"This is pretty tame for a Nadia party," Dante commented, twisting his head to check out the decorations. "I keep waiting on the big bang, the sky to fall. Something."

Before the words were even out of his mouth, Ronnie burst through the doors and ran over to Nadia. He whispered in her ear, and Dante watched her eyes light up.

"Be afraid," Waynie said tonelessly. "Be very afraid."

They both knew that look. Something big was going down.

Nadia ran over to Dante and grabbed his hands.

"Come here, come here, come here!" she said breathlessly, and tugged him to the nearest chair. She practically shoved him into it.

"I have a surprise for you, but you have to close your eyes first."

Obediently, Dante shut his eyes and leaned his head back.

"I'll be right back. No peeking!" she shouted.

"I wouldn't dream of it, princess," Dante replied.

A moment later, she said, "Hang on, we're coming."

Conversation died all over the room, and Dante started to get a little nervous. No telling what that girl was up to now.

"Okay," she said. "You can look now."

Dante slowly opened his eyes. He blinked once. Twice. What he saw nearly stopped his heart.

Nadia was walking toward him with a little black-haired girl in tow. He would've known her anywhere.

Lara. His daughter.

Dante was paralyzed, stuck to the chair as they approached. He tried to speak, but the words wouldn't form.

"Why is he crying?" Lara asked, peeking at him from underneath thick bangs.

Was he crying?

Dante touched his cheek, and was surprised when his fingertips came away slick with tears.

"Your daddy is just really, really happy to see you, honey," Nadia said.

She was crying too.

Dante felt so many things for Nadia at that moment, too many things to catalogue. He was afraid to look directly at her, afraid he'd bawl like a baby. It had taken finding Nadia to make him realize how lonely and wretched his life had been without her. His need for her was as essential as his need for water, for air.

He rose shakily to his feet, then dropped to one knee in front of them. All he could think to do was open his arms. With a tentative glance at Nadia, Lara wrapped her arms around his neck.

Dante hugged her, marveling at the feel of her little body in his arms. He'd never thought he'd see her again. Never thought he'd hold her. But here she was.

Thanks to Nadia.

He happened to glance at the doorway and saw Sharon standing there, watching them. She wiped a tear from her eye and whispered something to her husband, Brian.

"Nadia, I'm thirsty," Lara said, untangling herself from his arms.

"Well, come on, then," Nadia said brightly. "Let's get you some punch."

Dante stood and walked over to his ex-wife.

"Thank you," he said. He cut his eyes to Brian. "Thank you both."

"Thank Nadia," Sharon replied. "I have to admit, when she contacted us a couple of months ago, I wasn't sure about it, but she's very persuasive and—and she loves you a great deal."

"I love her too." Dante smiled and motioned Nadia over to join them. She poured Lara a cup of punch and left her with Ronnie while she walked over to join them. She linked her arm around Dante's waist and he kissed the top of her head.

"Dante, I want you to know that I'm sorry I kept Lara from you," Sharon said. "I've picked up the phone a thousand times to call, but the time never seemed right. The look on your face the day you came by our house . . ." Sharon shook her head. "It nearly killed me. What I did to you was worse than what my father did, because I knew you. I knew you were a good man, would be a good father to Lara, but I was a coward. I was young and scared, and I hope you don't hate me for it."

Dante glanced at his daughter, who was being entertained by Waynie. "No, I don't hate you."

"When Lara turned three, we even hired a private detective to find you. By then, you'd gotten into bounty hunting and were living in Japan. I thought you'd moved on, that maybe we could too. And the bounty hunting scared me. You were running all over the world, getting shot at . . . I only wanted what was best for Lara."

"I understand. But what changed your mind?"

"I think I can answer that," Nadia said with a smile. "I told them the bounty hunting was over and that I had thoroughly domesticated you." She held her hand to the side of her mouth and whispered, "He's practically a suit now."

"I heard that." Dante said, and swatted her behind.

Nadia grinned up at him.

"Nadia, Nadia come here!" Lara shouted. She held up a gold box and shook it. "This present has my name on it."

"So it does," she said, and winked at Dante. "Excuse me, guys. I have to go check this out."

"Lara loves her already," Brian said.

Sharon shifted and Dante noticed her bulging stomach for the first time.

"Oh, hey, congratulations," he said. "When's the big day?"

"Two months from tomorrow," Brian replied. "It's a boy." He hesitated and said, "You know, this baby put the whole thing in perspective for me. I tried to put myself in your shoes, imagine how you must feel. I love Lara like she's mine and it hurts to share her, but I realize you deserve a chance to know her too."

"I guess we'd better go now," Sharon said. "Nadia has

my cell phone number if you need me."

She must've noted Dante's surprise, because she said, "Lara's really comfortable with Nadia now. They've seen a lot of each other in the past two months, so I don't think she'll be afraid if we leave. One of us will be back to pick her up before bedtime. If you don't mind, I'd like to do a couple of day visits before she spends the night, to let her get used to being with you. Does that sound fair?"

"More than fair." Dante was grateful for any time he had with Lara at all.

"Once she gets used to the idea, we'll talk about regular visitation."

"Thank you," Dante said again. He extended his hand to Brian, who shook it and clapped him on the back.

Sharon tiptoed to hug him. "I'm glad you've found happiness," she said softly.

"I'm glad you have too," he said, and meant it.

With a wave, they left. Dante walked over to where Nadia was lighting candles on a massive white cake.

"Hey, where did they go?" Nadia asked with a frown. "We're about to get to the good stuff."

Dante ruffled his daughter's hair. "They said they'd be back to get her tonight."

"Oh, okay." She smiled at him. "So, do I throw a good surprise party, or what?"

Dante laughed. "Babe . . . you're amazing."

Nadia wrinkled her nose at him and lit the last candle. She

shook out the match and said, "There! Now, make a wish."

Ignoring the candles, Dante took her in his arms and kissed her.

What good were wishes when he had everything his heart desired?

For more information

about other great titles from

Medallion Press, visit

www.medallionpress.com